WHEN IT ALL WENT TO HELL

Stories

PHILL PAPPAS

Copyright

© 2015 Phill Pappas

First Edition, 2015

ISBN-13: 978-0692544662 (Phill Pappas)
ISBN-10: 0692544666

Cover Art: Kara Hemsworth
Cover & Book Design: Alex Pappas
Author Photo: Jamie Killen

AFTER THE SHOW — CONTINUED FROM RED.

"... I SAY, I SAY, WE ARE GATHERED HERE TODAY
TO ~~GIVE~~ PAY OUR RESPECTS TO ONE OF OUR FALLEN
(BUT NOT FORGOTTEN) "BROTHERS."

MADE A FIST

FOGHORN LEGHORN RAISED ~~HIS BALLED UP FIST~~ AND SLAMMED
IT INTO THE PALM OF HIS LEFT HAND. THE OTHER TUNES
STOOD ~~SILENTLY~~ WITH THEIR HEADS BOWED IN SILENCE. (HANDS BEHIND THEIR BACKS?)
"THE DUCK WAS A FINE GENTLEMAN, YA HEAR LORD?
I SAY, A FINE GENTLEMAN INDEED..."

THE TUNES NODDED IN AGREEMENT.
BUGS BUNNY, WAS DRESSED AS A WIDOW, AND HE BEGAN
TO WAIL, "WHY DID YOU HAVE TO TAKE HIM?" AND
THEN HE FAINTED INTO THE ARMS OF MARVIN THE MARTIAN
FOGHORN CONTINUED HIS SERMON.

"HE WASN'T A SOUTHERN GENTLEMAN, LORD, NOR
A BAPTIST OR A LUTHERN, COME TO THINK OF
IT, HE MIGHT HAVE BEEN A JEW OR AN ATHEIST, (POINT'S THE CASE)
LORD, WHICH I WOULD ASK YOU, LORD DON'T HOLD
THE LATTER AGAINST HIM NOW..."

TUXEDOED

THE RAIN ~~ON STAGE~~ CONTINUED TO POUR ON THE SHADOWS OF THOSE
NOTED THE QUALITY OF THE SET DESIGN AND EFFECTS. PRESENT. STETSON

"DOES THE DUCK'S ~~RELIGIOUS~~ RELIGIOUS AFFILIATION MATTER? NO,
DAMNIT, IT DOES NOT. WHAT MATTERS IS THAT
HE WAS KILLED IN AN ACT OF TERRORISM,
(NOTE: GOD "AND" OR HATE MOST ALL OF THE "ISMS") TERROR, I SAY, ISM. SO LORD I ASK YOU
TO BESEECH AND CONDEMN THOSE RESPONSIBLE FOR
THIS ACT OF TERROR, LORD — PUNISH THEM!"

THE PROCESSION SHOUTED, "PUNISH THEM" (HE WENT INTO CONVULSIONS)
FOGHORN RAISED HIS ARMS ~~ABOVE AND SHOOK~~ AND HIS BODY SHOOK.
"WE ASK FOR RETRIBUTION LORD, FOR JUSTICE!"
"FOR JUSTICE," THEY YELLED.
"WE ASK FOR THE BLOOD OF OUR ENEMIES TO

THREE OF THE FOUR WALLS WERE ADORNED WITH ~~FUR~~ LARGE MIRRORS,
LIKE THOSE FOUND IN BARBERSHOPS OR BACKSTAGE AT STRIPCLUBS.
BENEATH THE MIRRORS, COUNTERTOPS - WHITE, ENAMEL - VERY UNEVENTFUL.
TUCKED INTO THE CORNER, TO THE RIGHT OF THE ENTRANCE SAT
AN ~~BY VERY NICE VERY STOCKED~~ IMMACULATELY CARED FOR BAR - CLEAN
AND FULLY STOCKED.

WILLIAM TAFT (NO RELATION) BELIEVED THAT AFTER THE SHOW, THE
ACTORS SHOULD BE ABLE TO UNWIND A BIT IN THE SPIRITS OF
THE ADULT PLAYGROUND. THE BAR WAS, ~~THE~~ QUITE CLEARLY, THE NICEST
THING IN THE ROOM.

"NOW, AHH, WHAT'S YOUR NAME?" FOGHORN SAID, SWIRLING
A DRINK IN HIS HAND.

"UHA, HI THERE, MR. LEGHORN, ~~IT~~ IT'S A REAL..."

"I ASKED YOU FOR YOUR NAME BOY, YOUR NAME!" FOGHORN
TURNED TO SYLVESTER WHO WAS SPRAWLED OUT ON ~~ONE~~ THE
~~Ə~~ LEATHER COUCH NEAREST THE DOOR, TO THE RIGHT, "THE BOY DON'T
KNOW HOW TO ANSWER A SIMPLE QUESTION."

SYLVESTER WAIVED HIM OFF. HE ~~HELD~~ WAS HOLDING AN ICEPACK ON HIS
FOREHEAD.

"L.P. STETSON, MR..."
"YOUR FULL NAME, BOY," FOGHORN SAID. "GIVE ME YOUR FULL
NAME, I HAVE NO ~~NEED~~ NOR DESIRE NOR ~~TIME~~ FOR ABBREVIATING.
~~THE~~ UMM, LATIMER PARNASSUS STETSON, MR. LEGHORN, ~~STETSON~~.
~~YOU'RE TELLING ME THAT~~
"OKAY, WELL NICE TO MEET YA, LATIMER PARNASSUS STETSON.
MY NAME IS FOGHORN DILLENGER ROCKAFELLER BOONE LEGHORN,
BUT YOU CAN CALL ME FOGHORN."
"YOU CAN CALL ME L.P."
"OKAY L.P. WHAT CAN I DO FOR YA?"
"I'M THE THEATER ~~CRITIQUE~~..."
"HE'S THE CRITIC YOU DUMB FUCKIN' CHICKEN," BUGS SAID,
~~POINTING AT THE~~ LOWERING HIS HEAD TO THE COUNTERTOP AND

STETSON LOOKED AT HIS WATCH, AGAIN, AND HE BEGAN WALKING TOWARDS THE CAST LOUNGE — WHICH WAS DOWN THE HALL FROM THE MAIN ENTRANCE TO THE THE THEATER, THROUGH A SIDE DOOR THAT ~~LANDED~~ *LED TO A HALLWAY* ~~THAT RAN~~ ADJACENT TO THE STAGE, AND FINALLY A RAMP ABOUT THIRTY ~~FEET~~ FROM THE STAGE CONNECTED BY ANOTHER *SMALL* ~~HALL~~ *WERE TWO*. THERE ~~WAS THAT~~ EMERGENCY EXITS THAT ~~CONNECTED~~ *LED TO THE* BACK OF THE THEATER RAN FROM THE BACKSTAGE AND THE CAST LOUNGE.

~~STD~~ STANDING STEADFAST AT THE ENTRANCE TO THE HALLWAY WAS FRED, THE USHER.

"HEY THERE, L.P." SAID FRED
"HEY."
"WELL, WHAT DID YA THINK?"
"I'M STILL TRYING TO MAKE SENSE OF IT," L.P. SAID, "YOU?" ~~REALLY~~ ~~FIRST DECRYPTED THE ~~ ~~INSIDE~~
"A BIT HEAVY HANDED, I THOUGHT," FRED SAID. "I WOULDA LIKED TO HAVE SEEN SOME MORE ~~OF~~ OF THEIR TRADITIONAL BITS."
~~MAYBE WERE JUST TOO OLD NOW~~

"YEAH, OKAY, FRED," STETSON SAID, ~~RAISING HIS~~ GLASS AND GIVING *THE USHER* A NOD AS HE ~~WALKED~~ OPENED THE DOOR ~~AND WALKED~~ AND MADE HIS WAY DOWN THE HALLWAY.

AFTER THE COURTROOM VERDICT, THERE WAS A LONG SCENE IN ~~OF~~ WHICH SYLVESTER AND FOGHORN, DRESSED AS HIGH-RANKING MILITARY GENERALS ARGUED THE PROS AND CONS *(MERITS)* OF PERSUING TERRORISM WITH MILITARY ACTION, SPECIFICALLY, WHETHER OR NOT YOU COULD EVER KILL ENOUGH PEOPLE TO KILL AN IDEA, COMPLETELY. THE ~~ARGUMENT~~ ARGUMENT CRESCENDO IN A FEATHERED AND FLUFFY FRENZY, THE TWO GENERALS WRESTLING ON THE GROUND, AND FINALLY ENDED WHEN FOGHORN MOUNTED SYLVESTER AND STRANGLED HIM, ~~THE~~ THE LAST WORDS OF THE SCENE WERE FOGHORN'S, GRIMLY, ~~CONF~~ ASSUREDLY, "THAT'S HOW YOU KILL AN IDEA, PUSSY."

THE FINAL SCIENCE OF THE NIGHT ~~WAS~~ PORTRAYED YOSEMITE SAM AS A ~~THE-EMBODIMENT-OF-EVIL-TYPE~~ SLAVE OWNER. THE REST

THE ADJUSTMENT ~~BEAD~~ BUREAUCRACY

A MAN ~~IN~~ A ^WEARING GRAY, THREE-PIECE ~~GRAY~~ SUIT AND A TOPHAT STOOD OUTSIDE OF TERRY RUNKLE'S HOUSE AND SPOKE QUIETLY/SOFTLY TO A RACOON NAMED FRED.

IT WAS 11:00 P.M, EXACTLY.

TIME WAS IMPORTANT BECAUSE TIMING WAS IMPORTANT, TIMING, YOU SEE, WAS RELATED TO THE PLAN. WINDOWS OPENED AND CLOSED, DOORS REVOLVED, AND PEOPLE MOVED THROUGH THEIR LIVES ON VARIOUS PATHS AND AT VARIOUS PACES.

~~THE MAN IN THE SUIT WAS TASKED WITH~~

IT WAS THE MAN IN THE SUIT'S JOB TO MAKE CERTAIN THAT CERTAIN MARKS ARRIVED AT CERTAIN PLACES ^AND AT CERTAIN TIMES (IN ACCORDANCE WITH), ACCORDING ~~TO~~ THE PLAN.

THE MAN IN THE SUIT'S ^REAL NAME WAS BILL GLASS, BUT SINCE HE HAD JOINED THE AGENCY EVERYONE CALLED HIM AGENT PERCY STANBRIDGE, OR SOME VARIATION/COMBINATION OF THOSE THREE TITLES. HE ~~WAS ASSIGNED~~ ^A MAN NAMED PETER THE NAME PERCY STANBRIDGE TO BILL GLASS UPON HIS ~~ARRIVAL AT~~ ^ABDUCTION. BILL HAD STOOD IN FRONT OF PETER, AND PETER HAD SAID, "BILL GLASS, NICE TO MEET YOU. YOU'RE ABSOLVED. FROM THIS DAY FOREWARD YOU WILL BE KNOWN AS PERCY STANBRIDGE. PLEASE REPORT TO THE AGENCY FOR TRAINING."

BILL PREFERRED THE NAME BILL TO PERCY, BUT THERE WAS NOTHING HE COULD DO, THE CALL HAD BEEN MADE FROM ON HIGH, AND ^FROM THEN ON, HE WAS PERCY.

~~TO HELP BILL IN HIS QUEST FOR ORCHESTRATION~~

BILL RELIED HEAVILY ON ~~THEIR~~ FOLDERS. EACH MARK HAD A ~~A~~ FOLDER ASSIGNED TO THEM UPON BIRTH, AND THAT ^ONE FOLDER CONTAINED THE MARK'S PRESENT AND FUTURE PROJECTIONS. THE PRESENT PROJECTION INDICATED WHAT THE MARK WAS DOING AT THE PRESENT MOMENT - WALKING, TALKING, SLEEPING, INTERACTING, ETC. THE FUTURE PROJECTION INDICATED WHERE THE MARK WOULD BE IN THE IMMEDIATE FUTURE, AND IT ~~RELATED IMPORTANT~~ ^ALSO INDICATED WHETHER OR NOT THE PROJECTIONS, BOTH PRESENT AND FUTURE, ALIGNED ~~OR~~ CORRECTLY, ACCORDING TO THE PLAN.

THE FOLDERS RESEMBLED ^THE MANILA FOLDERS ~~FOUND IT COMMONLY~~ ^COMMONLY FOUND IN FILE CABINETS, ~~SINCE THE EIGHTH.~~ ^THE INSIDE OF THE FOLDER RESEMBLED AN IPAD (TOUCH-SCREEN USER INTERFACE) ~~THE FOLDER~~ THAT DESPERATELY NEEDED ITS OPERATING SYSTEM UPDATED. THERE WERE LAGS, GLITCHES, ETC., REGARDLESS OF ITS CALIBER.

WHEN IT ALL WENT TO HELL

Stories

PHILL PAPPAS

CONTENTS

For my brother, Alex.

"I came up with a new game-show idea recently.
It's called The Old Game.
You got three old guys with loaded guns onstage.
They look back at their lives, see who they were, what they
accomplished, how close they came to realizing their dreams.
The winner is the one who doesn't blow his brains out.
He gets a refrigerator."

- Chuck Barris,
                        Confessions of a Dangerous Mind

AFTER THE SHOW

ACT I

Stetson's hat was a part of his identity. He'd worn a fedora every day of his adult life. Shortly before becoming a reporter for the Missoulian, Stetson had changed his name from ____ to Stetson. He felt that his new name was much cooler than ____, and he credited his success as a theater critic, in part, to how his new name looked in print: L.P. Stetson. The byline commanded respect–the brevity of staccato in the final moments of an article's melody. A portrait of Stetson in his hat always accompanied the byline. He'd once considered changing his name to Fedora, but felt that it was too feminine or too Italian.

Stetson justified the contradiction brought by having the last name Stetson yet brandishing a fedora, with a roundabout explanation that a majority of Americans knew that a Stetson was a type of hat, but they were likely unaware as to what type of hat exactly. They'd think that maybe it meant hat-maker or hatter, or that Stetson had come from a long and illustrious bloodline of hatters–which was, much like cobbling or spearfishing Stetson thought, an honest profession. And maybe the people would make the connection that out of all the generations of hatters, Stetson was the only one, or rather, the first one to get out of the family business and pursue a different career. Therefore, Stetson always wore a fedora to honor his family and those who came before him. This was how Stetson had justified changing his name to one type of hat while wearing another.

The truth was that nobody but Stetson gave a damn about his name or his hat. The only people who actually paid Stetson any attention were the readers of his weekly column. But even those avid readers were unconcerned with his name or his hat; instead, they chose to focus on the too often incendiary, aggressive critiques that appeared on the front page, below the fold, each Monday.

Theater news was big news in Missoula. Well, not exactly big news. It would have been no news or the same amount of news as it had always been, but these days one man owned both the paper and the theater. A man named William Harrier. Harrier made theater news important by hiring an opinionated critic with a deep-seated hatred for his fellow man. Then he slapped that column, with little oversight, on the front page of the Missoulian each Monday.

Harrier had never noticed the contradiction that was Stetson's name vs. hat situation either, but if the conundrum had somehow worked itself into Harrier's consciousness, he too would not have cared.

The week Stetson was hired he'd received word that the column was going to appear on the front page, below the fold, weekly. Stetson attributed this change in frequency and location of the column to Mr. Harrier's recognition of his immense talent.

This assumption was incorrect, of course, as the change was the result of the simple coincidence that Harrier had hired Stetson and purchased the Civic Theater in the same week.

Stetson, privy to the knowledge that Mr. Harrier had just purchased the theater, chose to believe that the 500 words allotted to the theater critic were upped in notoriety because of his unrelenting geyser of talent. He even toyed with the idea that Mr. Harrier had purchased the theater *because* Stetson *deserved* it, what with his keen eye for truth in theater and all.

These associations, although completely ludicrous, assured Stetson that he'd made the right decision by changing his name, regardless of what kind of hat he wore. *I'm not even here one week*, he'd thought, *and Mr. Harrier has already bought me a theater.*

It was true that Stetson's career was going well as a theater critic, but as previously noted, that had nothing to do with Stetson's name, hat, or the size of his penis (which was perfectly average, but a man in the throes of a solipsistic binge is liable to jump to any conclusion). His star was rising. Because Stetson created conflict, people reacted. His reviews and critiques were controversial, and readers, performers, and other critics alike viewed Stetson as a bully (a crass, juvenile know-nothing who yelled from atop his soapbox).

Harrier liked Stetson, because he *was* controversial. Conflict and controversy sold papers by drawing a line in the pulp and asking readers to pick which side of the ink they were aligned. To Harrier, selling more papers meant potentially growing the number of theater patrons in Missoula, and both of these meant higher profits. Profit was a name that Harrier did care about.

Stetson entered the auditorium of the theater and handed his ticket to the usher, a man who looked exactly like Wilfred Brimley crossed with an emperor penguin—a small oddity in the Big Sky state.

"Hello again, L.P.," the usher said.

"Hello, Ray," Stetson said.

"Excited for the show?"

"We'll see if they've still got it," Stetson said, "after all these years and all."

"If how I feel's any indication," Ray said, opening his arms and inspecting his own girth, acknowledging his failings in old age, "then I'd say those old boys are spent."

Stetson nodded. "I'll see you after the show," he said.

He walked down the aisle of the auditorium, with regal carpeting underfoot and tender ambiance overhead, stopping at row 27 and then shuffled over to seat F, it was in the rear of the theater.

The location of his seat relative to the stage was an important point for Stetson. So important that he had spent the previous week's column trashing a performance based mainly on his seat's location in relation to the stage. The previous week's play was an adaptation of a biography of Nelson Mandela called *It's Dark in this Room*. The performance was dull, he'd noted, but he'd enjoyed how the actor had made the prison cell seem both paradoxically, spacious and suffocating. It was a good thing that the actor playing Mandela could pantomime, could emote passionately with his physicality, Stetson had written, because from row 25, seat H:

I spent the entire show wondering, questioning the director's choice to make Mandela, a man known for his immense prowess in the oratory, a mute. It was then that I realized that the ac-

tor was not a mute by choice but merely blessed with the vocal chords of a deceased iguana. With a prison sentence of nearly 30 years, Mandela must have considered suicide on a daily basis, and after witnessing a truly pathetic version of It's Dark in this Room, with a lead who ought to consider switching professions to, let's say, poster child in support of late-term abortions, yours truly has been seriously considering taking a trip down river with the razor of theatrical justice.

The lead, Albert Mondiav, had committed suicide shortly thereafter. His untimely exit from the stage of life had generated a cacophony of noise and protest from readers–a series of letters and phone calls that passed over the blind eyes and deaf ears of one William Harrier, because sales had also spiked approximately 37% that week.

Stetson sat and waited patiently, meekly, for the house lights to dim. Theater guests filed into the auditorium. Lights flashed at a count of three, a simplistic visual Morse code meaning three minutes until curtain. L.P. Stetson sat, waiting. He was waiting like everyone else for the house lights to drop, waiting for his childhood heroes to take the stage. With the influx of guests into the theater, the temperature had spiked causing the already plump and over-perspiring Stetson to sweat more. He pulled the coral-pink kerchief from his jacket pocket and dabbed at his forehead. The beads of sweat had formed along his brow like the tiny bubbles that existed, briefly, at the bottom of a pot of near-boiling water, and when he wiped at them the kerchief brushed against the edge of Stetson's scar. In the midst of all those people he was alone, and then his mind began to drift. And when his mind drifted, Stetson thought of one thing–the incident.

Always the incident, never the accident or an incident–it was *the incident*. During the quieter moments of the day, the least spectacular ones (opening a can of tuna fish in a mid-afternoon lull or removing a pebble from one of his brown loafers), his mind recreated snippets of the incident. A series of intrusive thoughts, annoying, like when you've been driving on the interstate and consider, for no particular reason, giving the wheel a good jerk at eighty miles per hour, wondering if you'd skip across the median like a stone or spin into a death roll, or would you regain control of the vehicle after a sharp slide and then make it out unscathed?

Fitz Myron pushed Young L.P.____; pushed him into the playground's dirt. Fitz dragged him. Young L.P.____ saw the underside of a car and a wheel next to his face. He felt Fitz kick him. It all happened very fast. Fitz's foot came down again, and Young L.P.____ was unconscious.

Stetson wiped his brow again and took a few deep breaths. His pulse had quickened.

The official report of the incident was a bit more grotesque than what even Stetson could remember. The official report was what expelled Fitz Myron from FDR Elementary, and it was filed with the school system and also as a police report. F. Myron was charged as a juvenile with attempted murder.

The day of the incident, during recess, both reports read, other students observed F. Myron teasing, pushing, and slapping Young L.P. ____. Children had noted that Young L.P. ____ was a frequent and favorite target of Myron's misguided anger and frustration. After a few minutes of antagonizing, the report added, Young L.P. ____, non-violently standing his ground as teachers and parents had repeatedly instructed him, had reached his limit. The boy began to cry, and he retaliated by pushing Myron. A third grader named Eddie Velasquez, who was the principal witness in both reports (a second generation Mexican-American with a slight lisp), said that Myron had pushed Young L.P. to the ground, grabbed him by the hair and dragged the boy. The boy, who had apparently curled into a fetal ball at that point, was dragged over to a navy-blue Buick sedan parked adjacent to the school, and had his head kicked into the wheel of the car approximately twenty-five times. Myron's sneaker forced the crown of Young L.P.'s forehead into the rim of the car and onto the concrete, splitting his skull at the point of impact with the steel. It was around this time that the Gym/Social Studies teacher, Mr. Dugars, saw Myron in action, restrained the youthful sociopath by force and instructed the other kids to tell a teacher to call 911. Police noted that upon their arrival they had assumed that Young L.P. was dead–his pint-sized body lying in a pool of blood, jammed under the wheel well of a Buick, like a worn leather boot lying curbside in a static puddle after a heavy rain.

Young L.P. almost died en route to the hospital–his loss of blood so extreme. Fitz Myron was whisked away to the Joe DiMaggio Juvenile Detention Center, and the students at FDR Elementary never saw him again.

When Young L.P. awoke at the hospital on the day of the incident, his mother and father were standing over their bandaged and woozy son. After gathering partial wits about where he was and what had happened, Stetson reached for the wound. The wound, wrapped carefully in gauze and bandages, was covered. He let his hand rest on the bandages, tenderly, for a moment. He wanted to feel it.

After a month had passed, Young L.P. returned to the fifth grade. He wore a hat–a Seattle Mariners ball cap, as Montana had no baseball team. The ball cap covered a truly awful scar. Plump, red skin that looked like a pair of large cartoon lips ran from the mid-line of his forehead over the crown and six inches onto the top of his head. In between the giant lips of the scar was the stitching that held together what could have been mistaken for ground chicken–pink, white, and yellow bulbs occupied space where there was once skin and hair.

The first time Young L.P. saw his scar, in the bathroom mirror on the first floor of his family's home, his mother stood at his side. Her hand gently trembled as she unwrapped the bandages. Her touch was delicate, measured. She was reminded of a moment days after her wedding when she was opening a friend's gift. She knew it was going to be a blender, wished it wasn't a blender, and felt that feeling of obvious disappointment when it ended up being a blender. Young L.P. winced after a few layers of gauze had been removed, the fibrous cloth tugging at the threads and knots of exposed stitch. He stared into the mirror during the unveiling, and he tried not to blink. He had thought that perhaps watching the process in its entirety would make the outcome better.

His mother, Sheila, pulled the last piece of yellowish gauze from his face. L.P. was spellbound, but he slowly came to terms with what he saw. Sheila was worried; he was staring so hard, she thought, so she said, "Honey?" When L.P. averted his gaze and met her eyes, Sheila clenched her jaw, and her eyes welled. She recognized not a loss of innocence but an acceptance of cruelty. Maybe they're the same thing, she'd thought. They were not the same, and with that realization something inside her broke.

The theater lights dimmed and then went dark. Stetson adjusted his hat one last time, grabbed both armrests and slouched into a more comfortable position within the faded red felt of his seat. A spotlight flooded the curtain, and the crowd applauded. The curtain rose. The spotlight went black for a moment.

Bugs Bunny stood in the middle of an empty stage upon the spotlight's return, shielding his eyes from the flood of the light with his left hand. With his right hand, Bugs chomped on an oversized carrot.

Stetson made a mental note that Bugs looked tired. Bugs was tired. The rabbit finished his carrot and rubbed his hands together, and then he relaxed, his arms loose at his side. "Ehh, what's up, Missoula?"

The crowd burst into applause.

"We got a hell of a show for yous guys tonight," Bugs said. "The whole gang is here: Marvin, Foghorn, the bird and the cat. Daffy and that cowboy, Yo-se-Mite."

Bugs scratched his head and said, "Ehhh, let's see, who else we got?"

A deep Southern drawl boomed from backstage, "You tell that dumb fuckin' rabbit the name's Yosemite, fer the last God dang time!"

Collectively, the audience's reaction was hesitant.

"Yo-se-Mite, relax," Bugs said.

"Oooooooo, I'm gonna kill him," the disembodied voice said again.

Bug's turned towards stage right, "Shut up," he said, "I'm doing the monologue." A pair of gunshots echoed from backstage. Blam-Blam. The crowd jumped and then fell silent. Stetson shifted in his seat a bit and then leaned forward.

"Like I was saying, ehhh," Bugs said. "We got that coyote and the rocket bird, too, and last but not least we also brought that autistic, bald hunter fellow, Elmer. So, get ready for a show," he said, spreading his arms in a theatrical Ta-Da, and the spotlight extinguished.

ACT II

At the end of the show, Stetson remained in his seat. He was unimpressed, well not necessarily unimpressed, he thought, more confused. Stetson was struggling to grasp the differences between the performance he had just witnessed and the one that he had expected his childhood idols to perform. He was trying to bridge the chasm between the two iterations, and as he struggled with these thoughts, the theater emptied.

After a few minutes, Stetson stood and made his way to the main lobby. He wanted to give the Tunes a chance to settle into their post-show routine, whatever it was, before joining them in the cast's lounge. Over the past year of interviews, Stetson had noted that a good 15 to 20 minutes should pass from the final curtain to the time he entered the actor's lounge. This gave the actors time to pour a drink, change, smoke, or whatever. And it gave Stetson time to use the restroom, grab a drink from the bar, and digest the performance.

Stetson went to the bathroom, a standard theater quality affair (quaint, Nuevo Utilitarian). At the urinal his mind drifted, and when it drifted he thought of *the incident*. Standing at the porcelain depository, Stetson moved his penis in clockwise circles and figure eights, thereby affecting stream trajectory around and across the red urinal cake that read "Olé!" He thought of this one time when he couldn't exactly remember why, but Fitz Myron had snuck up behind him in the bathroom and shoved him into the urinal. Then he imagined a boot kicking his face, and he closed his eyes as if he was capable of ridding the thought from his mind.

The school kids didn't point or laugh at Stetson after the incident. They saw the ball cap, and they knew what it meant. They hardly acknowledged Stetson after the incident. They tried to ignore it and him.

While drying his hands, Stetson studied his reflection. He inspected his green and gold-striped tie (cinched at the neck in a tight single-Windsor). After running his index finger and thumb down the length of his tie, Stetson adjusted his hat and came to the conclusion that he looked good. *This* was debatable, as everything about his outfit was terrible—colors, patterns, and textures all clashing. He wore a light purple, almost lavender collared shirt. The top of his tie touched an oversized belt buckle that said "CRITIC" in bold, silver lettering. The belt attached to the buckle was an odd maroon, which held up a pair of light, grey-blue jeans. The jeans, too short for even Stetson, exposed his sockless ankles and brilliant brown loafers.

He made his way through the lobby of the theater to the bar at the end of the East Wing. As he walked, the musings of a critique began to coerce his mind into the isolated realm of ideation. He wondered, *what did I just witness?* Stetson approached the bar, ordered a Manhattan, looked at his watch, noting that he had ten minutes to kill, and he tried piecing together the unique act. Stetson stood in the corner of the bar, between a planter and a janitor's closet.

After Bugs' introduction and the spotlight had returned, an upright piano was rolled out from stage right, stopping just as it passed fully into view. Then Daffy Duck, costumed in a black tux-edo, hands clasped behind his back, entered and bowed. He was wearing a monocle. He paced back and forth a few times, muttering something to himself, and then he took his seat at the piano.

Daffy raised his arms, like a small child would raise his or her arms to be picked up by their mother or father, and then he yelled, "Just give me a reason," and his hands dropped to the keys. 'Bwanggggg,' went the piano. "Just give me a sign," 'Bwangggg-gg.' "A jui-cer and some limes," and then he played Bom-bom--bim-bim-bom---bam-bum----be-bum. Daffy stood from the piano, bowed, and said, "Normally when I hit that last no," but before he could finish his sentence the piano exploded.

Daffy's limbs shot into the first few rows as if Gallagher had sledgehammered a Duck à l'Orange. Stetson felt the heat from the pyro-techniques. Then there were sirens, and Sylvester and Tweety drove on stage in a vintage hearse with the paint job of an ambulance. Dressed as EMTs, they stepped out of the car and approached the scorched spot where the piano had been–the blast point.

"Theems to me, there'th been an act of terrorithm, Tweet," Sylvester said.

The little yellow bird and the cat began a tap routine. They sang out in unison, "I thought I thaw Al-Qaida, ear-lier today, dey *wired up a pia-no bomb, and blew the duck a-way." They were a couple of natural hoofers; Sammy Davis Junior came to mind, playful and energetic.*

Halfway through their song and dance number they stopped, and Tweety said, "Puddy, we should go to da funeral."

The stage lights went down, thunder cracked over the speakers, and the orchestra began playing 'Swing Low, Sweet Chariot.'

When the lights came up, the set had been transformed into a cemetery, rain fell, and the Looney Tunes, dressed in black, stood solemnly around a casket. Those gathered split down the middle, and a giant chicken dressed as a priest stepped forward.

"I say, I say, we are gathered here today."

Foghorn paused, choking back some tears.

"We are gathered here today to pay our respects to one of our fallen brothers, fallen but not forgotten."

Foghorn slammed his fist into the palm of his left hand. The other Tunes stood with their heads bowed in silence, their fingers interlocked behind their backs.

"The duck was a fine gentleman, do ya hear me, Lord? A fine gentleman, indeed." He looked up at the rafters of the stage.

The Tunes nodded in agreement.

Bugs Bunny was dressed as a widow, and he began to wail. "Why?" he cried. "Whyyyyy?" Then he fainted into the arms of Marvin the Martian.

Foghorn continued his eulogy.

"He wasn't a Southern Gentleman, Lord, nor a Baptist or a Lutheran. Come to think of it, he might have been a Jew or an Atheist, Lord, and if that's the case, Lord, I would ask of you, now, don't hold the latter against him, now ya hear."

The rain continued to pour onto the suited shoulders of those present. *Stetson had noted the quality of the set design and special effects. A spectacular graveyard, swamped with lifelike trees and a woodland backdrop, soaked in rain that fell from the rafters above the stage and made its way into some type of gutter system, just short of the orchestra's pit.*

Foghorn continued, "Does the duck's religious affiliation matter? No, dammit, it doesn't. Now, what matters is that he was killed in an act of terrorism, terror, I say, ism. Ism, Lord. So Lord, I ask you to beseech and condemn those responsible for this act of terror, lord, this act of terror and our collective hatred for all of types of isms. Punish them!"

The procession shouted its response, "Punish them."

Foghorn held his arms out and his body shook.

"We ask for retribution, Lord. For justice!"

"For justice," the procession yelled.

"We ask for the blood of our enemies to flow like the mighty river of the Ganges, or the Mississippi, Lord, I say I say, flow like one of those two rivers, Lord. Whichever river's bigger, Lord, I do not know at the moment, but that's besides the point."

"Besides the point," the procession yelled.

"Bring these poisonous perpetrators of incredulous injustice for, ahhh, for, until we have justice, Lord, what choices will we have but to seek our own brand of justice. I say, I say, our own brand of justice."

And the lights went down.

Stetson gulped at his Manhattan, which, he noted, was quite stiff. A pair of pleasant-looking brunettes in their mid-to-late thirties walked past. The lady nearest Stetson looked at him. Stetson smiled and raised his drink, feeling rather good about being noticed, and then he heard her whisper a bit too loudly to her friend something about a "ridiculous outfit" and "that doughy man." As the ladies continued making their exit, they laughed.

Stetson drank and told himself that maybe she was talking about a different doughy man in a ridiculous outfit. He looked over the room, searching for some other sad sod who may have been at the end of the lady's barbed remark. There was none.

Taking note of the time and realizing that he still had a few minutes before heading over to the dressing room, Stetson replayed more of the performance.

When the lights hit the stage again, the set had transformed into a mock courtroom. Marvin the Martian presided over the courtroom as judge. Below him, stage left sat the defendant, Roadrunner.

"Time for your closing arguments, gentlemen," Marvin said. "Prosecution first, please."

Wiley E. Coyote, wearing a nice grey suit, white shirt, and a thin black tie, stood and approached the jury. The jury consisted only of Bugs Bunny, who was sprawled across the empty wooden seats of the jury box like a pile of clothes strewn around the hamper in the room of a sixteen-year-old stoner.

The Coyote stood in front of Bugs and began miming his closing argument. He pointed at the roadrunner, then flapped his arms and shook his head back and forth, violently. Then he faked a heart attack, and after lying still for a moment he popped back up to his feet. Wiley, running, circled the stage three times, stopped again in front of Bugs' jury box, folded his arms across his chest and tilted his head. Then the Coyote returned to his seat.

Bugs looked out at the crowd and said, "Ehhh, I'll buy it."

"And now for the defense," Judge Martian said.

Elmer Fudd, wearing his usual hunting garb, approached the jury.

"Waydeez and gentumen of da jury. On da behalf of justice I pweed wit you to find the defendant innocent. He's no more guilty than I am of eating this tange-a-ween." Mr. Fudd then pulled a tangerine from his pocket, peeled and ate it. "I west my case, y'onor."

The honorable Judge Martian slammed his gavel and asked for the jury's decision.

Bugs hopped onto the railing of the jury box and began to pace. He scratched his head while he walked, his soft, fluffy feet silent against the ornamental railing of the jury box.

Stetson had noted the crowd's discomfort–they'd been quiet, and he noticed the shifting of shoulders and movement of heads and arms, the crowd seeming uncertain. The Tunes had been un-predictable up to this point, and so they were threatening. When the audience has trouble following logically, they are at the mer-cy of the performance. Their emotions exist to be manipulated. *The trick, Stetson had thought, was that they must not bewilder the audience, mustn't confuse or confound. If they went too far, they'd lose their edge and slide into the idiotic waters of absurdi-ty. Real and unpredictable, that was how you got them.*

A shotgun fell from the rafters above the stage, and Bugs snagged it from its free fall with deadly precision. He swung around towards the witness box and fired. The birdshot ripped through the Roadrunner's face in a burst. The bird's small purple head spray-ing pieces of brain and skull against the back of the witness stand, *her long, thin neck swaying coup-counter-coup and then crashing down onto the front of the stand. As the bird's mangled head came to rest, a chunk of skull and rubbery grey-matter dislodged and fell to the floor of the courtroom.*

Bugs yelled, "Guilty!" and then Wiley E. Coyote, Foghorn Leghorn, the honorable judge Marvin the Martian, and the rest in attendance leapt from their seats and yelled and whooped and hollered and applauded.

Stetson looked at his watch again, and he began walking towards the cast lounge, located down the hall from the main entrance of the theater, through a side door that opened on a hallway that ran adjacent to the stage and ended at a room about thirty feet from the stage. The lounge was connected to the backstage area of the theater by a small corridor.

Standing steadfast at the entrance to the hallway was Ray, the usher.

"Hey there, L.P.," Ray said.

"Hey."

"Well, what'd ya think?"

"I'm still trying to make sense of it," L.P. said. "You?"

"A bit heavy-handed, I thought," Ray said. "I woulda liked to have seen a few more of their traditional bits."

"Yeah." Stetson raised his glass and gave Ray a nod, and then he made his way down the hallway.

After the courtroom verdict, there was a long scene in which Sylvester and Foghorn, dressed as high-ranking military officers, Silver-Starred Generals, argued the pros and cons of pursuing terrorism with military force–specifically, whether or not you could ever kill enough people to kill an idea completely. The argument rose in a crescendo. The two generals ended up in a wrestling match, which was finished when Foghorn mounted Sylvester and strangled him. The last lines of the scene were Foghorn's, grim and with assured wickedness, "That's how you kill an idea."

The final scene of the night portrayed Yosemite Sam as the-embodiment-of-evil-type slave owner. The rest of the surviving cast were shackled, wrists and ankles, to the floor. Resting on their hands and knees, they faced the audience.

At this point people began walking out of the theater.

Yosemite Sam whipped one of the Tunes every time someone got up and left, as if right on cue.

"Oh, you can't take it?" he said.

Crack.

"Too much for ya? I see."

Crack.

"When will ya learn?"

Crack.

"Hurts don't it?"

Crack.

"You think I'm getting any pleasure outta tasting this par-tic-u-lar shit sandwich?"

Crack.

The tunes were writhing in agony. Their faces twisted and snarled from the pain of the lashes.

"If you aint gonna learn," Yosemite said. Crack. Crack. Crack. "Then I'm gonna have to keep teaching."

Crack.

Curtain.

No applause. Just mumbles, and the muted shuffles of disap-

pointed feet.

After Stetson knocked on the door to the cast's lounge, Foghorn's voice boomed out, "I say, whomever may be at the door, please, you are more than welcome to, ahh, come in, come in."

Stetson did just that. He walked into a room that was filled with his childhood idols. As he shut the door behind him, he tugged down on his hat–a quick adjustment.

The room was familiar. After all, he'd been there interviewing various actors, week after week, for the better part of a year.

There were four couches in the center, black, leather, that sat back-to-back, two-by-two. Three of the four walls were adorned with large mirrors, like those found in barbershops or backstage at strip clubs. Beneath the mirrors, countertops–white, enamel, uneventful. Tucked into the corner, to the right of the entrance sat an immaculately cared-for bar. Clean and fully stocked.

William Harrier believed that after the show the actors should be able to unwind a bit in the spirits of the adult playground. The bar was, plainly, the nicest and most well kept thing in the room.

"Now, ahh, what's your name?" Foghorn said, swirling a drink in his hand.

"Uhh, hi there, Mr. Leghorn. It's a real–"

"I asked for your name, boy. Your name." Foghorn said, turning to Sylvester, who was sprawled out on the leather couch nearest the door. "The boy don't know how to answer a simple question," Foghorn said, thumbing towards Stetson.

Sylvester waived him off. He was holding an icepack against his forehead.

"L.P. Stetson, Mr.–"

"Your full name, Boy, gimme your full name," Foghorn said. "I have no need nor desire for abbreviated introductions."

"Umm, Latimer Parnassus Stetson, Mr. Leghorn."

"Okay, well nice to meet ya, Latimer Parnassus Stetson. My name is Foghorn Dillinger Rockefeller Boone Leghorn, but you can call me Foghorn."

"You can call me Stetson."

"Okay, Stetson," Foghorn said. "What can I do for ya?"

"I'm the theater–"

"He's the theater critic you dumb fuckin' chicken," Bugs said. His interruption garnered a shot of disgust from Foghorn. Bugs lowered his head onto the enamel countertop and sniffed at a line of white powder through a twenty-dollar bill.

Foghorn whipped around.

"Now wait just a minute there, bunny," Foghorn said, his enormous frame towering over the seated rabbit. "How about you keep from jawing and sit there like the disgraceful, I say, disgraceful fucking junkie that you are."

Bugs slapped the countertop and bounced onto his feet, standing on the vanity's chair. He swiveled his hips and swung the chair around, standing now at an equal height to Foghorn.

Stetson took a seat next to the bar in the corner of the room and casually added a bit of whiskey to the melted remnants of his Manhattan. Stetson noted that the tension that he'd felt during the performance had failed to dissipate after the show.

"Oh, I see how it is," Foghorn said.

"Yeah, do ya?" Bugs said.

"You think 'cause you can look me in the eye now that you're tough?"

"Tough," Bugs said.

"Either that or that damn powder got your furry memory a bit shook from the last time I beat you, huh?" Foghorn said. "Beat him bad, too, ain't that right, boy?"

Bugs grabbed Foghorn behind the ears and planted a kiss on the rooster's beak. After the kiss, the bunny pulled away and slapped Foghorn.

"Damnit," Foghorn yelled. "You silly faggot."

He wound up and threw a series of punches at Bugs, but Bugs dodged them with ease, slickly, like Archie Moore in his prime.

Tweety and Marvin the Martian poked their heads up from the couch that backed up to where Sylvester lay. In the reflection of the far wall's mirror, Stetson saw that the pair were reading magazines and sharing a glass of white wine. They were a bit removed from the escalating situation.

"Would you two knock it off," Tweety said. "Can't we have just one night where you two don't get under each other's skin?"

Bugs bounced off his chair and onto the counter and walked over to Daffy Duck, two seats along the mirrored wall.

"Well," Foghorn said, "I'm tryna act civil, ya know, gentlemanly like." He pointed at Bugs, "but that damn–"

"There'th nothing thivil about calling him a faggot," Sylvester said.

"Well I'll be damned," Foghorn said. "Look at this, I say, look at this turncoat son-of-a-bitch. Siding with the drugged-up hippie."

Daffy, who looked far more exhausted than the rest of the Tunes, lifted his head off the counter. Stetson had assumed that Daffy had been napping.

"Don't you think it's a bit hypocritical for a lush like yourself, Foggy, to call names and point fingers?" Daffy said.

"So I'm the villain here?" Foghorn said. "We have transcended rhyme and reason, rhyme and reason here," shaking his head.

"You cannot possibly compare a dirty drug like cocaine to a cocktail, one of life's simplest pleasures. Sam, Sam, help me out he-ah."

Yosemite had been tossing playing cards into a hat on the floor. He and Fudd took turns. They sat to Stetson's right, two chairs down, and until now had been minding their own business.

"I'd say ol' Foggy has a point," Yosemite said. "Not all vices are creee-ated equal."

Stetson sipped his drink. He couldn't believe what he was witnessing, what was unfolding. He thought about a potential opener for the paper: *The only people that may hate the Looney Tunes more than the crowd in attendance for Saturday night's performance, a particularly dark and nonsensical show, may be the Tunes themselves.*

"Thank you, Sam," Foghorn said. "A voice of reason in–"

"Would you shut the fuck up already," Daffy said, the duck, apparently, at his limit. "I'm tired of that gaping hole you call a mouth."

Bugs stood, and he grabbed a pair of scissors from the make-up kit that lay open on the countertop. Stetson noted that Bugs looked wild, on a cusp of some-sort.

"Oh no," Foghorn said, holding his hands up, feigning fear. "The bunny wants to get real." He started laughing. "You gonna find out how real, real gets," Foghorn said, putting his fists up.

Wiley E. Coyote jumped up from the couch and, stepping into Bugs' path, tentatively restrained the rabbit.

"Wiley, don't get involved," Roadrunner pleaded. Her concern seemed marital, was marital, Stetson thought.

Wiley shot her a look, and she stopped honking. The Coyote held onto Bugs' wrists, pleading a bit with the rabbit to halt his aggression.

Foghorn laughed. Stetson drank, nervously.

"If yah can't, ahhh, manage the Coyote's muscles, bunny, you must be, I say, what hope can you possibly have against these?" He bobbed up and down, and threw a couple of quick punches.

The giant rooster was shadowboxing.

"I shouldn't even acknowledge your scummy presence, you low-life, you insignificant two-bit, I say, two-bit junkie," Foghorn said. "You ain't nothing but common trash. Your mother thumped her way through all the dick and jizz west of the Mississippi before you popped out."

Bugs lowered his head and began butting it into the Coyote's chest, his advances juiced by an imaginary needle of adrenaline.

"And then," Foghorn continued, "And then she discarded you, bunny, because, and trust me, I say, trust me on this one," bringing his hand to his chest in sworn testimony, "Because you are of no value, intrinsically, bunny. A thing to be discarded, over and over, again and again. Trash."

Bugs twisted his hands and then snapped them free from the clutches of the Coyote. He shoved Wiley E. into the side of the nearest couch, took three quick steps towards Foghorn, slipped to the inside of the rooster's haymaker, and stabbed Foghorn in the thigh with the pair of scissors.

"Owwwwwweeeeeee," Foghorn yelled. He grabbed the bunny's neck and began peppering his face with a series of short, stiff blows. A gash appeared. Blood began flowing out of the cut. Bugs' head snapped back, and his grey fur turned crimson.

Daffy stood, yelling, "That's enuff." He joined the melee, climbing onto Foghorn's back and bopping him over the head (bop-bop-bop). The bops did no damage, but they served to distract Foghorn enough that he released his grip on the rabbit's neck.

The others sat and watched. Stetson assumed that their mild interest in the altercation could be due to frequency–the broken record of familial altercation (thanksgiving dinner twice a week, every week, for fifty years).

Bugs and Daffy wrestled Foghorn to the ground. Punches flew, arms and legs flailed, and the fight began resembling a dust devil of limbs. Tumbleweed dotted with protruding extremities. The ball moved closer to Stetson, and as it approached he scooted his seat away from the action. Stetson was backed up against the bar. The fight moved closer yet again, and so Stetson stood and squeezed his body against the bar stocked with bottle after bottle of Gin, Whiskey, Vodka, mixers, etc.

An errant limb shot out of the cartoon ball and struck Stetson in the face. He wobbled and turned his head in hopes that he'd be able to disappear into the bar.

A rabbit's foot struck him. A solid shot this time, and he fell back into the bar. Bottles broke. Bottles crashed. Stetson's legs went limp. His hat fell from his head.

Sylvester, Elmer, Marvin, Yosemite, Tweety, Roadrunner, and Wiley E. Coyote gasped, as the contents of the bar seemed to explode into the corner of the lounge.

Stetson's eyes burned from the liquor that ran down his face, surprise and shock jolted his spine.

Foghorn lay on the ground two feet from Stetson, his mouth wide open in awe.

"I'd ask you if you were okay, there, boy," Foghorn said, "But it appears that you, that during the altercation there, that your head magically grew a vagina. Spontaneous Labi-uption!"

Sylvester started to snicker.

Stetson, still a bit dazed from the blow, didn't understand the reference until he felt his face, at the behest of Foghorn's pointing, and he felt his scar. Slightly drunk and dazed, Stetson reached for his hat that lay on the ground a few feet away.

"Now waaaiiiiit jus' a second there," Yosemite said, grabbing the hat from the floor and tossing it across the room to Sylvester. "Maybe we should call a doctor in to examine your parasitic face-intestine."

Stetson felt small.

"What in Sam hell is that thing anyways?" Yosemite said, leaning in for a closer look.

Bugs stood up and walked over to his post at the mirror, pulled a duffel bag from underneath the counter, and he started rummaging through a collection of costumes.

"Please," Stetson said, "Can I have," he swallowed, his mouth and throat felt parched and tasted of bile, "my hat," he finished. As he moved his hands over his scar, trying to cover it, Yosemite grabbed an arm and pulled it away.

"Don't stop the show jus' yet," Yosemite said, "We gonna git a doctor in here to ans-ah a few questions!"

"What?" Stetson said.

"I wanna know if I can fuck it?" Yosemite said.

"I want to know if after I fuck it, will it ecspechth me to call it in the morning?" Daffy said, his hand on his chin, staring in wonderment.

Foghorn and Daffy stood, their wrestling match now officially over.

"I, I just would like," Stetson said. He looked at the Tunes towering over him–deviant smiles waxed and waned on their faces, their eyes trained on the weakling before them. "My hat."

"Is it considered a homosexual act, I say, now, if you fuck a man's face-vagina? Does that make you queer?" Foghorn said.

"Only if you enjoy it," Marvin the Martian said, stepping into the semi-circle hovering around Stetson.

Bugs walked into the group wearing a doctor's coat, a stethoscope hung around his neck.

"Now, ehhh, what seems to be the problem, doc?" Bugs said, plugging the stethoscope's buds into his ears, and then pressing the drum onto Stetson's scar.

"Never mind," Bugs said. "I see it now."

Stetson eyes began to well.

"Yep. Your face-pussy is healthy," Bugs said.

"Can I fuck it, Doc?" Yosemite said.

Bugs nodded. The Tunes were all laughing now.

"It looks like the rebel leader, Kuato, from Total Recall," Sylvester said.

"Quaaaaaaaaaaid," Foghorn said, howling out the classic line from the sometimes coveted and often forgotten Schwarzenegger classic. He brought his arms tight to his sides, his fingers creeping out like the tentacles of an alien who was also an accomplished dancer of interpretive jazz.

"Quaaaaaaiiiiiid," Foghorn yelled, again.

Yosemite dropped his pants and approached Stetson.

"No," Stetson muttered. "Please. Stop."

"Quaiiiiiid," the Tunes all yelled, their laughter a collective howl.

"Hold still now," Yosemite said, and the tiny, old Southerner, naked from the waist down, hopped onto Stetson's head, his penis resting comfortably in the middle of Stetson's scar.

The Tunes fell to the ground, rolling with laughter.

"Qua-Qua-ah-ha-ha-ha"

"Qua-ha-aiiidddd"

Stetson began to weep, yet he remained quite still, almost disregarding the small, naked man thrusting atop his head. Stetson sobbed. Yosemite continued humping the plump scar, pointing at the other Tunes and flexing his biceps while laughing.

Stetson began to shake, and then he was bawling.

The laughter started to subside.

Yosemite dismounted.

Stetson cried.

The Tunes stopped laughing altogether now, and then they regarded each other. Stetson rested in shambles, his hands over his eyes, drool seeping from his open mouth. He existed, at that moment, in another place and time.

The room fell quiet. Only Stetson's sobs were heard.

Finally, Bugs broke the silence. "Hey, ehhh," Bugs said, tapping Stetson's knee. "We didn't mean nothing by it."

"Yeah, yeah," Sylvester said. "Just horthing around."

"Buck up, boy," Foghorn said.

Yosemite finished buckling his pants and apologized. "I just got caught up in the moment is all," he said. "Didn't mean nothing by it." Sylvester handed Yosemite the hat, and he placed it on Stetson's head. The grown man stopped crying. The Tunes continued to apologize effusively until Stetson had left, and then they turned their attention back to one another–the ribbing, the jokes, the insults.

Stetson exited the theater and stepped into the cool, dark summer evening. He passed through the parking lot, crossed Main Street, walked two more blocks, and turned left. Stepping carefully as his feet passed over cracks in the sidewalk, he made his way home under the soft glow of weak, flickering streetlamps from a bygone era.

Two days later, William Harrier's newspaper ran Stetson's article on the front page of the Missoulian, above the fold. The article started, "When I attended the fifth grade, at FDR Elementary, I was terrorized daily by a boy named Fitz Myron." The article never mentioned the theater, the performance, or the Looney Tunes. People paid attention to Stetson after that, and, much to his surprise, their intrigue had absolutely nothing to do with the hat that he had always worn.

COCINEROS

"Fucking Simón's late again," Drew said, looking at his watch. A ticket started to print, errr, errr, errr–burger, mid-rare, side of fries. Drew read the time-stamp on the ticket, "Eleven-oh-two. That fucker." The restaurant opened at 11:00a.m. Drew was always pissed at the first ticket of the day, regardless of when it came in.

I reached into the lowboy, unwrapped a half-pound, pre-formed patty from its 38-degree drawer and threw the burger on the grill. "He'll get here," I said, "always does." Drew was at the beginning stages of making our in-house salsa. He had all of the ingredients laid out at the ready, jalapeños, tomatoes, garlic, etc., but he hadn't actually started anything yet because he kept getting distracted by the sound of his own voice. Drew was a manager, and what he managed to do, mostly, was talk.

"He probably spent the whole night driving around selling that shit to all the fucking amigos," Drew said. "That's why he can't get here on time, man, I swear."

I grabbed our in-house seasoning (a blend of salt, sugar, and chili pepper) and doused the patty with enough mix to extinguish a small brush fire.

"Whatever, man," I said. "You know he closes down Vine's after he gets out of here, and they don't stop service until midnight."

The printer errr-ed out another ticket–burger, mid-well w/fries, and two chicken sandwiches w/side salad/ranch–and I hung the ticket on the rail. I opened the low-lowboy, grabbed the pair of tongs that hung on the railing of the oven, plucked two boneless skinless, butterflied chicken breasts from the nine pan, sprayed the grill with a bit of oil, slapped the breasts down onto the fire, kicked the low-low closed, opened the burger drawer, unwrapped a patty and threw it on the grill next to the birds.

"Bullshit, dude," Drew said. "You don't know?"

"Know what?" I said, walking over to the fryer and grabbing three handfuls of fries. I dropped the fries into the mesh basket, and then headed back to the grill where I seasoned the three pieces of protein that I'd just laid down. Drew cut the ends off of one Roma tomato–the first of forty sitting in the 12 quart in front of him.

"Man, I'm telling you, Simón sells cocaine, man," Drew said.

"No way."

"Dude, fuck yeah he does. I've seen that shit go down."

"What do you mean you've seen it?"

"Man, I've seen that motherfucker talking to some sketchy ass dudes in the parking lot after work. Like, and I know, I know, I just know, because I used to be big into that shit."

I flipped the first burger and then dropped the basket of fries into the oil.

"Man, that doesn't mean shit," I said.

"Bullshit, man," Drew said, pointing his knife at me instead of the skin of another tomato. "I'm telling you, that fucker sells cocaine. I promise you."

"The guy works like 90 hours a week, man, when the fuck

would he have the time to sell cocaine?"

I pulled four buns from the stainless steel shelf above the make-line and built them up with some good-looking LTOPs (lettuce, tomato, onion, pickle). The printer made its incessant noise again, errr, errr, errr. Chx Ten/FF/R. I walked down to the freezer at the end of the line and grabbed four pre-made, frozen chicken tenders from the hastily ripped plastic bag that rested on the middle shelf. Walking back towards the fryer, behind Drew, I dropped the tenders into another basket, submerged the basket into the oil, pulled up the basket of fries that I'd had going for tickets one and two, slammed the basket against the backstop of the fryer (forcing extra oil to spray off the fries), threw them into a bowl, added seasoning, tossed the bowl and fries around, plated the fries for ticket number one, grabbed my turner, flipped ticket number two, plated number one, topped the burger, grabbed the first ticket, walked back behind Drew, slid the burger into the window, and hit the bell.

Ding.

"Look at that car he drives, man," Drew said. "You can't tell me that thing doesn't scream drug money."

Drew was referring to Simón's Lexus.

"I mean, yeah. Okay. I'll give you that much." The car was sick. It had tints, a system, slick rims, nothing ugly, smooth, proper, and clean.

"See, man," Drew said. "There's just some shit that doesn't add up. And he always looks fucking so high when he gets here, man, his eyes are all red, and he's always sniffing back man. That's the drip. I used to do a lot of that shit, man, and I know when someone's kicking back a drip. I know that much."

I plated the fries for order number two, grabbed the three

pieces of protein off the grill with the turner, topped the buns, spun together a quick side salad with ranch, hit the bell, tossed the tenders in the bowl, plated the tenders and fries, grabbed a ranch, hit the bell, walked behind Drew, grabbed the two tickets from the rail, walked back behind Drew, threw the tickets in the general direction of the window and hit the bell again.

"I don't," I said, "I don't see it."

"They're all into some shit," Drew said.

"Who is?"

"Man, fucking Mexicans!" Drew said.

Simón was Guatemalan, but I didn't bring it up because it would have fallen on deaf ears.

One of the surly, daytime servers walked up to the window and begrudgingly grabbed the tickets and began plating her tray. Daytime servers were always pissed they worked days because days were slower, and slower meant less money. But daytime servers were also pissed when they had to work nights because the restaurant was busy, and when the restaurant was busy they had to work harder. Daytime servers believe in this strange equation that they deserve maximal income with minimal effort. A lot of people around here think they are better than what they're doing, so they view mild inconveniences as egregious transgressions.

"You forgot a ranch," she said. She was new. I didn't remember her name.

"Sorry," I said, opening the lowboy next to the window and slapping the ramekin of ranch on the counter. Drew was staring at her, his eyes filled with contempt. She walked away, and I started scraping down and seasoning the grill. Drew turned to me.

"What a fucking bitch," he said. "And dude, don't fucking apologize to her, man, who the fuck is she? Fucking slut. She probably looks that beat up from all the fucking dick she takes, big fucking hogs too, nailing her around the eyes, fucking her face up."

Drew started laughing and slapping his own face with limp hands as if they were giant dicks. I oiled up the grill and smiled. He was a complete asshole but also kind of funny in that sick and twisted, hate-filled kind of way.

Maria, the bartender, poked her head into the kitchen and said, "Guys, we just sat two ten tops, two six tops, and the patio just filled up so get ready for it." This was lunch, on a Thursday.

"Goddamnit," Drew said, as if this wasn't the job. "I'm never going to get this fucking salsa done. Where the fuck is Simón?"

"I don't know, man?" I said. "What do you want, grill or fry?"

"I'll take the *fucking* fryer," he said.

The printer started making its errrs, and it didn't stop for a while. Life during a rush looks like this 2CB/FF/R, 6CHX/3SS/3FF/6R, 4CT/FF/R, 6CB/86 TOM&ON/FF/R, APP PLATE, CB/SS/R side of CHED "CHEDDARONTO," but for two hours at a time.

I stared at that last ticket and looked at Drew.

"Dude, what the fuck is a Cheddaronto?"

"What?"

"This ticket," I said, laughing, holding it up to Drew, "says Cheddaronto."

Drew turned and yelled, "Maria!"

Maria poked her head into the kitchen. "Yes," she said.

"What's the new girl's name?" Drew said. "Never mind, it doesn't fucking matter. Get the new girl back here."

"Gina," Maria said. "Hold on."

Gina walked into the kitchen, "Yeah," she said.

"What the fuck is this?" Drew said, pointing at the ticket.

"What?"

"What the fuck is Cheddaronto?" Drew said.

"Oh, I wrote 'cheddar on tots.' There must not have been enough room or something."

"Oh my god," Drew yelled. "The next time you have some stupid fucking request, please, just walk back here and tell us, so I don't have to decipher the fucking ticket like it's some sort of hieroglyphic pyramid, I'm not Gandalf, alright, I don't have a fucking wand."

"Excuse me?" Gina said.

"I'm not a fucking magician," Drew said. "Do you see a wand in my hand?"

I was praying that she didn't try to answer that question.

"When you modify something, come back here and let us know exactly what you want, okay, your job isn't that fucking hard."

Drew was being pretty harsh on her, which, honestly, was Drew's style.

"Now go back to your tables," Drew said.

Gina walked out of the kitchen, clearly frustrated. I would have been too. Drew hung the ticket back on the rail and said, "Cheddaronto, I'll show you a fucking cheddaronto," grabbing his crotch and smiling. "Seriously, man, you don't think I will?"

"Please don't whip your cock out."

"I'll do it, man," Drew said, beaming.

Ten minutes later I looked at the rail, there were two tickets left hanging. It was the end of the rush, close to one-thirty. I asked Drew if I could go smoke, and he nodded. He was still steamed about the whole cheddar on tots thing. I knew he was still steamed because he hadn't shut up about how stupid Gina was and how many dicks she probably sucked every day, since their interaction.

I walked out the back door and lit a cigarette. Took a couple of drags. It was quiet out back, and the breeze felt fresh compared to the salty, hot confines of the kitchen. I watched Simón turn into the lot in his black Lexus. Simón had the windows down and was bumping some Spanish crooner music that featured a heavy dose of tuba. I leaned against the building, nodding my head at Simón as he parked his car in the space directly in front of me. He left the car running and got out.

"Qué onda, guey?" he said.

"Nada amigo," I said. "Tranquilo."

Simón had this piece of toilet paper sticking out of his left nostril.

"What's up con eso?" I said, pointing at his nose.

"No sé. Fucking bullshit." Simón pronounced bullshit like, boo-chit.

"Is Drew mad?"

"Yeah amigo," I said. "Cuidado."

"Okay," he said, sticking his fist out.

We bumped fists, and he walked inside. I took a drag off my smoke and looked around the parking lot. Simón's car was definitely the nicest. I didn't have a car, but if I did I'd want it to look like Simón's. A few minutes passed. They were good, quiet minutes. The chaotic churn of service was the yardstick by which life in this kitchen was measured, and moments of peace were found out back, in the parking lot, in the time that spanned the length of one cigarette.

Simón came back outside as I was finishing my smoke.

"Fucking bullshit," he said.

"What happened?"

"Terminado."

"Seriosa?"

"En *serio*," Simón said, correcting my Spanish.

"Damn, amigo." I shook my head. "Lo ciento."

Simón shrugged his shoulders, and then his phone began to ring. He took the phone out of his pocket and said, "Hola." He looked at me, "Sí, a, one second, please." He held the phone out for me to take, and he said, "Please, hablas. Por fa."

"Who is it?" I asked.

"El doctor."

I took the phone. "Hello." The voice on the other end said, "Hello, I'm calling from Doctor Snyder's office, and I'm trying to confirm an appointment today for Simón Nuñez."

"One second," I said, pulling the phone away from my mouth. "Ellos quieren confirmar your appointment para–"

I put the phone back to my ear. "When's the appointment for?" I asked.

"Mr. Nuñez has an appointment for 4:00pm, today."

"Para las quatro, hoy," I said to Simón.

"Sí, necesito cambiar."

"Hi there," I said.

"Yes."

"Mr. Nuñez is wondering if he can reschedule his appointment today, for–" I looked at Simón, "Quando?"

"Oh, no importa. Dos semanas. Tres."

"Could he reschedule for two or three weeks from today?"

"Okay," she said. "Does the 17th work?"

"El dies y siete?" I asked.

"Sí, está bien."

"That will work just fine," I said.

"Okay, thank you. Tell Mr. Nuñez that we'll see him on the 17th at 4:00p.m."

"Okay, bye."

"Goodbye."

I handed the phone back to Simón.

"Thank you, guey," he said.

"Yeah, man. Sin problema."

"I already cancellar, like, tres veces, three other times."

"Oh yeah?"

"Sí," Simón said. "No quiero que piensen que soy pajero."

"They wouldn't think you're a liar. People cancel that shit all the time, no big deal."

"Okay, guey," Simón said as he getting back into his car. "Thank you."

"Si, amigo. Sin problema. Why couldn't you go?"

"Fucking ir al otro trabajo, very busy tonight, mucha gente."

"Okay, amigo. Maybe I'll see you later. Give me a call or tex-to."

"See you," Simón said.

He pulled the car out of the spot, turned the music up, and sped out of the parking lot. I walked back inside. There were no tickets hanging from the rail, I opened the lowboy below the grill and took a look at the depleted ranks of uncooked meat.

"You fired him?" I asked Drew.

"Had to, man. Did you see him? Fucker's nose was all bloody probably from snorting fucking lines all night. Can't do that shit and then show up three hours late and expect not to get fired."

"True," I said. "I'm gonna stock some stuff up."

"Okay," he said.

I closed the lowboy, and as I passed Drew on my way to the walk-in, I saw him cutting the ends off of his second tomato.

Around 4:00p.m, the guys working the dinner shift started trickling into the kitchen. They made themselves some food, darted out of the kitchen to eat a quick meal, and then reappeared fifteen minutes later smelling like a combination of Red Bull, weed, and cigarettes. I told them that Drew had been in the office meeting with the owners for about two hours, and that he'd fill them in on the night when he came back. I told them he fired Simón.

"Balls," Nick said. "That means one of us is going to have to start working more fucking mornings."

Geoff and Mickey mumbled something to show solidarity with Nick's disapproval of the possibility of more early shifts. I told them to have a good shift, and, almost in unison, they told me to go fuck myself.

After clocking out, I started drinking at the bar. Shot and a beer. Shot and a beer. I've always preferred establishments that pay you to work, and then, when you're off the clock, let you give back the money you just earned. Day shifts that turn into a seven-hour drinking session have the tendency to make me feel like I'm winning, losing, and breaking even all at once. I blew through my day's pay with a determined zeal. Losing. Gina, the cute-enough new server, grabbed a seat next to me and started pounding margaritas. Winning. Shift beers turned into an open tab with Gina, who, predictably, looked much more attractive as the afternoon turned into the evening and surface-level pleasantries flowed into deeper conversation, fed by a shared desire to establish a connection, quickly. Breaking even.

Sometime after ten while Gina and I were out back smoking one thing led to another, and we wound up in her car and then she blew me in the parking lot. I was too drunk to focus on her or admire her technique, so I just leaned back in the worn, black leather seat of her pickup and stared off across the lot, at the cars, the restaurant, and the moonless night sky. Her head bobbed up and down, in and out of my peripheral. Her hand felt cold against my penis, and I wondered how heavily she smoked and if she suffered from poor circulation. The parking lot was dark, and I could barely make out the smoke billowing up from the hood vents that jutted up from the roof of the building, above the kitchen. I wondered how the night guys had handled service. I grabbed Gina's hair and felt the swell of elation mutilate my senses for exactly three seconds—a moment of clarity in the midst of boozy confusion. She swallowed, wiped the corner of her mouth with the back of her hand, and then told me she thought I was cute. I laughed and asked her if she said that to all the guys. She smiled like a cat that'd just caught a sparrow and said, "Maybe."

A Tribe Called Quest was playing on her stereo, and we smoked a couple of cigarettes and talked. She seemed like a good girl, maybe too good. She was in school, had a dog, and talked about her future with an ease and certainty that made me shift uncomfortably in my stupor. I heard my sister's voice on the phone, "Of course she seemed cool to you, she bought you drinks and blew you in the parking lot while you guys listened to hip-hop." I wondered if that made me shallow and obvious, and then I forgot about it. She gave me her number and said goodnight. As I walked across the lot to the bar, I heard the hesitant revving of an engine as Gina drunkenly pulled out of her parking space and made her way to the street. I glanced over my shoulder as she hung a right out of the lot, heading, I imagined, home. Another conquest that was sure to lead nowhere and mean nothing, ending before it began, like all the others, land lost to apathy before ever being truly explored.

It wasn't ten minutes later, after another shot and half of my new beer, that I got a text from Simón. "Dónde?" was all that it said. I told him I was still at the restaurant, and that I needed to go home. I drank and waited for his response. He said he was off work in fifteen, and that he'd pick me up. I finished another beer and smoked a cigarette before he arrived.

I could hear the Simon and Garfunkel blasting from Simón's car before he turned the corner. Simón loved Simon and Garfunkel, Leonard Cohen, and Hall and Oates, aside from all the mariachi and romantic shit that he listened to. I hopped into shotgun, and slapped Simón's hand.

"Qué onda, amigo?"

"Fucking boracho," I said. "Drunk."

"Dónde están las chicas?" he said, as he put the car in gear and floored it. When he hit the gas the car lurched, and my stomach reeled. I thought about telling him to take it easy on the Jimmy Johnson shit with me being this drunk, and that I didn't want to hurl anywhere in the vicinity of such a nice car, but I couldn't think of the words in Spanish, so I forgot about it.

"You just missed 'em," I said.

"No más?"

"You see any with me right now?" I opened my arms and looked around the car just to make sure I hadn't hidden any women in the back seat when I got in. Simón started laughing.

"Ahhhh, s'okay," he said. "Quieres ir a la casa? Home?"

"I don't know, man. I should. Fucking voy a abrir el restaurant mañana. I've got to open that shit tomorrow."

Simón started shaking his head, smiling, and then he rattled off a slew of obscenities in Spanish followed by the refrain from Scarborough Fair.

"Puto mierda pinche restaurante parsley sage ros-a-merry and thy-me."

I started laughing.

"You're fucking funny, man. I mean it."

"No, Charlie, you," he said.

"No man, I'm drunk, you're funny. There's a difference."

"Okay, Chaaaaaaaa-lie," Simón said, turning onto Paradise Ln. a nice, wide, six lane road that split Millville, north/south. He slammed on the gas, shifted from second to third, and before I knew it we were doing sixty.

"You want come to mi casa?" Simón asked. "No hay fiesta grande, pero mis amigos tienen cervezas. Small party."

"I don't know, man," I said.

I thought about it for a second, picturing myself opening the kitchen in the morning with bloodshot eyes, the same clothes as the day before, no shower, Gina's lipstick caked to my dick, hung over, or, more likely, still drunk. I watched as tomorrow me flipped on the lights, unwrapped everything from the walk-in, set up and stocked the line–a routine I'd done thousands of times. I saw tomorrow me operating on autopilot. Working. Getting through the day without concern for the one that came before it or the one that would come after.

"Yeah, fuck it. Let's fiesta."

"Okay, Chaaaaaa-lie," Simón said, and he slapped my thigh.

I'd been to Simón's house before, or, at least, I'd seen the outside of it from his car. I knew he lived with his brother, Victor, but he never told me that there were nine of them living in that two bedroom house. When we walked in, he briefly introduced me to everybody out in the backyard and then gave me the grand tour. Each room had two bunk beds, like the kind Irene, my sister, and I had when we were kids. When we got to the living room, Simón explained that the couch folded out and that was where Miguelito slept–Miguel, the youngest of the crew was a slender, hundred-and-twenty-pound-soaking-wet kid from El Salvador.

Christmas lights bordered the frame of each window throughout the house, lending a festive vibe to the whole place. A random thought about fire safety struck me, but I didn't bring it up. The house was a house like any other I'd ever seen in Millville, a small, ranch-style home with a nice back yard. The guys were hanging out back. Simón grabbed a couple of Modelos from the fridge, and we walked outside.

Discarded aluminum soldiers were scattered about underneath and beside each chair. Everybody was pretty drunk, myself included. Simón, it seemed, was the only guy who looked or could be considered sober. I recognized Simón's brother, Victor, and said, "Que onda, Victor?"

"Oh! El pinche güero habla español?" one of the guys yelled, and everybody started laughing.

"Claro," I said. "Pero, solamente un poquito." I held up my fingers, showing them exactly how much Spanish I spoke.

Simón grabbed a couple of extra chairs, and we slid into the group. I had caught their names at the beginning–Nico, Tomás, Edgar, Miguel, the small guy with a Mohawk, Victor, and they mentioned the two guys that were still at work–but right after they'd told me, I'd already forgotten who they were or where they worked.

We had been drinking for a couple of hours. Music was playing off one of the guys' phones through the Bluetooth speaker that rested on top of a case of beer in the center of the pack. It turned out that it was Nico's last night in the US. After fourteen years of working two jobs in the States, he was heading home for good. Conversation melted from one topic to another with natural ease, like we'd all been friends for years.

We had covered countries of origin (Colombia, Mexico, Guatemala, El Salvador, and Panama), coyote stories (three day walks across the border, evading agents and patrolmen, linking up with rides to anywhere and everywhere in the US), soccer teams (club, CONCACAF, Barcelona, Real Madrid, the upcoming World Cup), restaurants we'd worked at over the years, cities that they had worked in (NYC, LA, San Francisco, Houston, Minneapolis, Chicago), hot newscasters on Univision, girlfriends, wives, children, the state of boxing, World War Two, North, Central, and South American Politics, and just as we were getting into the subject of immigration, one of the guys, I think it was Tomás, pulled out a little baggie, opened it, took out his set of keys, dipped a key into the baggie, brought the key up to his nose, and he sniffed back a bump of what I was soon to find out was good fucking cocaine.

Each guy took two bumps out of the bag, one for each nostril, and when it was passed to me I did the same. A shock of electricity hit my head, first, moved down into my chest where I felt its heat, and then it grew up from my chest back into my eyes. I felt a switch flip and my thoughts and sight went from transient and malleable to solid and focused.

"Wow," I said.

"Te gusta?" One of the guys asked.

"Yeah man," I said, passing the bag over to Simón. "Si, está bien. Muy, muy bien."

Everybody laughed, and one of the guys said something to the effect of crazy white boy. Simón passed the bag to Miguel who took his two bumps and kept the rotation alive. I lit another cigarette, cracked open another beer, leaned back in my plastic chair and took a deep breath. Two bumps were all it took, and I felt beyond sober. Empowered. Lifting a beer to my lips became a secondary motion to lifting the key to my nose. The bag moved quickly around the circle, and before I knew it it was my turn again and again. When the first bag was finished, Thomás pulled a second one out of his pocket and then a third.

"What was I saying before?" I said.

"About immigracion," Simón said.

A couple of the guys were having side conversations in Spanish of which I was tuning in and out the way somebody eavesdrops on a phone call happening next to them at a café.

"Yeah yeah," I said. "Si the problem y lo ciento if mi español es terrible, ummm, but the problem is la majoridad de las personas no recuerden que ellos estan immigrantes tambien. They don't remember because too much time has passed. Eso es una pais de los immigrantes but people forget that because some of them of them they, uh, they think that they aren't. Their families have been here for too many generations and they think that somehow they're different from los immigrantes que vienen aqui ahorita."

The baggie came my way again, and I sniffed at the key.

"But why," one of the guys asked, "why do they hate us?"

"They don't hate you," I said. "They're just stupid."

"Pero," he said, and then he blazed through a couple of sentences to Simón of which I didn't understand.

"If there's nobody to do the work," Simon said, "then why make it so hard for people to come work?"

"I don't know," I said. "It shouldn't be. But you have to understand I think that the greatest lie ever told was that this country was about something other than making money, at all costs. Forget all the shit about moral high ground and freedom and all that bullshit that el gobierno likes to talk about. This country is about making fucking money, and that's all it's about, making money and apparently war, never-ending war."

I trusted Simón with the translation of what I'd said, and when he relayed it to the guys they seemed to take my powder-fueled tirade in stride.

"You know," I continued, "every country has problems, and we're no different. We have a shitload of problems. But, I don't know, I mean, we're all making money here, right?" The drip slid down the back of my throat and I shook my head.

The baggie came around again, and I took my bump. The powder bit into my face like a needle. I felt it in the back of my nose, then behind my eye, and the sharp burn settled into the center of my head for what seemed like two minutes but was probably only fifteen seconds. I passed the baggie to Simón. With my left hand, still holding my beer, I rubbed my left eye. My eye watered until the pain subsided.

"Whoa," I said, shaking my head back and forth. "That shit has some bite."

Simón passed the baggie to his left, and the conversation turned away from whatever it was we'd been talking about to a series of random moments, which I cannot exactly remember.

There was talk about money, of which I didn't have any, and Simón pulled out a couple of twenties and handed it to one of the guys. There was talk about changing the music, when I said that we should change the music, but that idea went to conference and, aside from me, was unanimously voted down.

I had lost the focus that I'd had earlier, and I found myself drowning in and out of the conversations, as if I was watching a movie and kept falling asleep, intermittently. Simón had caught me gazing off into space a couple of times and asked me if I was okay, to which I replied with a toothy grin and an emphatic, "Tranquilo." In what had to have been an incoherent mess, I told the guys of my family's own history, my grandfather's immigration, how he'd come from Ireland to the States, how he'd met my grandmother, how he'd worked at The Mill for thirty years, put my mother through college, and then promptly died of a heart attack at 50. How I still felt connected to the land my grandfather left, although I'd never been there. I tried to explain the meaning of the expression "blue collar to blue collar in three generations." After I'd lost my train of thought for the twentieth time, however, I decided to shut up for a while.

The bag came around again, and I took a bump, and again it seared some part of flesh in the back of my nose, in between my eyes, but even harder than before. My eyes were shut as I passed the bag to Simón. I drank from my beer and lit another cigarette. I watched the smoke drool from the tip of my cigarette and in the distance, behind the trail of smoke, I noticed that the sun had partly risen and was tacked on the edge of the horizon like a brilliant lemon wedge.

"Shit," I said. "What time is it?"

Simón looked at his watch.

"Son las seis," he said.

"Fuck, dude, I have to work in three hours."

"You okay?" he said.

"Yeah, man. Estoy bien."

The baggie came my way again, and I took another key bump. The bump made me cringe. Everything went blurry for a second, and I heard Simón say something. It was too quiet to understand.

"What?" I said.

He responded again but I didn't hear him.

"What?" I said, again.

"That's it, Charlie," he said. "That's it, no more. Finito."

"Okay," I said. "Finito. That's it."

"Done."

"Yeah, man. I'm done."

"Seguro?"

"Si, guey," I said. "Seguro. Man, that last shit bit so much harder than the stuff we were doing earlier."

A couple of the guys started talking.

"Es diferente," Nico said. "Cómo se dice, Simón?"

"It's crystal," Simon said. "Diferente."

I sat back in my chair, my arms loose at my side, and I tried to comprehend what the fuck they meant by different. I looked around at the guys. Everybody was laughing, talking. The pink and yellow light of the early morning spilled through the trees in the back of Simón's yard, and I tried focusing on each face before me, but with every passing second that I stared, cheeks and eyes grew puffy and bulbous. I realized that I was high out of my mind and might as well just gaze off into the distance and smoke another cigarette.

My thoughts wandered as I smoked and smoked, and I over-heard the guys talking about their families back home, their kids, their farms, their wives, brothers and sisters, and their plans for the future. I lifted my head from my shoulder as Nico was telling Edgar about how excited he was to go home, to Colombia. He spoke of his plans to open a music school and spend time with his children. Nico pulled out his phone and passed it around the circle. When it came to me, I looked at the three little faces on the screen–his wife, and their two daughters. The girls were striking poses like seven-year-old girls do, arms and legs flailing, mouths roaring, and his wife stood in the middle of the girls, smiling, her long brown hair hung over her shoulder across her chest in a braid. I managed to tell him that they were beautiful before passing the phone over to Simón. I tried thinking about my plans, my future, but all I could muster was to take my pack of cigarettes from my pocket, find my lighter, light one, and smoke as I watched the sun crest, fully, from behind the trees, in all of its beauty. And for that moment that was, and had to be, enough.

Nico had been gone from the circle of chairs in the yard for I don't know how long, and when he returned to his seat he was holding an accordion and wearing a patterned black and white hat, both of which made me chuckle for some incomprehensible reason aside from being the last two things I would have expected to see then and there. Nico sat on the edge of his chair, propped the accordion on his knee, looked straight at me and said, "Güero, listen."

He started to tell me a story about the music of his family. He explained that the waters of two rivers, the Cesár and the Guatapurí, flowed through the city of his birth. His city was called Valledupar, and the music of his family was called Vallenato. "It was only by chance," he said, "that Vallenato music came to feature the accordion." Generations ago in the days of his grand-father's father, a ship transporting various goods through the region of La Guajira, headed to Argentina, supposedly, fell victim to a tumultuous storm and sunk into the bed of one of the rivers, near the coast of the Caribbean. The goods, from the bowels of the capsized ship, flowed downriver, traveling twenty, fifty, one hundred miles, no one knows exactly how far. In some places jewels washed up along the shores of the river, and in others weapons and gold. But on a set of rocks in the Guatapurí, a series of wooden crates had traveled further than any of the jewels, weapons, or gold, and when the villagers fished the crates from the river and broke them open they discovered that inside each crate was an accordion. "It had seemed," he said, "that the destinies of Valledupar and the accordion were as intertwined as the fibers of my Sombrero"–his Vueltiao. And then Nico pulled his arms apart, and the accordion showed its colors like a peacock beckoning to a captive audience.

I'd never understood the accordion until I heard Nico play, and I'd never heard a singer, I mean a true singer, until I heard Nico. His fingers lit buttons and danced across the keys with a simple grace. His voice bellowed, crisp and strong, and he seemed to sing in all octaves and pitches. When it was time for the chorus, he puffed out his chest and let the words glide out half-open lips. And when he pitched high, Nico slowed the movements of his arms and hands, and the accordion became almost silent, a nearly imperceptible accompaniment to the delicate vocals. I was dumbstruck. I tried to remember if I had ever heard anything as beautiful in my life, and I couldn't come up with an answer. The tears burned my eyes, as if a callous had been removed and the tender flesh beneath had been revealed. The tempo grew faster, Nico's voice rose to a boom, the instrument writhing under the force of his hands. The sound was incredible, inescapable. And then just as quickly as he had started, Nico stopped. For a moment, we were all silent.

"Esa," Nico said, taking a deep breath of morning air in through his nose. "Esa, es la musica de mi familia."

I couldn't find the words. I had nothing to say, so I walked over to Nico and nodded. He looked me in the eyes and shook my hand.

Then it was time to leave, and Simón helped me get to the car. I sunk into the stiff, shiny seat of his Lexus, and when he turned the key Simon and Garfunkel came blasting out of the speakers. The boxer. We made a couple of turns, and then we pulled into a gas station. Simón handed me a coffee. I sipped at it as we made our way down Paradise, North, back towards the restaurant.

"I'm surprised you can drive so well after a night like that," I said, although I'm pretty sure the words fell out of my mouth, languidly. My head was slumped to the side, and I watched as we zipped by strip malls and used car lots, banks and fast food joints.

"No me gustan las drogas," Simón said. "Just a little cerveza."

"What? I was passing that bag to you all night."

"Sí," he said, "but I passed it. Solamente passed."

"Come on. Seriously?"

"En serio," he said. "No me gusta."

We pulled into the parking lot behind the restaurant where my days always seemed to begin and end. As I turned to Simón to tell him to take it easy, I noticed that he had another wad of toilet paper plugging up his nostril.

"Are you going to go see a doctor for that?" I said, pointing at his nose.

"Not today," he said. "Necessito buscar otro trabajo."

"You need to get that shit checked out, man. That's not normal, might even be more important than finding a new job right now, comprende?"

"Si, Charlie," he said. "Claro."

I thanked him for the night and the ride, and I stumbled towards the back entrance to the kitchen. As I approached the door, I had a feeling that I'd been gone from this place for a measly five minutes, the span of a cigarette. I opened the door and walked into the kitchen.

"You look like shit!" Drew said. He was standing near the dish tank, talking on the phone. "Clock in, grab some coffee, do whatever you have to, and then let's open this bitch. The fucking new guy I hired is already late. He was supposed to be here at eight, what kind of shit is that? Fucking Simón, man. He totally fucked me yesterday and now today. What a dick."

I stared at Drew for a second, without speaking, and then I walked over to the computer and punched in my employee number. The printer erred out my time stamp. 9:15a.m. I was late. As I poured myself a cup of coffee, I considered the hand that I'd been dealt and whether or not, someday, I'd start playing.

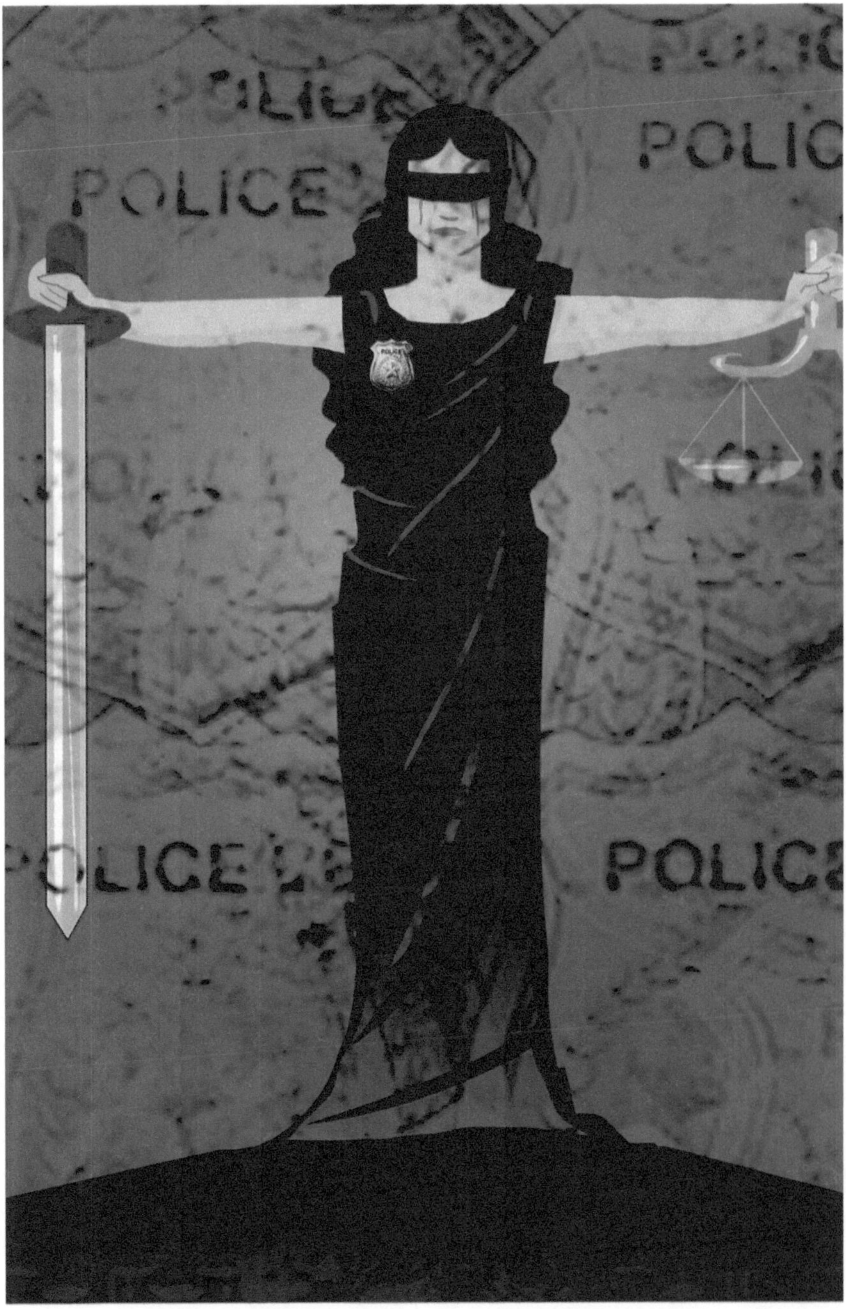
POLICE

RANK

Back before I made Detective, it was Officer Canela. That was about seventeen, eighteen years ago. And no, if you're asking, they haven't flown by. I feel every bit older. The kids are all grown up, Eddie and Teresa. My wife, Nancy, she's older. Nancy looks good though, you know? She's kept it together. Still hits the gym in the mornings with me, which I appreciate. Too many guys in the force let themselves go once they get past fifty. Not me. And I admit I'm pretty happy that Nancy has joined me on this whole staying healthy kick we've been on for a few years. We're a pretty good unit as a family. Nobody hates each other, and I'm thankful that we've been blessed to have it as good as we do—a good mix of making the right decisions for the family and the coin flipping our way with all that.

Nancy still doesn't like the work that I do, but she knows I'm only a few years away from my pension. It wouldn't make sense to quit until I've hit my thirty. She's got sense like that—can tell when someone in the family is making the right move for everybody, all of us. Plus Teresa's off at Penn, and even with the loans we qualified for that's taking a stack out of the mattress. Eddie's still got a couple of years left at home before he flies the coop. He'll probably get a scholarship somewhere anyways, and I promise you I have no idea where the kid got the brains. I'm not saying that Nancy and I aren't smart. I mean, I read The Daily and Nancy teaches, but still, Eddie, he's playing with a stacked deck.

I've always had a pretty natural disposition for police work, I guess. There wasn't really ever a calling, though, not like you see in movies. I didn't grow up thinking that I wanted to be police, nothing like that. I grew up thinking I wanted to be a jazz player. Piano. With my hand to God, I used to love the sounds of The Duke–he was the best. After playing as a kid, and in some mix-matched bands in high school and that sort of thing, it was pretty obvious that I was never going to be a jazz musician. I never figured myself as too serious a guy, but hey, it is what it is. I still like listening, though.

When I got out of high school, I already had Nancy. We got married straight out, and my father asked me what I was going to do for work. I told him I didn't know, so I went and worked construction for about seven years. Made some good money in that time, but man oh man those were some tough years. We didn't have the kids yet, thank God. I would've been too tired to pay any attention to them if we had. Then Nancy took a look at me one morning, towards the end, and she saw me lying in bed, and I must have looked something real awful because she said, "Honey, I think it's time you gave it up." She always had a good sense for what we needed to do to keep it together, the two of us.

So that's when I decided to become a police. Went through the academy and all that. Got assigned to a beat. This was back when you'd walk the beat. Not everybody had cars yet–especially not in Philly. You didn't need them. I had that beat for about, oh, I don't know, five or six years maybe. Good beat. I spent my days walking through Queen Village along the Delaware River. Even in the eighties, with all the recession going on everywhere, the neighborhood was the neighborhood, you know? Lots of families, lots of good people, couple of misfits and stuff like that, but I never really had to use my service weapon. Couple of arrests here and there, sure, but nothing some of the other guys had to deal with. I never had any run-ins with the mob. Most people in the neighborhood got to know me pretty quick, so if there were ever any problems, I'd get a phone call, or a quick wave to come on over and chat for a second. "Officer Lou," they'd say, "I think I know who broke into so-and-so's house the other day." I'd say, "Okay, what do you got?" That was pretty much the extent of it. Sometimes guys turned up and I took them in, and sometimes they didn't. Leads were handed off to detectives for anything more serious, and I didn't really get in anybody's way. Teresa was born when I started on the Queen beat, and Eddie a few years later.

So anyways it must've been about fifteen years ago now, because Teresa had already started in the Scouts. I came home to Nancy after walking the beat all day, and Nancy tells me not to take my shoes off yet, and I'd better not even think about relaxing, because I was about to head back out there and sell some cookies. I remember it clear as day. "Come on, Babe," I pleaded with her, "I just got home, and I've already been walking around all week. How about I just do it on the weekend?" "No," she said, "you've been saying that all week, and it's five o'clock now which is a great time to start, go out and catch people coming home from work. They'll be all happy that it's the weekend, and you'll be standing there with some cookies from the Girl Scouts of America. You'll sell them like hot cakes, I promise. And anyways, I told Teresa and Jane to stay at the park until six, and then I'd pick the two of 'em up, but since you'll be out walking around selling cookies you can pick them up. She'll love it. See her daddy in uniform at the park."

I mean what could I do? The woman was unrelenting. She knew what needed to be done, and she'd made up in her mind that I was the one to do it, so who was I to argue any further? If there's anything I've learned about marriage over the years, it's that when one of you has strong convictions about something in particular, and one of you could care less about it either way, then there's no sense in arguing. You just have to heed to whoever feels stronger. Did I really want to go sell cookies door to door after a full ten hours on my feet that day? No, I did not. Did I really want to piss Nancy off for the rest of the evening? No, I did not. So what did I do? I went and sold some damn cookies for the Girl Scouts of America, so I could come home to my wife of however long we'd been married at that point and hope to get lucky that evening. And man, would I get lucky.

It was all unexpected, of course, you wouldn't believe it, and I hardly believe it to this day. I'd left the house still in my uniform, the "Neighborhood Blues" as Nancy called them. I thought about changing into some casual threads, but Nancy convinced me that it was a rock solid idea to head out in uniform. "When they see that you're a police, and you're trying to sell cookies for your daughter, how could they not buy a box of Thin Mints?" I figured, hey, why not? The captain might have looked down on it if the circumstances had been different, but things played out the way they did, thank God. "Take the wagon," she'd said. "Head out like that, Lou. Oh my God, you look great! Wait, let me take a picture of you in front of the house." Nancy grabbed the old Kodak camera that we had, and she took this picture of me standing on the sidewalk in front of our house in my Neighborhood Blues, holding onto the Radio Flyer wagon that was filled with boxes of Girl Scout Cookies. I've got this big grin on my face, because Nancy was in stitches the whole time telling me I look great, like a true hero. Nancy still has that photo in a little, silver frame next to the bed, and she says it's her favorite photo of me. I like the one of me and my old man, when we'd spent the whole week out at Cape May, on the coast, fishing, and we're sitting there on the pier, and the old man's all bald and I got on a sailor's hat, and we're holding beers, and the old man has his arm around my neck like he's going to carry me with him wherever he goes. That's my favorite, and then a photo from our high school prom, Nancy and I, that comes in second. The day I made rank ranks third, if I had to rank them.

So I headed out back into the neighborhood on Pemberton just off the corner of South Front, a block off the Delaware Expressway and two blocks from the river. It was a pretty funny sight, and I knew it was. A handful of neighbors were hooting and hollering as I walked by. "Hey Canela," they yelled from the stoop, "nice wagon." I'd wave at them and yell, "Yeah, yeah. The wife's got me working overtime today." So I started stopping at every house on Pemberton. Most of the people I knew, the Gioras, the Maltos, I went to school with most of them, or their brothers, or they went to school with Nancy, or their cousins did. When you've been in the neighborhood as long as us, for as many generations as we had, you knew everybody, that's just how it was. Of course Nancy was right, I was selling cookies like they were made of solid gold. I was halfway through the wagonload before I even made it three blocks. Thin Mints were the most popular, with Shortbreads and Peanut Butter Sandwich coming in second and third.

I pulled my wagon to the corner of Pemberton and South Second and headed north. Then I cut left on Monroe St.—the park where Teresa and Jane were playing, Starr Park, was about ten blocks north-west of our place, up over on Lombard, so I headed in that direction. Anyway, the first row house I came to, I left my wagon at the bottom of the steps, walked up to the door, and I knocked. I checked out the brick building as I waited for someone to answer the door. Someone yelled, "Who is it?" And without even thinking, I said, "Police." I should have said, "It's Lou Canela, from down the street over on Pemberton, I'm selling cookies for my daughter, Teresa." But I didn't. I yelled, "Police." The sun had been beating down on me all day already, and I was tired from the long week, and I guess I just forgot exactly what I was doing, because before I knew it, I was doing police work.

"What do you want?" the voice said, from inside the door. I told him that I just wanted to speak with him for a minute, that I was walking around the neighborhood asking for a favor from people, and I was wondering if he could talk to me for a minute. That must have convinced him. The guy opened the door.

I know he saw the wagon filled with cookies at the bottom of his steps, because he looked confused as to why I was standing there. "Are those yours?" he asked me. "Yes," I said, "those are mine." He poked his head out of the door, and when he did the door opened a little wider. This pungent smell hit me dead in the face, like a pile of rotten meat stuffed inside some unwashed gym socks, except maybe worse than that.

"Are you selling cookies?" He asked.

"Yes, I sure am," I said. I put my hands on my hips to show him that he had nothing to worry about. "They're for my daughter's girl scout troupe."

He hadn't stepped out of the doorway yet, but from his head and neck poking out of that crack in the open door he looked real weird. Strange like. Bug eyes. Long neck. This skinny, pale arm that kind of swung loose at his side. And let me tell you, that arm was white—like he hadn't seen the sun that year, and if it had been winter I might have believed that he could be that pale, but it wasn't, it was July, and in July in this city people got some sun, one way or another.

"Well," he said, "I'll take a couple boxes of Thin Mints."

"Okay, sure," I said, and as I was about to turn around and fetch some cookies from the wagon, he stepped out from behind that crack in the door and plain as day I saw that his shirt and pants were covered in blood.

There are a few things that you learn over the course of training and working as a police that help you deal with, you know, tough situations or delicate, emotionally charged climates and all that. One of those things that they teach you during all that training and that you learn through all of that experience is how to assess when a situation demands that you pull your service weapon. Demands. Well, when I saw that young man standing there covered in blood, something inside of me either listened to my training or ignored it. But either way, what happened was that in the blink of an eye, and I do mean as fast as I could blink, my hand to God, I had drawn my pistol and shot that man in the chest. It happened fast, and then as it was happening time slowed down, like the slow-motion replay that you see on the baseball games. That was what it was like watching him fall backward into his house, as if time was sticky like molasses or something. Even though the laws of nature or physics or what have you wanted him to fall backwards, everything had slowed so much that there was a brake on the whole inevitable process. When I realized exactly what it was that I'd done, I was already dragging his legs into the house and closing the door.

I checked his pulse. Nothing. I wondered how that could be, and then I saw where I'd shot him, straight through the heart. He must've died instantly. Not that it mattered, but that was what I told myself. I stood over him, looking down at this pale, bloody mess of a guy, and I tried to figure it out. What I'd done, I mean. Trying to process it, I guess. I told myself that I needed to breathe, and so I took a few seconds and took some deep breaths. In, then out. In, then out. And every time I took a breath, things got clearer. I took a breath, and I thought about Nancy. I took another, and I thought about Teresa and Eddie. I took another, and I thought about my old man. Get a grip, Lou. Wrap your head around it, Lou. I took one last breath and opened my eyes.

The kid was still dead, if that's what you were wondering. So I turned my head, you know, away from this poor guy, and there was this deer carcass hanging in the middle of his living room. Now, I don't know where he got this deer from, or how he got it there, or why, really, but that must've been why he was all bloodied up. That's why there was that smell I smelled. And that was why I shot this guy, because of a misunderstanding. This poor idiot, carving up a deer in his living room and now look what had happened. I couldn't believe it. There were tarps all over the floor, and there below the carcass was what I thought was a blanket but was actually this deer's skin or hide or whatever, all bundled up. I couldn't believe any of it. I thought of Nancy. I thought of what she'd say in a situation like this. "Just make the right decision, Lou. Just do what's right, Lou." I wish I'd have had her there with me at that moment, I can assure you that would've been one way to test our relationship.

After maybe ten minutes had passed, I'd calmed down some. The right decision was easy to make, I had a family to think about. I walked over to the front door, and I put my hand up against the old oak and leaned my head against it, praying to God that nobody was out there in the street, that nobody had heard anything or maybe had heard but paid it no mind. And then I opened the door.

The fresh air hit me like a wave washing away some putrid, stagnant tide-pool that lived inside this guy's house. The street was quiet. I walked down the steps, closed the door behind me, grabbed my wagon, and I started walking home. I only had a few blocks to go, but in that short span I experienced more emotion than I had since my old man died. I felt anxious and upset, I was shaking, and then I was laughing at how ridiculous everything seemed—like with enough thought maybe it would all go away. I thought of my family, again, of Nancy, and I cried. I thought about how there are no take backs and second chances are myths. I thought about what happens when a guy like me does what I just did, gets put in a spot like I just did, and I wondered if what I did next would define me. I thought about how thirty minutes ago I was one person, I was a police, and I wondered if now I was something else altogether.

When I got close to the house, Nancy started yelling at me from where she was sitting on the stoop. "No way, Officer," she said. "You've still got cookies in that wagon, and you didn't even pick up your daughter from the park." I told her that I got radioed into the station, and that I wasn't sure what it was about. I told her that I'd take some more cookies in the car with me and stop by on the way back home to a few more houses. I gave her the money that I'd made, and I told her that I loved her. I told her that I was sorry about not picking up Teresa and Jane, but that I really had to get going. Nancy could tell that something serious must've been going on, because of the way I was acting, so she just said, "Okay, Lou. Call if you're going to miss supper." And then she gave me a kiss. I grabbed a stack of boxes from the house, threw them in the trunk of the Cadillac, and drove off towards Frank's.

Frank was a friend of mine since grade school. We grew up together and had the same history. Our families had been in the neighborhood for as long as anybody could remember. Frank ran a small metal fabrication plant in South Philly, a fifteen-minute drive from our house. If anyone could've helped me right then without asking any questions, it was going to be Frank. And if anyone had the stuff that I needed, it was going to be Frank. So, Frank's was where I was headed.

On the drive over, I prayed that Frank would still be there, that he hadn't gone home for supper. So, I'm sitting at this stoplight, right, heading on down to Frank's, and I started thinking about my old man. Maybe it wasn't as clear as day as that. I had been thinking about the kid, and what I'd just done, about how stupid he was for not saying, "Sorry, Officer, I'm a bloody mess right now, because I've been carving up this deer." I was in the car, driving, yeah, but at the same time I felt myself hovering over the kid. That poor kid. Me standing over him trying to fold his legs far enough into the house so I could shut the front door. The best I can explain it is that my mind was projecting flashes of what had happened onto the windshield of my Cadillac, like I was sitting at the Drive-In Movies watching the replay of what I had done, over and over, right there in my car. The kid kept opening that door and stepping out all bloodied up, and I saw my gun come into view and fire. Then it would restart. He opened the door again, and I fired. And after a few minutes of watching this, my hand to God, my old man opened that door, and I raised my gun and fired. The old man was calm as hell, even had a beer in his hand. He didn't react when I shot him, just stood there. But his eyes hurt. Understanding. Disappointment. Like he'd been in my shoes. He was staring right at me from the screen of my windshield. Maybe I was hallucinating, I don't know. Maybe it was the adrenaline. Whatever it was, at that moment when I needed him, like always, the old man was there.

"In the war," he said. The old man had fought in the Pacific. He was one of six from his company that had survived four years of fighting. "We did a lot of terrible shit. A whole mess of nastiness that I ask forgiveness for every day, you understand that?" I nodded. The light turned green, and I kept driving towards Frank's. "But I don't ask forgiveness from any man, because nobody who wasn't there could understand. So, I look up, towards God, and I ask Him for forgiveness. You hear me, Lou? Let the Lord be your judge, and until the day of your judgment is upon you, do what you must to make it home to your family."

I pulled into Frank's lot. Now, I can't remember exactly what I told Frank, but you'll have to believe me when I tell you that I was as honest with him as I could be. I looked him in the eye and said something like, "Frank, I killed a man today. It was my fault, and he didn't do anything to deserve it. But now I need to get rid of the body, and I need some chemicals that can help me do that." I went on talking about how we'd known each other our whole lives, and that I'd never asked him for anything, but he cut me short and told me to shut the hell up and follow him into his garage. Frank rummaged around for a second and grabbed two big metal cans, they were about three gallons each, if I'm remembering correctly. Just as he was explaining to me that alone each liquid couldn't do more than strip the paint off of some sheet metal. Alone, they were inert, that's what he said. Well just as he was saying that, my radio kicked on.

Dispatch said that Nancy had called in to the station and was hysterical about something, yelling that I needed to call her right away. I remember feeling a spike in my heart, like something in my chest had burst. It's over, I thought. They found the body. Somebody saw me shoot that poor boy, and they waited until I left the house. They saw that it was a cop and then they followed me home before they called the police. Every idea flashed through my head like a maze of lightning, except that in this maze there were no false starts or dead ends. Every path led to a cell.

I used Frank's phone and gave Nancy a call. When she picked up, I could hear how frantic she was by the way she was breathing and rambling. For a second, my heart sank. I took a breath. "Calm down," I said. "Nancy, calm down. What's wrong?" "Teresa's not at the park," Nancy said, "and neither is Jane." I held the phone against my ear and looked up. "They probably just ran off to Jane's house," I said. "Did you call Tim and Jennifer's?" Nancy was screaming into the receiver, "Call Tim and Jennifer," I said, "I wont be much longer," and then she started sobbing.

I told her not to worry. They were kids, and they were probably out chasing an ice cream truck. We lived in a safe neighborhood. They probably just walked off down the street. Just take it easy, I told her. I'll be back soon. I told Frank I owed him one. I threw the cans that Frank gave me into the trunk of the Caddy, next to the boxes of Girl Scout Cookies, and I tore out of there for the house where I was fixing to do something awful.

I had seen the machete lying on the floor next to the bloody hide. The room was already covered in tarps. I figured I could chop him up a bit, quarter him, and then halve those limbs at the joints. It might take all night for the chemicals to do their trick in the bathtub, but Frank guaranteed that it would work. Stop up the tub. Put the limbs and torso in. As small pieces as you can manage. Pour the two cans in. Lock up the house and come back in the morning. Use something to release the stopper and that was that. No more body. No more worries. He's just a guy that took off on a whim. Let the landlord figure out that his tenant is missing when the rent is late. Get back to walking the beat and raising two kids. Get back to being a police.

The sun was starting to set when I got back to the kid's house. Dispatch called my radio again, and told me that Nancy had called the station, again, and that, again, it sounded urgent. I told them that I was going to sell a couple last boxes of Girl Scout Cookies for my daughter, and then I was heading home where I'd help Nancy deal with whatever it was she was going through at that moment. I sounded calm over the radio, but really I was scared shitless at this whole mess. Terrified. Thinking of Nancy and the kids was the only thing that helped me steady my nerves. When I pulled up to the kid's house, I almost threw up. I parked the Cadillac. There were no take backs, I thought. No second chances.

I walked around to the trunk of the Cadillac, popped it, pulled out a few boxes of cookies and walked up to the kid's house. I knocked on the door and then waited for a second, in case anybody was watching. I said, "Hello," as I opened the door, starting a fake conversation. There he was, crumpled in the doorway, right where I'd left him. I said, "Sure thing," into the empty house. Nobody replied, not even the deer. I put the cookies down on the floor and fetched the two cans that Frank had given me. "Oh yeah," I said, as I walked back outside into the neighborhood, "I got more cookies right here." My radio crackled and dispatch started again. "Officer Canela, you need to call your wife. You need to call your wife. Officer Canela, you need to call your wife."

I put my hand over the speaker of my radio so that nobody nearby could hear dispatch yelling my name. You know, in case they were listening. I got back into the house, and responded to dispatch. I told them to tell her that I was busy, that I couldn't call right now. I told them that I was doing what she told me to do, that I was selling God Damn Girl Scout Cookies, and that Nancy needed to calm the hell down, and that I'd be there soon. Dispatch remarked something about marital bliss and keeping my personal affairs out of the office.

As I dragged the kid into the living room, I told him I was sorry. I told him that I didn't mean to shoot him, and that I didn't want to chop him up like I was going to. I hoped he'd forgive me, but one of us was going to keep on living and the other, well, he wasn't. Since it was pretty clear who was who in that situation, I thanked him for letting me carry on with my life. He understood. I had a family and a career. He was some pale kid in a house that smelled like shit with a deer carcass in the living room. Who was he? Who the hell was he to ruin my life, to take away all that I had? He was nobody. He was nothing. So he had to go. And then I heard a bump from upstairs.

I dropped the kid's leg. I looked up at the ceiling. There it was again, *bump*. I drew my gun. Did I not clear the house earlier? Did I not even check to see who was there? I tried replaying what had happened after I shot the kid, and I couldn't remember the details. Now that enough time has passed, I can remember, but then, I couldn't. *Bump.* I crept over to the staircase. Visions of that cell at Holmesburg darted past my eyes. My heart rate climbed. Things started slowing down, again. That walk up the stairs must've taken me five minutes. I thought about what I was getting ready to do. How far was I willing to go to right my wrong, to try and put things back to normal? "It started as an accident, your honor," I swear, "I just wanted to take it back." "But there are no take backs," the judge would say. "I know," I'd say.

As I entered the first bedroom, the only thing I could hear was the bu-bump bu-bump bu-bump of my heart. I popped through the door, a quick glance. There was nobody there. A full-size bed on what looked like some antique frame sat in the middle of the room—ornate, with the big posts and everything. I kept my gun steady as I bent down and peered under the bed. There was nothing there. The kid had a big old dresser that matched the make and model of the bed, and on top of the dresser were some photos in little silver frames. The first was of the kid with an older man. Might've been his father. They were standing outside of the courthouse, on the steps, the ones that Rocky ran up in the movie, and both guys had their hands up like they were fixing to go twelve rounds right then and there. The other two photos were of the kid with a woman about his age, maybe his wife, eating dinner at a nice restaurant in one, dancing in the other. My heart sank. They looked happy. I walked to the closet, took a deep breath, praying that she, his woman, wasn't in there. I had my gun raised, and when I pulled that door open I pointed it straight into the closet, but the closet was empty except for clothes, jeans and tees that smelled like sweat and sawdust.

I turned and headed towards the second bedroom. I had heard something. I was certain of that much. I wiped my face with my forearm, focused, turned the handle to the second bedroom and pushed open the door. There was a single-bed frame in the room and nothing else. It had been cleared out. No mattress, no dresser, no desk. The closet door was open, and I shuffled against the wall towards it before peeking in. Empty. Then I heard that noise again, and I knew, I knew for sure, right then, that whatever it was, whoever was in there was in the bathroom.

When I opened the bathroom door, I froze. There, tied up like two little piglets, all gagged and bound, were Teresa and Jane. I recognized them immediately. My baby and her friend done up with duct tape and gagged with washcloths. Bandanas over their eyes. Their thin, fragile arms and teeny bodies snugged up together in that porcelain tub. I didn't understand why they were there. How. I couldn't move.

Now, I don't know exactly how to explain it, but, at that moment, right then, my spirit left my body and perched itself in the corner of the bathroom above the toilet. I watched from above as my body untied the girls, hugged them and told them that it was going to be okay, told them that they were safe. They started crying, and my body picked the both of them up, one in each arm, and carried them downstairs.

I followed my body downstairs, and then out to the car, and I watched as my body put the two girls in the Cadillac. Then, bam, just like that I was inside the house. I held my gun, pointed at that sicko, that sick fuck beneath me, and I emptied my pistol into his chest. Then I called it in. Shots fired. Suspect down. Request backup. Corner of Monroe and South Second. Call my wife, call Nancy, and tell her I found Teresa and Jane. I felt a pressure lift off of my chest and started to cry. Send backup. I killed a man.

When all the bells and whistles showed up, I had moved the canisters into the bathroom, and I was waiting in the car with the girls. I told everyone to head inside, and that I'd be in there in a minute. I wasn't leaving the girls until Nancy showed up. Captain Miller asked me what happened. I told him. Out here selling cookies and heard a peep from upstairs. Sounded strange. So I asked the guy what was that noise. Guy freaked out, tried slamming the door on me and then ran inside. I kicked the door in, saw him grabbing a machete off the living room floor, and I emptied my sidearm into his chest. Cleared the house and I found my daughter and her friend, Jane. Just dumb luck, I said. "You got instinct," Captain Miller said. "A lot of guys don't have that."

Nancy showed up in tears. I told her that everything was fine. She took the girls home in the Cadillac. Captain Miller said that it looked like he had planned to dissolve their bodies in some chemicals. "Makes me sick," He said. I told him that I saw those too, when I went up there, and that I didn't want to think about what would have happened had I gotten there twenty minutes later. "I look at this kind of thing," Captain Miller said, "and I think about the decline of the human race. That a man can do something like this, that a man can stray so far from the path of normalcy to do something like this makes me worry about the future, about the kind of a world our kids are going to grow up in."

I told him that I agreed with him. I believed that there was a line, and that once that line was crossed it couldn't be uncrossed. That there were no take backs. I lied and told him that you were either filled with good or evil, but that the final judgment was reserved for God. I shook Captain Miller's hand as he told me that now was as good of a time as ever to tell me about my promotion. Detective. I looked him in the eye and smiled. He told me that he was proud of me and that I was one of the good guys. I nodded and said that I wish he had the ear of the Almighty. And then I heard Nancy's voice in the back of my mind, what she'd always said to me everyday before I left for the precinct, "Make the right decision, Lou. Don't be no hero." Don't be no hero. Don't be no hero. And I knew, for sure, that I wasn't.

THE MEETING

It was time for Columbus Elementary's third annual teacher meeting since La Famiglia had taken over. Five teachers sat in the break room.

The school bell rang.

Ted, the rotund, silver-haired principal wearing a recently pressed grey Armani suit, sat at the head of the table. He fanned himself with a stack of papers.

"I want to welcome everybody to this annual teacher get-together thing. Some of youse I know real well, John, Tiny," Ted said, looking at the two men.

John was tall and thin, all arms and neck, like an Italian Kareem Abdul Jabaar. He wore a dark charcoal pinstriped suit with high lapels. Gaudy gold cuff links poked through the sleeves of his suit, like the yellow eyes of a great cat.

"Hey, Ted," John said with a quick nod.

"Hiya, Ted," Tiny said, his infantile teeth poking through his thin-lipped smile.

"And a couple of youse," Ted said, "I gotta be honest, neva seen before."

Ted acknowledged the other two present, protruding his jaw

and bending his puffy cheeks into a bulldog's countenance.

"Pete D'Amato," Pete said, "Ehhh, fit grade and computas."

"Melanie, Mel fa short," Mel said. "I head the library."

"Okay, Pete, Mel, Nice to have yas," Ted said.

Tiny wore black slacks and a loud, cream-colored silk shirt. Pete wore a tuxedo. Mel, a red sundress.

"If I may, Ted, I'd like to say something before we get down to business," John said.

"Sure thing, Johnny," Ted said.

Mel poured herself a glass of the chilled white, a Catarratto from the southwest regions of the motherland that rested placidly in a bucket in the middle of the table. She winked at Ted as she took her first sip.

"Okay, as Terry and Ted already know, two weeks ago I bought a new vehicle," John said.

"She's a cherry, Johnny," Tiny said, slapping John on the back.

The others nodded in agreement. Real nice, they thought.

"She was," John said, "Until yesterday when one of these no good bast-ads keyed her, and now I'm in the hole five macas for a new coat of the dipingere!"

John shook his fist. The cufflink on his right wrist clinked.

"I swear on my mother if I find the punk that–"

"Alright, Johnny, that's enough," Ted yelled. "Take a walk or something would ya?"

"I'm sorry, Teddy," John said.

While John craned his neck and adjusted his collar, gathering himself, Pete leaned over to offer his condolences.

"We'll find the punk," Pete said.

"Okay, anything else before we begin here?" Ted said.

He pointed at each teacher, one by one. The teachers shook

their heads. They knew it was time to get serious.

"First order of business," Ted said, "and this was brought to my attention by Tiny as still being an issue, and, of course, I'm speaking about Jimmy Spinoza."

Mel raised her wine.

"Yes, Mel," Ted said.

"Is Jimmy Spinoza the second-grader with the cowlick who always smells like gasoline?" Mel said.

"C'mon, Mel. That's Eddie Finarack," Tiny said. "The kids call him Alfal-foline."

"It's a play on words," John added.

"Jimmy Spinoza," Pete said, "and please correct me if I'm wrong here, is the kid, fourth grade, with the scar on his upper lip, and no matter when you see him he's only got on one shoe."

Everyone nodded in agreement.

"That's Spinoza?" Mel said. "I always see him standing next to the furnace room with his head against the door."

"Son-of-a-bitch loves the sound of a furnace," John said. "Whadda-ya-gonnado?"

Laughter.

"Okay, okay. Now that we all are familiar with whom Spinoza is, let's get down to it. Where is this kid's other freaking shoe?" Ted said.

Tiny cleared his throat.

"Ya know, I thought I seen a shoe outside the music room the other day."

"You talking Tuesday or Wednesday, Tiny?" Ted said.

"I'm thinkin' Tuesday."

"You know what?" Mel said. "I was passing by the music room Tuesday, I was on my way to go visit with Cliff, anyways, I heard

Anne talking to Albert Finnegan, second grade, about taking off his shoes during class."

"So, was it Finnegan's shoe? Or has the owner yet to step forward?" Ted said. "Because, I gotta be honest, I'm tired of this Spinoza kid walking around with one shoe all day."

"What's the big deal, Teddy?" Pete said. "Kid hardly's got the peanuts to know that he's even at school, let alone whether or not he's wearing the appo-piate number of shoes."

"Spinoza's a little off, ain't he?" John said.

"Reminds me of the batman, what with that dual-personality syndromes," Tiny said.

"Please tell me he hasn't started wearing a cape," Ted said.

"No cape, Teddy, just breaking balls," Tiny said.

Ted passed his meaty hand through his silver, conditioned hair.

"Alright, good. Keep an eye out for that shoe though," Ted said. "I can't take another year-and-a-half of the shoeless wonder standing outside the furnace room."

"There is something to be said about the low hum of a good furnace. Kinda like one of those Buddhist chants or something," John said. "Jus' saying."

Mel, Pete, Tiny, and Ted fell silent. They looked at John, deciding whether or not what he'd just said was in jest.

It wasn't.

"Watch out, Johnny's a good furnace away from losing his right shoe!" Tiny said, slapping his knee.

Tiny reached up and grabbed John's neck just above the collarbone and pinched—like an older brother adding a highlight of injury to the insult.

There was laughter. John shrugged off Tiny's hand, and then he crossed his arms.

"All right, okay, settle down," Ted said, calming his troops. "Next order of business, is it true that Stevie Reems, fifth grade, hit Carl Carlson, first grade, wit' a brick to the face?"

"Ab-so-friggin-lute-ly," Mel said. "I saw the whole thing happen."

"Okay, Mel, what's the word?"

"Well, they were playing tag, and little Carl called Stevie's mother a whore."

Pete and tiny hollered, "Hooooooo," in unison.

"Kids got some balls," Pete said.

"And then what?" Ted said.

"Well," Mel said, "Stevie, acting like nothing happened, picked up a brick, walked over to Carl and smashed him in the face."

John, still a bit upset over the shoe joke, rejoined the conversation.

"Hey, can you blame him? You call my mother a whore, and I'll slit ya friggin' throat," John said.

"Fuggitaboudit," Ted said.

"Can't blame the kid for that," Tiny said.

"Completely agree," Pete said. "You talk about family like that you gotta expect consequences. These kids gotta learn consequences."

"For the record," Mel said, letting the words sink in. "Johnny, your mother's a whore."

"Speakin' of balls," Pete said, nodding at Mel in a gesture of respect.

Ted, flipping his glasses up and down along the bridge of his nose as if trying to place the woman in the red sundress into focus, said, "Heyyyy, who we got running the library over there? Is that

Bobby De Niro?"

"Ya know, if you weren't a lady I'd crack you in the fuckin' head right now," John said.

"Heyy, take it easy tough guy," Tiny said. "She's just breaking balls."

"John, relax," Ted said. "Enough with the sensitive crap, it's getting on my nerves. Seriously though, should we suspend the kid?"

Pete, always a good consigliere, chimed in, "Nehhh, he'll learn his lesson one way or another."

"Alright, next issue, and without a doubt the most important. I been getting a lot of flack from the parents about having French toast as the staple of our before-school breakfast program."

"What's the problem here?" Pete said.

"I got about fifty inquiries into the nutritious value of French toast," Ted said, looking at the sheet of paper he held.

"Are they aware that Dolores makes it from scratch," Pete said, "bless her heart."

"That's a valid point Pete's got," Mel said.

"No, no, they know. Their problem is, apparently, with us giving the kids syrup," Ted said.

"This problem they have, it's with the syrup?" Tiny asked.

Ted checked his sheet, again. "According to 43 emails, yes, the syrup is the issue."

"What if we offer 'em waffles or something?" Tiny said.

"Yeah, waffles with, ehhh, jam or jelly?" Mel said.

Everyone nodded at the good idea.

"Already tried the jam and waffles approach," Ted said.

Tiny, Pete, and Mel sighed.

"Anyways they got a problem with the, the uhhh, syrup," Ted

said.

"What about pancakes," John said.

"I'm sorry, Johnny, you're gonna have to repeat yourself," Ted said. "It sounded as if you just said, 'What about pancakes?' That's what it sounded like. When we are clearly having a conversation about a proper substitute for syrup, you feel the need to bring up pancakes?"

"I'm sorry, Ted, I—"

"Oh, you're sorry?" Ted said.

"Doesn't make it right, Johnny," Pete said.

"But, Tiny just said waffles," John said, pointing at Tiny.

"What's with this guy?" Mel said.

"But I," John said.

"Friggin' idiot you ask me," Tiny said.

Ted started to yell.

"We're talking about appropriate French toast toppings, and you don't say, 'what about powda sugar, or straight butter,' but instead you start talking about pancakes, one of the lowest if not *the* lowest ranking breakfast food around."

"Friggin' pancakes, Johnny?" Tiny said.

"They always get so soggy," Mel said.

"I was just making a suggestion," John said.

Pete stood from the table and said, "Teddy, you want me to shut him up?

"Please," Ted said. He'd had enough.

Pete slapped John. Once forehand. Then backhand. And one more with the palm.

"Johnny, you're my friend a long time here, but you gotta go," Ted said. "You're fired."

John, realizing that Ted was serious, and fearing the worst if he stayed, began his exit. His long lanky body bobbed as he walked, like a pump car starting out on a set of train tracks. John shut the door behind him.

"I can't believe he brought up pancakes," Mel said.

"Whata-ya-gonnado?" Ted said. "Alright, guys, that's all I got for this year's meeting. I'll figure out the breakfast situation on my own. Pete, can you cover John's art class for the remainder of the year?"

"No problem, Teddy."

"I thought art programs was gettin' cut?" Mel said.

"Over my dead body they're getting' friggin' cut," Ted said.

"This comes down from the bosses?" Mel said.

"From the man himself," Ted said.

"Why?" Mel asked.

"Why?" Ted said. "Because these kids gotta experience everything. You think I give a fuck if some kid can't pass some rudimentary mathematics? Hell, I can't even pass rudimentary mathematics, and I don't need to. I got some accountant quack that deals with all my finances. But let's say that one of these kids keeps failing math class, doing real bad in all his classes. Let's say he walks into the art room one day and picks upa some clay, and he's hooked. Loves to do the pottery, and he's pretty good too. Well, if he keeps at it, he might be able to make a whole boatload of money off it, and then he can hire some accountant shmuck to deal with his finances too. And, Mel, we ain't taking *that* opportunity away from the kids. Not here. Not at Columbus."

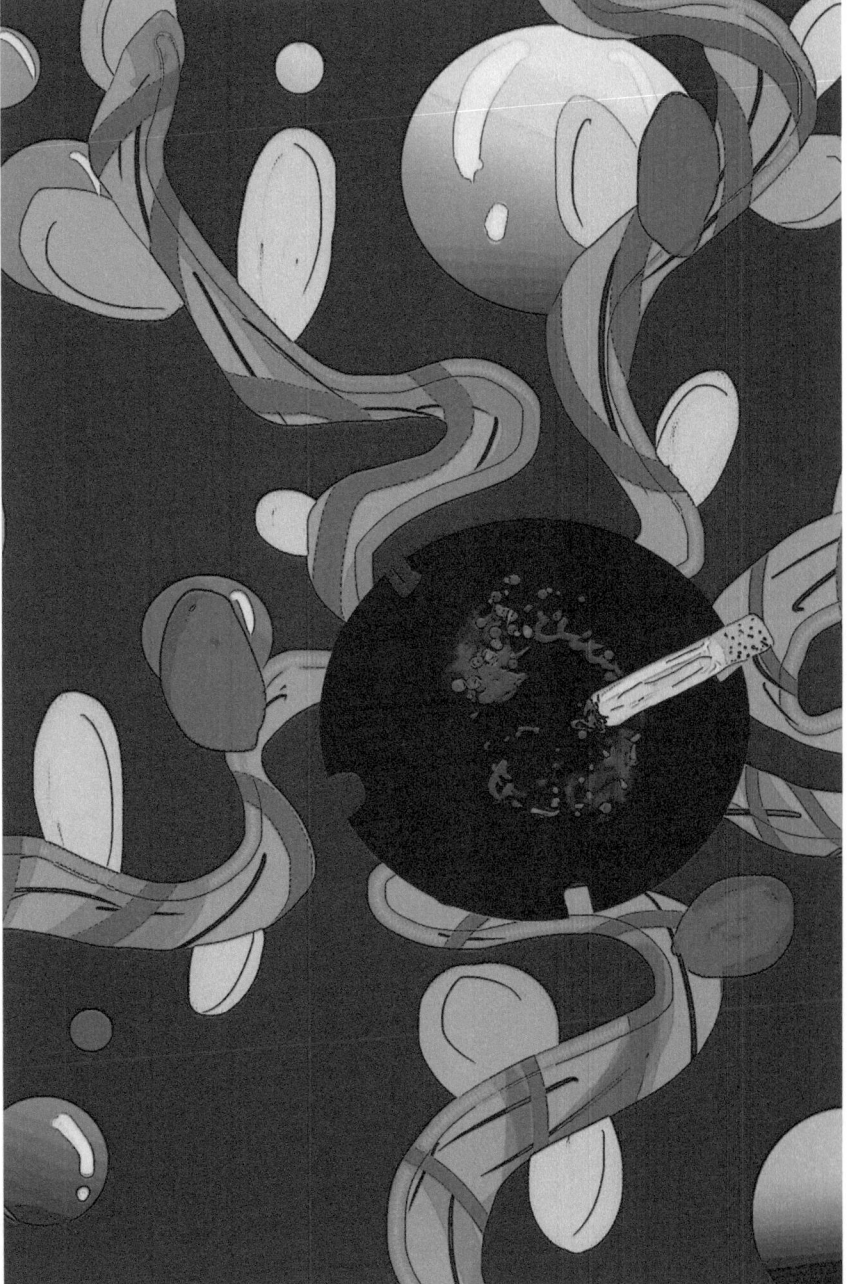

THE JADE

When Nikki got home from work and parked her rusted-out, '96 Honda in the driveway and climbed the steps, she found James laid out on the hammock with a copy of *Cyrano De Bergerac* split-turned on his chest, distracted from the play, observing the view. She sat in the beige, corduroy EZ chair that had seen better days, grabbed the wooden handle on the right side, and kicked back into a heavenly recline.

"What ya doing?" Nikki asked. She knew what he was doing, and James knew what she meant.

"I was reading but now," he said, looking out over the un-kempt lawn and warped sidewalk into the yards and trees across the street.

"Yeah," Nikki said. "You were reading. I see that, I mean what's going on around here?" She motioned towards the neigh-borhood.

"Hmm? Oh, I've been watching Benny's place for like three hours."

"Benny's place?" Nikki said. "Nothing ever happens over there."

"Not today, Nik. Not today." He paused. "Action today, Nikki, lotta action."

"You want a beer, Action Jackson?"

"Yeah, thanks."

Nikki reversed the wooden lever and, timing the violent kick from the mechanical release of the EZ chair, sprang to her feet–a skill that develops as the result of a long relationship with the same quirky, ancient chair, like a reflexive roundhouse kick to the throat of a would-be assailant after years of training. She opened the screen door and disappeared from James' sight. James gazed, still. A half-hearted sun bled through a weak bandage of clouds in the afternoon sky. What James had just described as a source of action was, at the moment, not.

"Pabst or High Life?" Nikki yelled. The neighborhood was accustomed to the sounds of disembodied voices hollering out varieties of cheap beer from the blue house with white trim.

"High Life."

The screen door kicked open and Nikki walked over to James. She handed him his beer and kissed him on the forehead.

"Hello, dah-ling," she said. Nikki grinned and turned back to her EZ chair.

"Hello, and thank you, my dear, dear Nicole."

Nikki pulled the wooden lever once again, and as she reclined her feet felt light and blood pulsed easily in and out of her legs, alleviating certain vertical pressures.

"So, what's happening over at Benny's?"

"I'm not quite sure yet," James said. He took a sip of his beer, and he turned his head toward Nikki.

"Oooh, dramatic effect," Nikki said. "Me likey."

"Shut up," James said. "Listen, I've seen eleven people park in front of Benny's house in the past, what time is it?"

"Four-Fortyish."

"I've seen eleven people park in front of Benny's house in the past two hours."

"So what," Nikki said, "he's probably having a bridge party or something."

"No, it's not like that." James swigged his beer and shook his head. "These people were all steaming mad when they got out of their cars, and I mean through the roof fucking pissed. All of 'em."

"And..."

"And, and then they go into Benny's house and after twenty minutes they come back out calm as a cool is calm can be, and they get into their cars and drive off."

Nikki laughed, and she drank.

"This is the action?" Nikki asked. "A bunch of angry, geriatric drivers walking into Benny's and leaving happy?"

"Yeah, as far as I can tell."

"I'm failing to see what's so intriguing, Dah-ling, it sounds so properly boorish to me," Nikki said.

"My dear, I'm telling you, something's amiss."

And they grew silent. They drank from their beers and stared out at the greens and greys of lawns and sidewalks that shifted into the browns and blacks of tree trunks and asphalt. Time passed between them without a word.

James heard Nikki finish her beer, and, without looking or mentioning or acknowledging, he rose from the hammock, walked inside, and grabbed two more beers from the trusty brown fridge (which they'd considered replacing every spring, wondering if the fridge would last through another summer), and he delivered Nikki a Pabst and kissed her forehead and said, "A cool beverage for my dedicated Southern belle," and as he turned toward the hammock Nikki said, "A gal should be so lucky to have a strong man, such as yourself, by her side." And they grew silent again, and they allowed their minds to locate the stillness that existed in that moment.

A late 90s, black Lincoln Town Car in mint condition and with a fresh coat of polish turned onto Canal St. with complete disregard for the stop sign on Dreymond St., about three blocks south of Canal, as if in a high-speed chase, with tires screaming and rubber marking–leaving dark streaks on dirty grey–and accelerated down Canal right past the blue house with white trim. The two disembodied voices on the porch let out a simultaneous "Holy shit." Nikki's mouth fell open when the Lincoln slammed on its brakes and tried to pull into Benny's driveway but careened over a curb and onto Benny's lawn. The taillights went into park, and clouds of dust and dirt rose from the street and sidewalk and grass into the air, hovering, like a harmless, overactive swarm of gnats.

James and Nikki remained silent.

The door of the Lincoln flew open and sprang back off its hinges so fast that it slammed against the small, corduroyed-leg that had poked out of the driver's-side door onto the lawn. A high-pitched yell came from inside the Lincoln.

A man who must have been in his late 70s based on his posture, frail body, and time-stamped outfit stepped out onto the lawn and exploded in hysterics.

"Goddamn, fucking, stupid, piece of shit fucking car door, hobo-sucking, commie red-devil son-of-a-bitch, bastard, unbelievable bastardized horse spawn of a greasy snake, yellow-bellied John-Wayne-hating fucking idiots who put these pieces of shit together, yeah, I'm talking to you, you piece of shit, you wide-turning, wide-turning boat. You boat. You giant Goddamn land boat!"

The old man took off his hat, threw it to the ground and began stomping and jumping on top of his golfer's cap while screaming, "Yahhhh kiyyyyyyyyyyyaaaa Unggggdddddddddddaaaaaa!"

And then, as suddenly as he'd started, the old man stopped jumping. He stopped yelling and grunting. He walked around the Lincoln and into Benny's house, slamming the front door behind him. His hat lay in the front yard right next to the dusty car—the driver's side door wide open.

James looked at Nikki, and she let out a snort and snarled out a laugh.

"Oh my fucking god!" Nikki said. "What the hell was that?"

"That, my dear, my love, was the action," James said. He smiled and, in a celebratory and inclusive manner, raised his beer in her direction.

"How right you were, dah-ling, indeed." She tipped her beer towards him and then took a sip.

"I'm telling you, Nik, it's been going on for hours, just like that."

"Just like that?" Nikki said.

"Well, okay, no. Almost," James said. "I mean he was by far the angriest."

"Did you see when he jumped on his hat and started groaning? He was like 'Unnnnnnnnngnggggggg!'" Nikki laughed at her impression of the man, which wasn't necessarily accurate, but captured the essence of the moment rather well.

"Watch," James said. "Because this is the part that's going to throw you for a loop. In ten minutes or whatever, old hat stomper is going to walk right out of that house like nothing ever happened, get into his car and drive away."

"I don't believe it," Nikki said. "No way."

She shook her head like a St. Bernard—emphasis in large sweeping motions.

"My dear, dearest Nicole, dost thou have no faith?"

"I just can't imagine a scenario," Nikki said, "short of that old man getting electro-shock therapy inside Benny's house right now, I just cannot imagine anything."

Nikki trailed off and paused for a moment before cranking the wooden lever to the EZ chair, springing into life, running into the house, grabbing two more beers, kicking the door open, kissing James on the forehead, and saying, "A precious nectar for my dearest Zhivago," bouncing back to the EZ chair and yanking the wooden lever once again.

The two roommates stared at the world in front of them, taking in the scene from the comfort of their wooden island. Birds chirped, trees waved with the passing winds, small creatures darted from bush to bush, children yelled in the distance, and engines and brakes and tires turned and squealed and thumped further down Canal St., but their eyes stayed focused on the stage.

James grabbed a pack of Lucky Strikes and a purple lighter that lay on the wooden end table next to the hammock. Before he lit his cigarette, James held the pack out at arm's length pinched between thumb and middle finger, his wrist dangling loosely, the way he imagined Joaquin Phoenix had offered his ring for Russell Crowe to kiss in the movie Gladiator. Nikki waved him off. "No thank you, Sire," she said.

James lit his cigarette and took a long drag. He placed the pack and lighter back on the table, and he watched the smoke climb from his mouth like some sort of ethereal genie slowly escaping its pulmonary prison. He reached over and tapped his cigarette against the ashtray.

The ashtray lay within the abnormal arms of a Jade plant. The plant was a gift from James, and the ashtray a gift from Nikki. It was only natural that both gifts quickly found their way outside, to the porch, and since the young Jade plant had looked like a small hand sprouting upwards from its potted earth at the time, James found it only right that he marry the ashtray to the Jade. An arm of the Jade grew and grabbed. Another turned and twisted, and after seven years the handmade ashtray was finally becoming a part of the plant.

"I can't wait any longer," Nikki said. "I have to know."

"What?"

"We have to go over there."

"No no," James said. "We wait."

"Fine," she said, a bit miffed.

But after another few moments had passed and another cigarette had been smoked, the urge was too strong. The old man remained inside.

"I thought you said he'd be out by now?" Nikki said.

James looked at Nikki and began nodding. He spun his feet over the edge of the hammock and said, "Let's go." Nikki looked at James.

"Really?" She said.

"Yeah," James said.

"Fuck," she said, waving her hand in front of her face. "I just got all nervous."

James started towards the steps.

"Come on, Miss Drew. Let's go solve this thing," he said.

Nikki popped the lever on the recliner, shot out of her seat, and followed behind. As the two roommates stepped onto Canal St., James turned his head and looked back at the blue house with white trim–their house. It seemed distant. The porch was almost invisible from the street. James felt the uneven pebbles of weathered asphalt crumble beneath his sneakers, and he grabbed Nikki's hand. The blacktop smelled like burnt shingles. Nikki's hand was soft and smooth.

They stepped onto Benny's lawn, peering into the Lincoln's windows as they passed. Nikki bent over and picked up the old man's golf cap. She brushed it off. Motes of dust and dirt flew into the air, and James turned his head to avoid the approaching puff. He observed Benny's house. The old man's place looked brighter from this side of the street, alive.

"Just in case we need a peace offering," Nikki said.

"A mighty fine idea, indeed, Doctor," James said. "On an expedition of this magnitude, you're truly in the dark as to whether or not the natives will be restless."

"Perhaps we should return to base camp and procure some of the cold, malty beverages to offer as well," Nikki said.

"Nonsense," James said. "We mustn't give the elixir of life to the savages."

James and Nikki stepped onto Benny's front porch, if you could call it that. It was a simple slab of concrete with two, thin columns that protruded upwards from the slab and supported a tiny black, shingled roof. Nikki looked at James, expecting him to make the first move. He closed his eyes while shaking his head. Nikki knocked on the door. Nothing. She knocked again. They heard the door's top bolt turning, and they took a half step back. Benny opened the door.

"Hello," Benny said. "Oh hi there, you two. Hello."

James shot a subtle eye at Nikki.

"Hi, Benny," Nikki said.

"Lovely, lovely. More guests," Benny said. "Please, please

come in."

"Ummmm, we were just wondering if the guy who drove that car," Nikki said, pointing at the Lincoln, abandoned in haste and resting on the lawn, "Is okay?"

"What's that?" Benny said.

"Is the man that drove that car okay?" James said.

"Madrigal?" Benny said.

"Who?"

"I think that's Madrigal's car," Benny said. "He's fine, but you'll have to ask him yourself, he's a bit decapitated... discapacitated... incapa–"

"Incapacitated?" Nikki said.

"Yup. That's it," Benny said. "Come on in."

Benny turned and walked back into his home, leaving the door wide open. James whispered to Nikki as she passed him, then he entered and shut the door.

The hallway was painted a bright, fire engine red. There was a window on their left that allowed in a sharp beam of western sunlight. The light hit the wall and set the red paint ablaze. The house smelled a bit dank, moldy, like a wet Labrador that'd been resting in the bed of a rusty pickup in the summer's heat. James and Nikki followed the hallway to the left, towards the voices.

They entered Benny's living room. The living room was sterile, composed–wooden floors, tasteful furniture, and colorful walls. Gathered around a tree trunk, which acted as a coffee table, seated on the couches, were four elderly couples–four men and four women. As they stepped further into the room, Nikki recognized the old man whose hat she held, whom Benny had called Madrigal. The elderly couples sat, in a docile state, holding on to thin rubber hoses that connected to a glass vase in the center of the coffee table, in the vase, a dark-red liquid, and beneath the vase, a flame. Benny sat cross-legged on the floor, opposite James and Nikki, and he was adjusting the flame's intensity.

As the burgundy ooze simmered, a bit of steam rose from the lip of the vase.

"These are my neighbors," Benny said, without looking up. "Neighbors, these are my good friends."

Nikki leaned forward, and then she gasped. She saw that the old folks weren't holding the rubber hoses at all. The lines were connected to needles that drew blood from the wrists of the elderly and then drained into the vase.

Only the four men connected to the vase. The women tended to small plastic valves just down the line from the wrists of the men. They'd turn the valve open, allowing a slight stream of blood into the tube, and then they'd close the valve. They did this every so often as they saw fit. The blood ran its course and entered the carafe, where it joined the bubbling molasses and slowly turned to steam. The men looked exhausted, and if not for their wide, toothless smiles, one would assume they were in pain.

The ladies who turned the valves spoke words of encouragement.

"That's it," They said.

"I'm here," They said.

"You're okay," They said.

Benny ceased tending to the flame and looked up at James. He smiled, showing his spotted and stained teeth.

"So glad you are here," Benny said. "Would you like to join?"

"Uh, I don't know about that, Benny," James said.

"Oh," Benny said.

"I'm not even sure what, ha, exactly, you're doing here,"

James said, laughing.

"Why, we're letting blood?" Benny said. "Can't you see?"

Nikki watched as a few larger blood bubbles popped and sprayed onto the walls of the vase. There, the droplets met their coagulated colleagues and formed into gelatinous pustules. Their color darkened against the vase–from a deep rich red into a shade of black–like bloody asphalt under a well-lit moon.

Nikki imagined herself tending to a valve.

"Yes," James said. "I can see that much. But–"

"But what?" Benny said.

"But, why?"

"Ahhh, why?" Benny said, contemplating the faces of his elderly companions, as if their expressions were enough of an explanation for the young man.

"Uhhh," James said. "Yeahhhh, so this is weird. Like, really weird. Strange even. I was expecting something strange, but this? Benny, this?" James clapped his hands together, "Man, Benny, you win this one."

James looked at Nikki for agreement, but she wasn't paying attention. Nikki was imagining how the plastic would feel under her fingers as she opened a valve, solid. She thought of touching the tube as a stream of blood passed within the rubber cylinder, warm. She smelled the vapors of the blood's reduction, a noxious scent like liquid rust caked against her nostrils. She imagined James with a needle in his wrist.

"Nic, Nicole," James said, grabbing her hand. "Time to go."

"Okay," Nikki said, snapping out of her fantasy.

Before turning to leave, Nikki reached out and placed Madrigal's hat back on his head. Madrigal turned towards Nikki, the skin on his face wrinkled and pocked, crows feet ran from his eyes like tributaries running from a canyon into a pale lake.

"One day," the old man said.

Nikki smiled.

"One day," She said.

James tugged at her hand, and he led her out of Benny's house. As they walked outside, Nikki felt them approaching the blue house with white trim as if they were floating. She didn't feel the crunch of the asphalt beneath her feet, and she felt closer to the house, now, at the base of the porch. They walked up the stairs, and Nikki lay out on the hammock. James threw open the door and grabbed a couple of beers from the fridge. Upon his return, Nikki was smoking one of his cigarettes. James handed her a beer.

"What the fuck was that all about?" he said.

Nikki put her right arm behind her head. She took a deep, life affirming drag of the cigarette—tasting its smoke, replacing the scent of blood that had lingered in her mouth and nose—and then exhaled.

"You'll figure it out," Nikki said. "One day." And then she flicked the ash of her cigarette into the Jade.

THE DHOW

Alexis was young, well, younger than I was. She was nine-teen, and I was twenty-two. It wasn't that much of a gap, but back home at least I could drink, and she couldn't. Except, Alexis was from Windsor, Canada, somewhere near Detroit she'd said, so maybe she could drink. But I'd traveled a bit more than her. This was her first time out of the country, aside from the US, she'd told me. She was a sweet girl, that's why we'd hit it off. Alexis was pleasant, if a bit uptight, but I figured that was because she just hadn't been around as much as I had. Seen stuff. She was kind of funny, too. When everyone else was partying at the end of the night, having drinks or playing cards around the table, all of the people at the hostel, the Germans and Italians and Israelis, Alexis would seek the solitude of her tent and write, almost obsessively, about the day's happenings in her journal. She was taking the journal thing really seriously, which was fine, you know, to each her own. She said that she'd never done anything like this, and that she wanted to keep a truthful account of everything she did, and who was I to stop her? So I let her do her thing at night, and I did mine.

But we got along well enough, too, bonded even. We'd found

similarities in our childhoods, divorced parents, soccer, school plays and musicals. We'd even played the same role of Fastrada in Pippin during high school. After two lazy days of strolling the beaches and getting to know each other, we'd decided to go to Zanzibar together. She was flying back to Canada in a week, and I was heading down to South Africa for another two months of volunteering at an elementary school in Rustenburg. Traveling alone is great, but sharing the road with a companion you meet along the way, no matter how brief, can be a welcome reprieve from some of the more solitary aspects of going at it solo.

It had become apparent, however, that I was a little less reserved than Alexis. I guess we just had different goals for what we wanted to take away from our travels. I wanted to experience everything, as much as I could, and it seemed after a few days of getting to know her that Alexis mainly wanted to observe. Not to say that she didn't get involved, but even when she did, she always seemed to slide a few steps behind everybody else or retreat to the edges of the circle, often giving her the appearance of a vulture, spiraling a pack of lethargic critters.

On the second day of knowing her, I told her that she ought to try to break out of her shell a little bit. When she said, "What do you mean?" I wasn't exactly sure so I said, "I don't know, live a little," which is easily one of the lamest things I've said to anyone in recent years, like something someone screams at the nerdy, bookworm character with bad hair and an overbite who ends up becoming prom queen in one of those teen rom-coms that I used to love when I was twelve or sixteen.

The night after I'd said what I said (I would've taken it back if I could have), Alexis hung out later than normal for her, and had more than a few drinks with me and Tierry, John, and Eli and Mita, the other travelers from the hostel. When Eli and Mita, the married couple who were so fucking cute it made you want to throw up but also so nice that you couldn't do anything but love them, started a drinking game that took the night in a direction none of us had expected. The object of the game was to build a structure from empty beer bottles, shot glasses, and playing cards. Whoever had the tallest building, won. Needless to say, in the pursuit of architectural glory we all got way too wasted. John ended up passing out at the table before his tower was even halfway done. Eli quit shortly after John fell asleep. He'd gotten the idea that he was going to start a fire on the beach, and Mita, lovingly, followed. Tierry, who was cute but not too cute in that tall and skinny, goofy sexy kind of way, stuck around, teasing me every chance he got about my inability to balance bottles on bottles, as if it was something I should have been practicing or, like, should have been innately good at. Alexis burst up from her seat at one point and went and threw up next to her tent, which wasn't in as secluded a location as, I'm sure, she had hoped, because Tierry and I kept laughing at her with every heave. I know it sounds mean, but she kept trying to catch her breath and then right before vomiting again she'd yell out, "Ohh God!" We thought it was a riot.

Tierry and I walked to the beach to see what was going on with the fire. After a few minutes of trying to figure out where the hell Eli and Mita went, we saw them fucking in the ocean. I'd turned to Tierry to laugh with him, but when I did he put his hands to the sides of my face and kissed me. He was a smooth kisser, and I led him by the hand to my campsite. I left my clothes in a pile outside of my tent, unzipped the flap, and crawled inside. Tierry followed my lead. After a bit of kissing, I pulled out one of the few condoms I had left from the pouch conveniently located inside my tent, tore the packet open with my teeth and went to wrap him up. Based on his height, I would have guessed that Tierry would have had a big ol' dick, so you can imagine my surprise when I came face to face with what I thought was my thumb. Oh, and for the record, I do not have big thumbs. My hands are perfectly proportional to the rest of my body. The sex, the actual intercourse part of it, was lame. I had sand lodged in between my butt cheeks, and it was so fucking humid at night, so whenever we rolled around our skin would pick up sand from the floor of the tent, which, when our bodies moved and writhed created the effect that every wonderful sensation was immediately followed by the lingering tinge of a sandpaper burn. It wasn't until he went down on me that I started to have a good time, and then I had a really good fucking time. Tierry licked my pussy like he'd had one his whole life. I mean it. That handsome boy got his time card, punched in, and went to work. Fingers, lips, tongue, just, gah, perfect. God. I stopped counting after my third orgasm, and I was exhausted after a few more so I kind of lost focus, but I'm pretty sure that the night watchman came over to the tent and listened to me moan, because at one point I could see the faint traces of a flashlight through the nylon fibers of my tent, about ten paces away. It was either that, or through those moments of ecstasy my brain had released itself from its physical confines and elevated its way to an enlightened, otherworldly state and I'd found God in that flash of light. Which, in hindsight, felt like the unlikelier of the two.

The next morning, I snuck out of the tent to go brush my teeth before Tierry woke up, and Alexis was standing at the sink already brushing. I asked her how she was feeling, and she gave me a look like I was some sort of lunatic. She looked like she'd had a pretty rough night. I smiled at her, over her shoulder into the mirror, and she said, "What?" "Nothing," I said. "You know," she said, "maybe I'm just the kind of person who has fun in the background. Maybe I don't need to live like you. Maybe the path you're on doesn't sound fun to me. Maybe I'm not you, and maybe we have two very different definitions of what it means to live." Alexis shut off the tap, grabbed her tube of toothpaste, and then walked away without saying another word to me for the rest of the day.

I was a little shocked at how judgmental she had been. I really didn't expect such a severe reaction, and it felt like a pretty heavy-handed thing to say to someone that you hardly knew. I mean, really, I knew that she was insinuating that she had some type of moral authority over me, as if she was a fundamentally better person, or that her self-proclaimed "righteous" decisions would take her further than me in life, or something like that. Which, if that's what she'd been implying, was complete bullshit. But I decided to put a positive spin on the entire thing and look at it from the perspective that she was just being a bitch because she had been sick all night and was hung over.

Later that evening, before she turned in to go write in her journal, Alexis walked over to the hammock where Tierry and I were splayed, limbs intertwined like we were in the middle of some airborne game of twister, and she told me that she was sorry for what she'd said earlier. I told her not to worry about it, and that I had thought that it didn't sound like her, anyways. She said, "Thanks," smiled, and then she walked away. Tierry asked me what it had been all about, and as I grabbed the back of his head and gently bumped his face into my crotch, I told him that he should do less talking. In the morning Alexis and I were going to Zanzibar.

"My name a Popeye. Mine," he said, pointing towards the

Dhow. "Captain," Popeye said, pressing his right hand across his chest. Popeye had a wide smile, all teeth, and they were white and well cared for, which was something to note in Tanzania (it meant he had some money). Popeye pointed over to another man who was holding a rope tied to the bow of the Dhow. The man stood on the grass at the edge of the water–the Dhow bumped in time with the small waves that crashed into the five-foot dirt cliff–"Silver-Man, first mate," Popeye said. Silver-Man waved us hello, "Mambo mambo," Silver-Man said. "Poa poa," Alexis and I said in unison (we'd been conditioned to the call and response of Swahili). Popeye pointed to another man sitting at the stern of the Dhow, next to the two motors, and he said, "He's Rudy, cabin boy." All three men laughed, and Alexis and I laughed too.

The sun was just beginning to rise over the Indian Ocean. The Dhow was this little, old rickety thing that was like twenty feet long and maybe five feet wide. It had a roof over the bench seat in the middle of the boat that was no bigger than a sheet of plywood. It was made of worn, wooden planks that looked as if they'd been nailed together, taken apart, and nailed together again, and then left to bake in the sun for twenty years without regard to the violent wear that salt, sun, and time might have on organic materials. But it was floating (at the moment, at least), and I took that as a good sign for Alexis and me.

All three guys, Popeye, Silver-Man, and Rudy were wearing these old khaki shorts and faded T-shirts. At least they'd decided on a uniform, I thought, at least they looked like a team.

"Okay, so thirty-thousand each to go Zanzibar, okay?" Popeye said. "Three maybe four hours," and Popeye pointed out at the open ocean, east. Alexis and I had decided, together I guess, that we were going to go to Zanzibar in the Dhow that the hostel owner, Gregory, had recommended. It was cheaper than trying to get all the way to Dar Es Salaam, and then taking the big ferry across that everyone had been talking about. It was certainly less expensive than flying from Dar. The Dhow was like twenty $20 US, apiece.

Alexis looked at me and said, "Can I talk to you for a second?" I reached into my pocket and pulled out a wad of colorful bills with numbers like 5,000 and 10,000 on them, and I handed my money over to Popeye. He smiled and said, "Asante-sana." "Can you give us a second?" I asked Popeye, and he said, "Hakuna shida" (no problem). He smiled at me and then went back to, I guess, making jokes with Silver-Man and Rudy.

Alexis and I walked a few feet away from the grass where Popeye was standing. "What's up?" I asked her. The sun wasn't even all the way up yet, and I was already sweating like a pig. I pressed my shirt in-between my boobs to soak up the few drops of sweat that were bothering me, and then I pulled my bandana off my head and let my hair down for a second. "I'm not getting on that thing," Alexis said, under her breath. Her gaze was fixed on the Dhow. I scratched the back of my head and ran my fingers through the length of my hair, which, after two months of traveling through Eastern Africa, was caked with salt and sweat and sand. I think the term rat's nest would apply nicely.

"What's the problem?" I asked Alexis, "They seem like nice guys, and Gregory recommended them." "Anyways," I said, chuckling, "the boat's not that bad." Alexis didn't find it amusing. "It's going to fall apart in the water," Alexis said, "and we're going to fucking drown in the middle of the fucking Indian Ocean." It was obvious that I'd been rubbing off on her a bit more than she'd wanted, because four days ago, when we'd first met, Alexis didn't swear at all.

"It's going to be fine," I said, tying my bandana back on. "No fucking way," Alexis said. "Okay," I said, and then I turned around to Popeye. "Popeye," I said, "How many times a week do you go across to Zanzibar in the Dhow?" Popeye perked up. I think he liked me, because he was staring at my chest. "Maybe, three four times ev-er-y week," Popeye said. I turned back to Alexis, "See," I said. "Popeye," I said, "How many times has the Dhow sunk?" Popeye looked out at Silver-Man who was holding the rope tied to the bow, and then he looked over the boat like he was putting some serious thought into my question, as if it had actually sunk before and he was trying to remember exactly when that had been (which, judging from Alexis's posture, would have been a deal-breaker, let me tell you). "This Dhow," Popeye said, "never. It's a good Dhow." "See," I said to Alexis, "it's a good Dhow, it's never sunk before." "Not even once?" I said to Popeye. "No," Popeye said. "It's a strong Dhow in the water."

"Come on," I said to Alexis, "we just have to get on that thing for three hours or whatever, and then we'll be lying on the beach in fucking paradise. These guys literally make this trip four days a week, back and forth. I mean, seriously, this is their job. Wouldn't you rather trust those three guys than some crazy big ferry out of Dar that depends on hundreds of people and all the shit that can go wrong with big companies in this country?"

And I guess that last part settled it for her, because Alexis gave Popeye her half of the money, and then she took Silver-Man's hand and dropped down into the Dhow. I said thanks to Popeye for being patient, and he said no problem in Swahili again (apparently nothing was a problem for anybody, ever, it was crazy), and then Silver-Man jumped into the boat. Rudy pulled the cord to start one of the pony-powered motors, we slowly reversed into the middle of the channel, and then we started heading out into the open water.

Rudy took our bags and rolled them into a giant tarp that he clamped shut with two long boards of wood that were jammed into the sides of the Dhow. He smiled at us and said, "Don't want water in there," pointing at the tarp. "Asante-sana," I said. The sun had risen pretty quickly, and since we were going to be exposed for a few hours I figured it was time to put on some sunscreen (the shit that I'd bought in Tanga that cost me almost as much as this boat ride). Popeye, Silver-Man, and Rudy must have been watching from the stern of the Dhow as I rubbed the lotion onto my already darkened arms and neck, because they went all quiet until I was done.

There was a fresh breeze coming off the water, and with every wave that the Dhow encountered, mist sprayed up to our left and the soft wind blew it into our faces. The Indian Ocean turned from a rich indigo into a deep emerald, depending on the angle that caught your eyes. Alexis wasn't really in the mood to talk, I guess, because she sat there with her eyes closed and her arms folded across her chest. She was breathing pretty steady, so I figured she was just meditating or something, trying not to think about the trip.

I turned around and started watching the three guys. Popeye manned the handle of the motor and was steering the Dhow. Rudy sat on a bucket to Popeye's right, and he was baiting minnows or whatever onto some fishing line. Silver-Man was smoking a cigarette and making Popeye and Rudy laugh. After ten minutes, Rudy threw the baited lines off the back of the Dhow. Why not fish? They were already getting paid to be out on the water. The tiny outboard motor had the number 25 in big white letters on its side. I asked Popeye what the second motor was for. He smiled and Silver-Man and Rudy laughed, and then Popeye said, "Backup."

Then I noticed a little bit of water sloshing around on the floor at the stern of the Dhow. Rudy's calloused bare feet were sitting in two inches of water as he tended to the fishing lines that dragged behind the Dhow. Popeye had his eyes set dead ahead towards the sun that was lit like a giant pineapple slice in the Eastern sky. Silver-Man smoked his cigarettes and cracked jokes that only the men could understand. Popeye and Rudy kept laughing, as Silver-Man's antics grew more and more animated. After a few more minutes, there was even more water in the back of the boat. Rudy's feet were completely covered and he had water up to his ankles. Silver-Man flicked his cigarette into the wind, and it flew away from the boat like a hummingbird changing directions mid-flight, and then it was gone. Silver-Man said something to the guys and nodded at me, and then he grabbed a big red bucket, one of those buckets that paint comes in, and he started bailing water over the side of the Dhow.

The noises in the stern of the Dhow had gotten louder over the past five minutes, and, as a result, Alexis came out of her tiff, her meditative whatever. She turned around and looked at the crew. There was Rudy tending to the fishing lines, and there was Silver-Man, with another cigarette dangling lazily between his lips, bailing water from the hull, and there was Popeye steering, making slight adjustments to the motor's handle as we whirred ahead into the shimmering whitecaps of the landless horizon. I looked at Alexis and said, "Every decision you've ever made has still led you here, with me. And regardless of what you think of me, we're here, in this moment, together. Get it?"

Alexis failed to respond or even acknowledge that I'd spoken, and after a minute of staring, mesmerized by the placid expressions of the crew, and with a shaky, wide-eyed look of uncertainty, she must have locked eyes with Popeye, because he averted his gaze from the horizon, towards her, waved, and said, "Hakuna shida. No problem."

BROKEN HORSES

Since we'd left the bonfire, we'd been watching the Puerto Rican men race their horses on the strip of road next to the parking lot. Luna, Taryn, Brian, and I had come to the car with the sole intention of retrieving the rum, but the thunderclap of hooves against the long, straight road in front of us was distraction enough to delay our return. And then Brian decided to roll a joint. The keg sat in a hand-dug pit at the edge of the sand under a bundle of palms, behind us, forty feet from the Caribbean, and it was running low. Streetlights as tall as the palms that lined the road's edge emitted their meager orange glow onto the otherwise dark stretch of asphalt–alongside the half-mile of road, I'd counted five of them. The men raced their horses, and when the horses ran their shoes sparked against the road, leaving trails of light in their wake with the same brilliance of the popping embers that rose from the heart of the bonfire, briefly, and then died and went dark before ever hitting the ground.

There were maybe thirty men in all–some of them old, some young. The youngest might have been twelve or thirteen. They were reedy, ratty kids, and they rode ponies–galloping alongside the strip–adjacent to the real action. The older riders looked well into their twenties or early thirties, and they rode the real muscle. There wasn't a cowboy hat, boot, or spur in sight. The men were all sporting clean Nikes (multicolored dunks, white Air Force Ones, or classic Jordans). There were a lot of basketball jerseys–Miami, Cleveland, Chicago, LA, and Boston. With the exception of one guy in a smooth pair of chinos, they all rocked baggy jeans or jean-shorts. Aside from the horses, it looked like a hip-hop show could've broken out at any minute.

Luna and I sat on the trunk of Brian's silver Toyota. Brian and Taryn were in the car, listening to music and rolling up. I passed Luna the bottle of rum, and as she took a sip two men barreled past us on horseback. They were in a jockey's crouch, and their white Nikes dug deep into the saddles' stirrups. One of the men was kicking the black horse with the heel of his sneaker while snapping a horsewhip against its chest. As they passed the street-light to our left, the men pulled back on the reins, and the horses scrambled to find their footing. They slid and then ran. Slid and ran. All the while sparking. All the while slowing. When they'd finally come to a stop about thirty yards past the streetlight in front of us, they were shrouded in darkness. The man on the black horse had won.

Each man guided his horse from the middle of the road to its edges as they turned around, and then they slowly cantered back to what Luna and I had decided was the starting line. As they came back towards us, two more racers sped down the middle of the road. The sides of the road were lined with guys waiting their turn for the main drag and kids on ponies in slower, sidebar contests.

Look at this guy, I said to Luna, and I pointed to a man in the parking lot sitting on a large brown stallion. The man was riding bareback, and his hands clutched at hefty clumps of the stallion's mane, which he yanked on mercilessly. The stallion bucked to the left, and the man silently pulled the horse's head downward, to the right. The horse spun, and the man pulled back on the mane with both hands. The horse walked calmly across the parking lot for four steps and then bucked and turned again, resisting.

Luna asked what the man was doing, and I said that he was breaking the horse. I told her that I'd seen my father do it many times over the years on our family's farm in Michigan. I told her that some were easier than others, and some could be stubborn. Very stubborn, I said.

Brian and Taryn joined us on the trunk of the car. The Misfits were playing on the stereo, and we sat smoking and passing the bottle of rum among us.

I hate watching this shit, Brian said. You know these motherfuckers don't even own the horses? Those aren't their horses. They fucking rent them. Can you believe that? They rent these horses and then they race them on the fucking streets. It's horrible, Brian said. Taryn asked Brian why they didn't race them on the beach, instead, and he said that he didn't know but that it was probably because they were all coked up and didn't give a fuck about what happened to the animals.

Who do they rent them from? I asked. They get them from the farmers, Brian said, or from the people who rent them to tourists for beach rides.

The caballero that had been trying to control the brown stallion whistled down to a man who was seated on a bench watching the racers. All the while the horse kept spinning in tight circles, and the man pulled at the horse's mane. The man from the bench walked over to his friend, spoke, and then he walked away nodding. The caballero kept tugging, and the horse stopped spinning to the right before bucking and circling to his left.

Two girls and a local kid named Peter whom we'd been drinking with at the bonfire made their way from the tree line that separated the beach from the parking lot and joined us. Luna passed the bottle of rum to one of the girls. The three locals stood with their backs to the races as if nothing intriguing was happening–business as usual.

Brian and Peter started talking about the waves that had been breaking earlier that day at Sandy Beach. The waves at Sandy jutted up against a sandbar, materializing in the warm and shallow waters of early February. That day there'd been seven-footers, and both Brian and Peter had taken full advantage of the four hours of lipped perfection that had broken in the late afternoon into the early evening.

The bench-guy emerged from a car just down the way to our right and walked over to his friend, the caballero. The caballero was still fighting with the stallion, and his friend stood out of harm's way and held out a bottle of liquor. The caballero turned his head as the stallion spun, keeping his eyes on his friend and the bottle of liquor. Each time the brown stallion turned his backside near the bench-guy, he stepped back to avoid being kicked. On the next rotation, the caballero reached down and snatched the bottle of liquor. The caballero's friend walked back down to his bench at the edge of the drag. Men were racing recklessly, pushing their rented animals to their limits with punches to the neck and heels to the side.

The caballero opened the bottle of liquor and took a tentative swig, like someone holding a cup of water during a footrace, trying not to spill. He tipped the bottle high, and when he was done drinking, he squeezed the bottle in the pit of his left arm and replaced the cork. The horse continued to buck and sway and turn, and the caballero raised the bottle again, but this time he brought it down, swiftly, with controlled malice. The bottle shattered on the brown stallion's forehead, just above and between the eyes. The horse made a noise that I'd never before heard an animal make. It screamed.

The four of us were stunned. We couldn't believe what the caballero had just done. I had heard of this method, but I'd never seen anyone use it. Then the caballero pulled on the brown stallion's mane, hard. He yelled, and the stallion resisted, and then he yelled and pulled again. The stallion shook its head, and finally submitted. The caballero pulled the horse to the right, and it went right. The caballero pulled the horse to the left, and it went left. Then they slowly trotted down to our right, to the far end of the parking lot.

That makes me sick, Luna said, and she shook her head and looked away. What's the big deal? Peter said, ripping the joint. It's an animal, and it needs to do what you tell it to do. It's just an animal, he said, puffing again, laughing. You have to train it to listen to you. It's cruel, Brian said, everything about this, this whole thing, he waved his hand over the racetrack in front of us, everything about this is fucked up. You just think that because you're not Puerto Rican, Peter said, this is normal; they're always out here on the weekends running the horses.

Two men finished their race at the streetlight to our left and continued at a slow gallop well into the darkness down the road lined with palm trees. I could see them when they reached the next light a quarter-mile down the road, and they turned and stopped. They waited, talking to each other. After a minute the horses burst from the dim glow of the light that was far down the road and entered into the darkness at full speed, heading towards us.

To our right we heard the clap of hooves, like the brr-app of an old Tommy Gun, and when I looked over I saw two men racing, pushing their horses, slapping, hitting, kicking, willing the animals to go faster. As they approached the night's agreed upon finish line, the streetlight to our left, the men racing in the darkness reappeared. The rider who was closest to us pulled back on his reins, and the horse's shoes skidded and sparked on the road. The horse turned its head at the last second, but they were going too fast and the animals collided. Their heavy, muscled bodies twisted and then flailed onto the asphalt with a dense thud, like when two children are on a playground running around and aren't paying attention to where they're going, and then they run face first into one another. Smack, but with more weight and intensity.

Holy shit, I said. Oh my god, Luna said. And we watched the man on the horse who'd tried to pull back on the reins fly into the air and then land at the base of the streetlight that was as tall as a palm. Two horses lay sprawled in the middle of the road. One was trying to get up, and the other lay still. The man that had pulled up on the reins was dragging himself to the base of the streetlight; his right leg was bent out at a ninety-degree angle from just under the hip. Neither man had made a sound.

A pack of fellow racers had dismounted and were running past us to the scene of the crash. There were five of them. Nikes, jerseys, fitted ball caps, and they were holding up the waists of their pants and shorts as they ran. When the group arrived to the man with the shattered leg lying underneath the streetlight, one of the men poked his head up from the pack and yelled, Ambulancia!

One of the horses got up, and one of the horses didn't. The other man involved in the crash, the nocturnal salmon, limped over to the crowd that had gathered around the man with the broken leg.

I hope the horse isn't dead, Luna said. Those guys deserve it, Brian said. I hope everyone's okay, Taryn said. The horse that had yet to move began stirring, and with the help of a couple of riders made it back upright. It began walking, but it kept its left, hind leg off the ground. They're going to have to kill it, I said, if it can't walk they're going to kill it. Animals, Brian said. We waited for forty more minutes, finishing the rum and watching the scene unfold in complete disbelief as to what we'd just witnessed. The Ambulancia was nowhere to be seen or heard.

When we finally left, walking back down the beach towards our apartment, I thought of two things. In the split second before the crash, when the man with the soon-to-be-broken leg pulled back on the reins and his horse turned its head to avoid certain death, its shoes sparking on the road like a metal grinder, I'd seen what had to have been fear in the animal's eyes. And I thought about the caballero, and how on a night in Puerto Rico I'd watched a man in a Chicago basketball jersey and a pair of shoes made in China–for a company that originated in Oregon–break a horse with a method used by Cossacks.

THE ADJUSTMENT BUREAUCRACY

I

A man wearing a grey, three-piece suit, whose dark hair was slicked back in a stylish 1950s coif, stood outside of Terry Runkle's house and whispered to a raccoon. The raccoon's name was Fred.

It was 11:00p.m.

Time was important to the man in the suit, because he dealt in a world of timing. Timing, you see, was related to the plan. Not a plan, but *the* plan. Windows opened and closed, doors revolved, and people moved through their lives on various paths and at various paces. People who were aware of time as a construct, however, were none the wiser of its relation to the plan.

It was the man in the suit's job to be certain that certain marks arrived at certain places at certain times in accordance with the plan.

The man in the suit's real name was Bill Glass.

Since he'd joined The Agency, however, everyone called him Agent Percy Stanbridge, or some combination of those three titles–Agent Percy, Agent Stanbridge, or even just Percy (his least favorite).

A man named Peter had assigned the name Percy Stanbridge to Bill Glass upon his sanctification. Bill had stood in front of Peter, and Peter had said, "Bill Glass, nice to meet you. Consider yourself absolved. From this day forward, you're to be known as Percy Stanbridge. Please report to The Agency for training."

Bill preferred the name Bill to Percy, but there was little he could do. The decision had been passed down from on high, and from that day forward he was Percy. Decisions and judgments were often passed down from on high.

Changing a name was important to The Agency. It was meant to distance the agent from what they'd known: give them a new life, a repurposed life.

Agents relied heavily on folders. Each Mark had a folder assigned to them upon birth, and that one folder contained a Mark's present and future projections. The present projection indicated what a Mark was doing presently–walking, talking, sleeping, interacting, etc. The future projection indicated where a Mark would be or what the Mark should be doing in the immediate future. The "sheet," as their record was called in The Agency, also indicated in real time, moment to moment, whether or not the projections, both present and future, aligned correctly according to the plan. *The* plan.

The folders resembled the cheap manila folders commonly found in the file cabinets of every office, since the conception of offices, paperwork, and folders. The inside of the folder contained the Mark's sheet. The sheet was one part divine and two parts touch-screen user interface.

Since joining the agency, Bill had handled 3,127 cases. That meant 3,127 different folders and 3,127 different Marks. It also meant 6,254 different trips to the agency's archives–6,254 different signatures on the office-mandated "in/out" form and 6,254 time-sucking conversations with the long-winded archivist Morton Piff.

For an agency that was so concerned with time, Bill often thought, you'd think that they'd have chosen someone a bit more introverted to run the archives than Piff.

Piff's real name was Greg Landers.

II

Fred the raccoon stood at attention on his hind legs and rubbed his thieving paws together in anticipation.

"So, what time do you want it done?" Fred said.

"5:32a.m.," Bill said. "Exactly."

Fred stared across Terry Runkle's unkempt lawn at three large metal trashcans. The cans were filled to their brims.

Bill looked over his shoulder, saw the trashcans, and then he turned back towards Fred, who was practically drooling.

"Until that clock in his kitchen reads 5:32a.m., don't even think about it," Bill said.

Fred stuck his paws out and turned his palms towards the sky above, as if to show Bill that he had nothing up his sleeves. The raccoon did not have sleeves–he was a raccoon.

"Think about what?" Fred said.

"Knocking those Goddamn cans over before 5:32a.m."

Fred dismissed Bill's accusation with the flick of a wrist.

"Don't worry about it, Percy," Fred said. "5:32. I'm your guy."

"I can't tell you how important it is that Runkle hears those cans crash down at 5:32, wakes up, and bursts out the front door," Bill said. "But, let's just say that it's imperative to the plan."

"Okay, okay," Fred said, "Cool your jets, Per-cy."

Bill felt the condescension in Fred's tone. He stared Fred down. Fred realized that he was a bit out of line. Here was Bill after all, just doing his job.

"I have to go check in at the office," Bill said, as he started walking away. "5:32, don't fuck it up."

Bill walked across Runkle's lawn, stepping over and around an assortment of discarded automotive parts that were strewn about the yard. He noticed the discarded front end of a '67 Mustang—the sight of which made him feel an uncanny nostalgia for reasons unknown, like seeing yourself in an old photograph but lacking any actual memory of the youthful snapshot. Bill walked down the short driveway and out to the street. Standing in the dim glow of the streetlight, Bill recited a haiku and vanished into thin air.

Fred scampered up a nearby tree, a maple. The tree faced both the kitchen window and the trashcans. The clock on the microwave in Runkle's kitchen read 11:09p.m. Fred glanced at the trashcans, licking his lips, and then he looked out across the yard and road for any sign that Percy was still there, spying on him. He looked back to the trashcans. Soon, he thought. Turning back to the kitchen window, he noted the time, 11:10p.m. One minute had passed.

III

As Bill ascended to The Agency, he questioned whether he'd made the right decision. Raccoons weren't trustworthy. Bill knew this. You should avoid delegating to a raccoon unless all other potential avenues had been explored and exhausted. Unless completely necessary. At least that's what the agency's manifesto on animal delegation, subsection 81-52.03, read:

Agents may find themselves in a pickle from time to time wherein two or more of their cases need/require intervention in present/future projection assimilation, concurrently. In times such as these agents must use their best judgment and available resources to ensure proper mitigation in their absence. This may include the delegation of occurrences to those animals or critters that the agency has determined, over the expanse of time, to be untrustworthy. These animals include flightless birds (incompetence), raccoons (impulsivity and lack of inhibition), and the common domesticated cat (apathy). Temporary employment of any of these aforementioned animals calls for a review of an agent's actions by a panel of his or her peers and the agent's supervisor, in accordance with agency reg. 2-04.39: 'An agent's actions that are in direct violation of any agency regulation, that has been stipulated, a priori, in the manual titled Agency Regulations must be reviewed by the agent's peers and direct supervisor at the first convenient time and date for all involved in the review process.'

In all his previous cases, Bill had only been up for review once. The circumstances surrounding his review were unfortunate. Dumb luck. Bill believed that his review had bordered on unfair. Bill had asked a turkey to spook a young girl. She would be walking in the woods, and the turkey was directed to pop out from under a shrub or small bush and yell, "dolololoololo!" Scare her. At least, *that* was the plan. The turkey, whose name Bill couldn't remember, had actually done a decent job of stalking the young girl. However, neither Bill nor the turkey had taken into consideration that it was October. It just slipped our minds, Bill had said during his review.

A hunter named Eddie Kelp had fired his shotgun twice. After all, bird season had just opened, and Eddie had thought he'd seen two birds. Eddie killed the turkey and the young girl, the discovery and admittance of the latter, on his part, altered Eddie's future projection assimilation for the rest of his adult life. Well, 20 to 30 years, to be exact.

The most trusted of animals, the manual stipulated, were birds of prey, rats, and all African ungulates (Kudu, Springbok, Oryx, etc.). Bill had only seen an African ungulate at a North American zoo while working on one of his cases in the late 20th century. He'd found the kudu to be pleasant enough, albeit a bit dumb, and he'd been rather perplexed as to why, precisely, they were held in such high esteem. Bill's query remained unanswered.

IV

Back at Runkle's house, Fred had descended the ratty maple and taken a seat at its trunk. He stared at the cans, overflowing with their beautiful, bountiful refuse. I could just go sniff it, he thought. His human-like fingers began to twiddle.

"Percy didn't say anything about no sniffing. All he said was, 'the cans must be knocked over at exactly 3:52a.m. Exactly.' There were implications, he said. Percy's a good guy. Right? Yeah, so he'd understand if I just went in for a sniff. Right? Of course he would. All I have to do is knock those cans over at 3:52, exactly."

Fred's paws got whatever was the raccoon version of clammy, and his skin went taut with goose bumps.

V

Bill arrived at The Agency exactly one minute after reciting his haiku. Agents traveled by haiku. Traveling by haiku always took one minute, regardless the distance. The agent must simply project his or her location to The Agency and recite an original, off-the-cuff haiku. One minute later, they'd arrive at their desired destination.

The explanation of travel-by-haiku, as it was known, existed in the manual titled, Agency Regulations 12-47.02, subsection Haiku:

> *If and when an agent finds him or herself in a situation wherein normal methods of transportation will not suffice, he or she is welcome to travel through haiku. Simply project a location, recite an original, off-the-cuff haiku, and one minute later the agent shall arrive wherever he or she desires. Agents must plan for this 60 seconds of travel, accordingly. The agency had considered allowing instantaneous travel, but after a period of deliberation it was believed that if an agent couldn't prove adept at even the slightest coordination of his or her own travels, then how could he or she be expected to manage caseloads or present/future projection assimilations of multiple marks?*

VI

The Agency looked like any and every part of a large office building: there were cubicles, phones rang, agents wore suits.

Bill walked by the front desk towards his office, passing his secretary, Agent Deborah Green (her real name was Lordana Fury).

"They're waiting for you in the big office," Deborah said.

"Jesus," Bill said, "I just got here."

Bill tapped Runkle's folder on Deborah's desk.

"Well, you know how the bosses like being kept up to speed."

"It's, mmmm," Bill said. He smiled at Deborah, holding his tongue, and then he continued walking towards his office.

"Good luck, Percy," Deborah said.

Bill waved Runkle's folder at her as he walked away.

VII

Fred approached the trashcans–lightly, quietly. He took his time to cross the yard, repeating the words, "Just gonna sniff, just gonna sniff, one lil' wiff, one lil' wiff," as he tiptoed.

The scent of the garbage engulfed his head like a wreath, no, like a space helmet filled with flavor gasses, he thought. Fred imagined himself delivering the Sermon on the Mount to a thousand raccoons below, holding a spaceman's helmet high above his head while his fellow masked-bandits went wild.

"Friends. Countrymen. Raccoons!" Fred said. "I have harnessed the smell. The one true smell, and it is good."

The raccoons below were hooting and hollering with wild approval, reckless abandon.

"Within this helmet are the most powerful scents in the known universe," he continued. "Within this helmet are dreams, and within this helmet are possibilities."

Fred was walking around the cans on his hind legs with a paw on his chest and a paw raised above his head. His eyes were closed. He was marching to the cadence of his imaginary speech.

"I present to you, all of you," he said, pausing for dramatic effect, "The Smell-met!"

A sea of raccoons bowed in the presence of greatness, and Fred raised his eyes, looking into the dark dome hovering above his head. Twilight beamed through the helmet's visor with a magnificent platinum sparkle. Then Fred lowered the Smell-met onto his head.

VIII

At that exact moment, the deputy police chief of Durmond County, Dave Crandorff, left the station. It was 11:15p.m., and Dave was headed home. It had been a quiet night in Durmond. Not too unusual for the sparsely populated area. There'd been no calls that evening, no nothing, really, so he'd decided to leave early. He'd said goodbye to Tom Agna–the only officer on duty during third shift–and then he'd split. Dave was driving down Lanning road, about ten miles east of Terry Runkle's house, and six more from his own. Crandorff's future projection had him leaving the office at 11:27p.m., not 11:15p.m. None of The Agents had anticipated that he would just quit working earlier than usual that evening.

IX

Bill dropped the Runkle folder onto his desk and entered the Big Office. Another meeting, he thought. Most agents hated meetings. Bill was no different. But, it said right there in the manual what was required of The Agents regarding communication and keeping the higher-ups informed. Agency Regulations, 72-14.82, subsection Meetings.

The conference room door closed behind him, and Bill took his seat at the table.

"Okay, priority cases," Lannister said. "Go."

A man named Gregor Yadlova stood. His real name was Tony Martuzzi.

"Sir," Gregor said.

"Case?" Lannister said.

"Edwin James. Corn farmer. Iowa."

"Father of five?"

"No, sir. Two kids, one of which was born HIV positive."

"Jesus," Lannister said. "How'd that happen?"

"Sir, according to his file, his wife contracted the virus before she was aware of her pregnancy while she was having an affair."

"Problems? Concerns?" Lannister said.

"Sir, Mr. James has developed a conscience. This development has placed his present and future projections at extreme odds."

"Explain."

"He's supposed to be the new leader of the Iowa Corn Farmers Coalition that will put pressure on state representative Tanner. Pressure that will result in Tanner's eventual loss in the upcoming election."

"Problem?" Lannister said.

"The coalition is pro-GMO and aligns with conservative causes, sir. Mr. James' sick child has changed his outlook a bit more than, uhh, expected." Gregor said.

"Guy got any brothers? Sisters? Relatives nearby?"

"No, sir, just the children."

"How old's the oldest?"

"Seventeen, sir."

"Prime beneficiary?"

"Yes," Gregor said.

"Okay," Lannister said, mulling it over for a second. "Here's the fix."

The room was quiet. When Lannister spoke, agents listened. He'd been assimilating present/future projections since time eternal.

"Mr. James will die in a freak accident of some type, or maybe a murder or some botched attempted robbery. The farm goes to the kid, the oldest. Younger brother holds on for a while, and then contracts some rare parasite, that, in coupling with his already questionable immune system, forces the inevitable, and the youngest dies. Now the oldest has nobody left, feels slighted by the universe, etcetera, questions his lot in life, blah blah blah, works himself to the bone to keep the farm going. Ummmm let me think."

Lannister spun a pen around the thumb and index finger of his right hand.

"Okay, Gregor, align an older farmer's path, who lives in the same area to cross with the young Mr. James Junior. Coalition still gets its young, fiery leader, except this one's even younger and fierier."

"Thank you, sir," Gregor said.

"Okay, Gregor," Lannister said. "But you guys need to do a better job, dammit. That should have been an obvious fix. And I keep saying it, and I'll keep saying it, think out-side the box."

Lannister kicked his feet onto the conference table, and he shooed at agent Gregor Yadlova to go away.

Gregor said, "Malicious bear claw, you are my favorite snack, cholesterol high." Then he vanished.

Bill smiled–he liked that one.

"Next," Lannister yelled.

X

Deputy Dave Crandorff was singing along with the radio. His car clunked along down the road. He was in no hurry. "There are stars in the southern sky, down the sev-en bri-dges ro-ad." Crandorff tapped out the refrain to the Eagle's hit on the top of the steering wheel. He bobbed his head along in time to the tune.

Dave was smiling. There was a good song on the radio (his opinion), he had half a sandwich in the fridge at home, and it was early enough that his wife, Kate, might still be awake. He turned up the radio. He thought about his wife, then the sandwich, then his wife, and again the sandwich. The car's headlights led the way home—home to Kate, home to pulled pork and coleslaw.

XI

Had Terry Runkle awoken at that exact moment and looked out of the kitchen window, he'd have seen a raccoon marching around his trashcans like a North Korean soldier on Dear Leader's birthday. Terry Runkle, however, was fast asleep.

XII

Lannister waited for the next agent to take the floor and give a progress report. While waiting, Lannister took stock of his troops. They looked tired, uninspired. They looked not like agents of the bureau, whose dedication and determination were unquestionable, resolve unflappable, but like modern American corporate hacks. Lackeys, even. They were bleary-eyed. Their hair disheveled. Lannister even noticed a few of the agents around him with wrinkled shirts, crumpled collars, and stained ties. All three in direct violation of Agency Regulation 3-28.01, subsection Wardrobe:

> *An agent must keep up all manner of appearances, including but not limited to the ironing of pants, shirts, coats, and vests, the immediate removal of visibly stained articles of clothing, the polishing and buffing of wing-tips, and the manicured maintenance of facial hair, hair hair, and the moisturizing of skin.*

The agents were expected to act and dress as if they were representing a wing of divinity. And, they were. But things had become a bit more complex over the past few millennia.

The population of Earth had grown, and the size of the agency had followed–it was as simple as that. What had once been a group of 27 agents was now greater than 10,000. And still, the agency was shorthanded. Earth's population exceeded twelve billion, not including every species of animal or insect. Every agent was overworked and overwhelmed, like public schoolteachers with classrooms of thousands.

Caseloads continued to grow with each passing minute. Manila folders manifested themselves in the file cabinets of the archives all day, every day. Morton Piff assigned each new folder to a caseworker without regard for his or her current caseload. Within each folder lay a new set of present/future projections. A life connected to the plan.

Doors needed unlatching so that toddlers could sneak out back and fall into a family's swimming pool. A brick needed placing in the middle of a highway so it could be jettisoned by a passing 18-wheeler into the windshield of a semi-truck following closely behind, instantaneously killing the driver and causing a massive pile-up–killing another ten in the wreckage, but giving an up-and-coming news anchor her big break. A bag of meth needed placing next to a fire hydrant where a recovering junkie would get high and then go on to rape a 13 year-old girl named Allison Tanner who'd been walking home from school.

The last of which was the hardest case for Bill Glass to oversee. He watched from behind a brown picket fence, in a docile suburban neighborhood, as Allison Tanner was knocked unconscious and brutally raped by the junkie. Bill stood by as Allison's present and future projections fell back into alignment.

This was the job. And once you were chosen, the job lasted forever. There were no sick days, no vacations, and there was no quitting. Time eternal.

After Allison Tanner's case, Bill felt a bit down on The Agency. He had become a bit overwhelmed by his caseload, the nature of the work, the infallible bosses, the endless paperwork, the archivist Morton Piff, and the meetings (the meetings!). They were the worst, Bill thought, talking about work instead of actually working. How many meetings? Too many. Interrupting the day's workflow so the higher-ups could opine, direct.

Most of the other agents shared Bill's sentiments.

XIII

Terry Runkle's case had been fast-tracked to priority status because of his ex-wife, Patricia. She had been and still was too good for Terry–miles beyond him. They'd been married right out of high school. Both children lived with Patricia in New York City, Manhattan, Upper West Side.

The kids, Scott and June, were too young to remember their

father, and (since Patricia's exit) it wasn't as if Terry had made any effort to reconnect with the kids (or Patricia, for that matter). Patricia and the kids had left nine years ago. Terry thought about the three of them, maybe, once a month. They'd cross his mind when he was standing at his kitchen sink, washing dishes. Looking out of the window, he'd imagine two kids running around the yard out front, playing. They were faceless beings that had no discernible characteristics other than their relative size. Terry would picture Patricia lying in the grass, reading, and then he'd feel a pit in his stomach, he'd swallow, and he'd go on forgetting what he'd lost.

Patricia had worked as a high school teacher during their marriage. She'd taught political science and introduction to economics. It seemed to many who knew them that Patricia was far too good of a woman to have married such a dimwit as Terry, but the reality was that great women often married defective men, and no one, including The Agents at The Bureau, could ever explain why. Since the divorce, Patricia had finished her Ph.D. at Columbia, specializing in modern campaign strategies and influence throughout the region known as "The Bible Belt," in the United States. Nowadays, Patricia taught *at* Columbia. Her colleagues respected her intellect. She spent her days immersed in life and work–at the university, raising two kids–and she'd just received an offer from one of two of the major political parties in the United States to help with their campaign strategy in the southern states. It was an offer for the upcoming national elections. The money was good, and Patricia was seriously considering the job.

The Agency needed Patricia to decline the offer. Future projections indicated her overall influence on the campaign as being *the* reason for the party's victory. The party's victory went against *the* plan.

Terry Runkle was going to find Patricia's phone number next to a strategically placed flight voucher to New York. He would buy a ticket, fly to New York City, and surprise Patricia with a phone call and the news of his arrival. Terry's mere presence would force Patricia to reconsider the job offer. Family, she'd be reminded, was more important than money. She'd consider reconciling, and she'd rescind the job offer.

Without her knowledge of political strategy within the Bible Belt, the candidate for whom she would have been employed would lose. This loss, politically, would make way for the rise of Coleman Dange. Coleman Dange would be known, historically, as the man who started World War III.

None of The Agents at The Agency had the slightest clue as to why WWIII was something that the higher-ups wanted, but, then again, none of The Agents even bothered to ask.

According to his future-projection, Terry Runkle was going to find the flight voucher and his ex-wife's phone number in a pile of garbage. The garbage would be freshly spilled, lying in his drive-way. Terry would hear a noise, wake, run outside, and see a raccoon scampering away from the scene of the crime. Through the intoxicating pink and orange light of dawn, and the shimmer of the dew and fog that rested on and above the damp morning grass, he'd see Patricia's number and a voucher, and he'd say to himself, "Fate."

XIV

Deputy Crandorff opened a can of Budweiser. He drank. It was crisp. He was thirsty. The Bud tasted good. He lifted the can again and again until it was finished. Then he threw the can out of the car's window. Turning the radio up, Crandorff opened another Bud. Waylon Jennings was on the radio. Crandorff sang along, "I'm eas-y come, eas-y go, easy to love when I stay." Crandorff thought about Dane's BBQ–the local Durmond joint where he'd gotten his sandwich. Dane's specialized in barbequed pork. He'd tried to recreate the sandwich, replicate the recipe at home, but he always came up short. It had something to do with their braising, he thought, that or their spices. Deputy Crandorff took another sip of Bud, and then imagined opening his own BBQ joint. Dave's Den, he thought, that's a good name. Crandorff's Bar-Be-Dorff, no, that one's dumb, he thought, throwing another empty can out of the window.

XV

Lannister stood, hunched over the conference table with his hands at their mark like a sprinter resting at the blocks seconds before the gun.

"Everyone I can see, here," Lannister said, gesturing to The Agents nearby, "looks like shit."

A few of the men and women present bounced around uncomfortably in their seats, as if they had itchy assholes.

"I know I don't need to bring up 3-28.01," Lannister said. "Or do I?"

He looked smug. Knowing.

"This is the job," he continued. Everyone present already knew that.

"This is the job you signed up for."

A hand rose.

"Yes," Lannister said. "Go."

"Sir, we were assigned to the bureau or, I guess, I was."

"That's not the–"

"I mean–"

"What's your name, Agent?"

"Delvin," Delvin said. "Wait, do you want my real name or my agency name?"

"Why would I want your human name?" Lannister said. Agents were pathetically attached to the past, he thought.

"I don't know."

"I wouldn't," Lannister said. "You are an Agent of the Bureau, for Christ's sake. Now what's your name, Agent?"

"Julio," Delvin said. "Julio Caesar."

"Jesus," Lannister said. "I've got to have a talk with Peter."

There was a spattering of chuckles throughout the Big Office.

"Listen, I don't know why any of you are still referring to yourselves with your human names, but if you are you need to cut that shit out. Right. Now."

Lannister looked at The Agents in front of him. He shook his head in a disapproving manner, like an equestrian's father, expectant and disappointed regardless of any outcome. The Agents held on to their human names, because it was all they had. They'd believed they would've been able to hold on to so much more.

"I need the level of professionalism around here to go up, okay?" Right now we're here," Lannister said, holding his left hand at his waist, "and I need you here." He moved his right hand just shy of his hairline. "Understand?"

"Yes, sir," The Agents responded.

"Take pride in your work," Lannister said. "You are an integral part of–"

Bill finished Lannister's lines under his breath. "An integral part of intricate plans, the plan, and we can't do it without your absolute–"

"Dedication," Lannister finished.

"Sir," another Agent said.

"Name?" Lannister said.

"Caesar," Caesar said.

"Another Caesar?"

"Caesar Chavez."

"Is Peter just fucking with me?" Lannister said, raising his hands in the air, surrendering. "Never mind, don't answer that, Chavez. Go."

"Sir, it might be easier to take pride in our work if we were given ample opportunities to actually do our work."

"What's that supposed to mean?"

Eyes darted back and forth across the conference table—flashes of concern. Curious agents wondered, "Was this conversation actually going to happen right then and there?"

"Sir, I don't know if you've noticed, but we spend the majority of our time either pushing paper, tracking down folders, or sitting in oversight meetings. I haven't actually monitored a Mark in, I don't know how long. Future projections? Forget it," Chavez said. "I haven't got the time."

"Don't give me excuses," Lannister said. "I don't want excuses."

"Not to mention the caseloads," Julio Caesar said.

"Yeah," Chavez said.

"Sir, do you have any idea how many cases I have on my plate?"

"Stop. Stop it right now," Lannister said.

Bill Glass wanted to speak up, but, no point in getting involved, he thought.

"Enough shit. Enough whining," Lannister said. "This is how it's done. This is the system, and it's always been and it will always be. So, you need to... Figure... It... Out."

Heads hung. Dejected. The sheep at the table nodded. Bill, for a moment, felt relieved.

"Okay, moving on," Lannister said. "Who's on the Runkle case?"

"Sir," Bill said, standing from his chair.

"Go," Lannister said.

XVI

Fred the raccoon had let his imagination get the best of him, again. He was in a world all his own. The Smell-met. A crowd of unworthy citizens gathered below him like the peasants of ancient Rome, yelling, reaching in awe of the power before them. Fred was finishing his speech.

"There will be no more hunger. No more fighting. No more failed attempts at lid lifting on modern, plastic receptacles. There will be only garbage for all. On demand. Such is the power of the Smell-met!"

Terry Runkle rolled over in his sleep, almost disturbed by the squeaking of a raccoon with an overactive imagination. "Squeek squeak squeak squeak squeak," went Fred.

"But does it work?" cried a small and crippled raccoon from the crowd.

"Of course it works," Fred yelled.

"Prove it," the cripple said.

"Prove it," yelled another.

"Prove it. Prove it," the raccoons chanted.

"I shall," Fred said, flipping down the Smell-met's visor. "Let it be so."

Fred gestured to the crowd to retreat, to part. And at his beck-on, they did just that.

Fred focused. He thought of trash. Garbage. Refuse. He thought of the Smell-met's strength. He envisioned a small pile of garbage, and then he reached out and projected the powers of the Smell-met onto the Earth before him. Energy surged through his body and the pile grew.

The pile of garbage became a heap, and the heap became a mound. The mound grew, more now, and it became a dump. The raccoons looked on in disbelief as this, this *God* manifested a landfill's worth of garbage from thin air–from nothing. The pile grew. And it grew more. And it soared towards the heavens.

XVII

Deputy Crandorff threw another can of Bud out of the win-dow. He reminded himself that he was an officer of the law, and as such he probably shouldn't be drinking. Just a couple, he thought, life's simple pleasures. A few cans on the way home. Loosen up a bit before I get home to Kate, he thought.

Crandorff was a simple man. Not a simpleton, just simple. His dreams and aspirations were exactly what he felt they should be for a high school graduate with a steady job in the force (a steady job that paid quite well, benefits, etc.). He had a mortgage, and a wife who loved him and whom he loved, too. Even the yet-to-be-named BBQ joint that he'd fleetingly considered opening would be simple–five seats at the counter, a couple of booths–nothing too fancy. Deputy Crandorff had little interest in being a part of a grand plan. Any plans other than his simple ones, really.

Unfortunately for the deputy, he had just made a right turn

down Choula Rd. and was only a few minutes away from Terry Runkle's house. Dave's wishes were of little consequence, because by leaving work early this evening he had altered the path of his future projection. Crandorff's folder, buried deep within Morton Piff's archives, reflected these changes.

There were no Agents present to witness these changes in Crandorff's folder. All of The Agents were in meetings.

XVIII

Bill cleared his throat.

"Sir," he said, "as of exactly 11:00p.m. Mr. Runkle was fast asleep. A row of garbage cans will crash to the ground at exactly 5:32a.m., jolting Mr. Runkle into consciousness."

"Continue," Lannister said.

"Mr. Runkle will run outside to address the racket, and as he approaches the downed trashcans, he'll see his ex-wife's discarded phone number sitting next to–"

"Yeah yeah yeah, sitting next to a flight voucher to New York," Lannister said, waiving his hand in a get to the point or get the fuck out manner.

"Sir?"

"You're telling me what I already know, Per-cy."

Bill cringed. He loathed the name.

"This is the update, sir."

"It's the same as," Lannister said. "Look, you're just telling me what you think is going to happen. But you need to fucking convince me, Per-cy."

"Okay, sir."

"What about his wife's projections? Are they in agreement with your plan?"

"I don't have her projections, sir."

"Why not?"

"I don't have the fol–"

"Why don't you have the folder?" Lannister snapped.

"Piff wouldn't give it to me," Bill said.

Agency regulation 5-37.14, subsection Folders, stipulated:

> An agent may only be in possession of one folder at all times. There are no exceptions to this rule. Folders must be returned and signed for, appropriately, with the archivist, before an agent may procure a different, assigned folder. Although this regulation may seem petty, The Agency cites the era known as the "Dark Ages" as evidence for the efficacious nature of adopting said regulation. The Agency must remain vigilant against losing or misplacing folders.

"Jesus," Lannister said, rubbing his temples. "So we're in the fucking dark, here?"

"Sir," Bill said. "It's, it's hard enough." He bit his lip. "I believe in the system, sir. The last future projection indicated that morning light, glowing on voucher and phone number alike would inspire Mr. Runkle to reconnect with his ex-wife. His phone call will take place at the appropriate time–the moment his wife needs to hear his voice. She will decline the offer. Future projections indica–"

"Okay, okay," Lannister said. "Show me Runkle's sheet.

Bill looked down. The folder wasn't there. Shit, he thought.

"It's on my desk, sir," Bill said.

"High-priority case, Percy, and you leave the sheet on your

desk!"

"One moment, sir."

Bill left the conference room. He passed his secretary, Deborah, who thought about asking how the meeting was going but then decided against it. He grabbed the folder from his desk. Fucking folders, he thought. Then he hustled back into the conference room. Bill tossed the folder at Lannister.

Lannister opened Runkle's folder and saw a flashing green line. The green line changed to a flashing orange line. The orange line turned red.

"Oh, fuck," Lannister said.

"What?" Bill asked.

The rest of The Agents in the conference room sat with dumb looks slapped upon their faces. Lannister turned the folder around revealing a big fat red line, as thick as painter's tape. The projections had changed.

XIX

Fred the raccoon stood before the landfill that he'd conjured. The powers of the Smell-met witnessed by the masses. He held his arms out wide and, admiring his work, took a deep breath.

"Lead us," shouted a believer.

"Lead us," another said.

"Climb," Fred said.

The believers nodded.

"Climb," he said again, pointing up towards the peak of the towering landfill.

Fumes of the steaming refuse escaped through the composting vents of the towering mass, like geysers of smoke puncturing through the cracking countenance of Vesuvius.

"Climb," Fred said, and then he began to leap.

XX

As Terry Runkle stirred in his sleep, a car's headlights shined in the distance. Deputy Crandorff was behind the wheel, slightly buzzed, singing along to Queen. "I like to ride my bicycle, I like to ride it well. I like to ride my bicycle, I like to ride it well."

XXI

"How's Runkle getting woken, again?" Lannister said.

"Trash, uh, trashcans," Bill said.

"Trashcans, how?"

"They're getting knocked over," Bill said.

"By who?"

Bill felt a slight pain in his side.

"Fred. By Fred," Bill said.

"Who the fuck is Fred?" Lannister said.

"Fred's the raccoon that lives in the maple tree outside of Runkle's–"

"Oh, you Goddamn moron," Lannister said.

XXII

Terry Runkle's eyes opened. He blinked twice. He thought that he'd heard a noise. Terry looked at the alarm clock that sat on the bedside table. The clock's numbers glowed yellow, and they read, "11:40p.m." The sound was coming from the front yard. Clang clang clang went the sound. Terry jumped out of bed and ran to the kitchen, looking out the window in disbelief as he watched a raccoon jump into and on three overturned trashcans. What in the hell? He thought. The raccoon looked like a hyperactive child bouncing on the bed of some cheap motel.

Fred and his minions had reached the peak of their landfill and were celebrating in a state of sheer, unbridled ecstasy.

"Mother-fucker!" Terry yelled, grabbing a green handled broom from the pantry. He ran outside and bee-lined it towards the raccoon. Terry swung the broom, missed, swung again, and the broom's handle made contact with the raccoon's midsection.

Fred snapped out of his hallucinatory state when something whacked him in the stomach. Lying in a pile of garbage, Fred looked up and saw a naked man standing over him. Fred knew the man. The man was Runkle. Runkle swung again, but Fred, now aware, dodged the broom handle with relative ease and ran through the yard towards the big maple tree that he called home. "Eeep, eeep, eeep," said Fred. "Son-of-a-bitch," said Runkle, giving chase.

XXIII

Deputy Dave Crandorff's car careened around a shallow right turn, and, while looking out the driver's side window, he witnessed a flabby naked man run through a yard, wielding what looked to be a sword. Crandorff slammed on his brakes. It's always gotta be something, he thought, putting the car in park and getting out. Runkle stood at the base of the big maple tree, smacking the broom handle against the bark, yelling into the leaves and branches clustered above.

"Hey, hey you," Crandorff yelled, his left hand out in front of his body like a crossing guard at a four-way intersection. With his right hand, he unsnapped the button at the heel of the gun holstered on his waist.

"Stop."

"Huh?" Runkle said, shifting his attention to the stranger walking towards him. "Who said that?"

"Police, sir." Crandorff drew his firearm and trained it on the naked man in front of him.

"Police? What's the police for?"

"I'm with the police. Don't make any sudden movements, sir."

Crandorff examined his surroundings for a moment. Junk in the yard, abandoned cars on the property, what looked like a pile of garbage to his right. Yup, he thought, this guy could be dangerous.

"Sir, what the hell are you doing?" Crandorff said.

"Ohhh I was just chasing this damn raccoon here that knocked mah cans down o'er there," Runkle said, pointing the broom towards the pile of trash.

"Where are your clothes?"

"Oh, well, I didn't have no time to put on them pants if I wanted to get that lil' fucker," Runkle said. "What the problem is? Man ain't gotta wear no pants on his own property any why no how."

"Actually, sir," Crandorff said, "You pretty much have to wear pants all the time."

"Bullshit," Runkle said. "Hell, I hardly ever wear pants."

"In public."

"This ain't public. This mah fuckin' yard."

"Listen, sir," Crandorff said. "If you go back inside and put some clothes on before the next time you come back out, I'll ignore this ever happened."

"Ain't telling me what to do, fuckin' pig," Runkle said, and he lowered the broom handle inches from the muzzle of Crandorff's sidearm.

Fred sat in the maple above and thought about how Agent Percy was going to kill him.

XXIV

"You and you," Lannister said, pointing at the two Caesars, "Let's go."

"What about me?" Bill said.

"Of course you're coming, Percy," Lannister said. "It's your fucking mess we're cleaning up."

"I'm sorry."

"Save it," Lannister said. He closed his eyes and said, "My catapult flies, your stone walls cannot stop me, kings we overthrow."

Lannister vanished.

"Virtue knew nothing, said the evil to the good, oh mighty magpie," Caesar Chavez said.

Chavez vanished

"Represent your hood, in this life and the next one, bang motherfucker," Julio Caesar said.

Caesar vanished.

"It was laundry day, and all my socks were dirty, not that it mattered," Bill said. Bill vanished.

XXV

After Runkle had swung the broom handle at Deputy Crandorff, Crandorff had wrestled the man to the ground, placed shackles around Runkle's wrists, and locked him in the back of his cruiser. Crandorff was upset; this lunatic, this ignorant hillbilly had ruined his night.

"Where you taking me?" Runkle said.

"Durmond County, you're spending the night, buddy," Crandorff said, swinging the cruiser around and starting back towards the station.

Crandorff turned the radio up, ACDC's "highway to hell" drowned out Terry Runkle's pleads for leniency.

XXVI

The four Agents materialized in Terry Runkle's front yard. Bill walked up to the big maple tree. The two Caesars headed across the lawn towards the house, and they peered into the dark windows hoping that Runkle would be home. Lannister sifted through the downed trashcans and pulled out a flight voucher and a piece of paper that had the word "Patricia" and a number on it.

"Fred," Bill yelled, from the base of the tree. "Get down here."

"No," Fred said.

"Now," Bill said.

Fred made his way to the Maple's lowest branch. He remained out of reach–Percy couldn't grab me at this distance, he thought. Lannister and the two Caesars made their way over to the tree.

"What the hell happened, Fred?" Bill said.

"It's all very complicated, and you'll probably never understand."

"Try me," Bill said.

"Well, first off," Fred said, "There was this helmet, well, a Smellmet, really, and it gave me these amazing superpowers. I was like a God. You should have seen it. And the others, they were all following me."

"That's enough," Lannister said.

"What?"

"Listen you little fuck-up," Lannister said, "you have no idea what you've done here, no idea! Now, where'd they go?"

"The police man took the Runkle away, because he was naked and he tried hitting the policeman with a broom."

"What police man?" Bill said, hoping that there was still a chance the ship could be righted.

A broom lay next to the maple.

"Durmond County," Fred said. "That's the last thing I heard him say before they drove off."

"Which way did they go?" Lannister asked.

Fred pointed down the road in the direction the cruiser had gone.

"Gentlemen," Lannister said, "Durmond County jail. Go."

Lannister and the two Caesars repeated their haikus and vanished.

Bill lagged behind for a second.

"You really fucked me over on this one," Bill said.

"Sorry," Fred said. "But, man, you should've been there. I was like a God."

"I have no idea what you're talking about," Bill said, shaking his head, "and I don't care. In the face of God, I question my existence, left unsatisfied." And then he vanished.

XXVII

Deputy Crandorff parked the cruiser and took the key out of the ignition. It's always got to be something, he thought, taking a deep breath. He opened his door and walked around to the trunk of the car.

"Hey, lemme outta here," Runkle said from the back seat.

"One damn minute," Crandorff said.

Crandorff pulled a government-issue safety blanket out of the trunk. He closed the trunk and opened the car's rear door. The parking lot was empty, save Tom Agna's cruiser.

"Here," Crandorff said, holding the blanket out for Runkle.

"Now, how ma sposed to grab that thang with these on?" Runkle said, turning to his right to show the bracelets that held his hands together behind his back.

"Right, right," Crandorff said.

"Well, hell, least you got me a blanket."

Crandorff draped the blanket over Runkle's shoulders and around his body, twice. Runkle was cuffed and encased like a sausage, or like a cat wrapped in a small blanket–all head and hind legs, no body.

They made their way to the station's entrance. Crandorff opened the door for Runkle, and then they stepped inside the building.

Durmond County was a small, tidy unit of police real estate–like an old man's studio apartment. Tom Agna stood from behind the only desk in the office.

"Well hey there, Deputy," Agna said. "We've been expecting you."

"We?" Crandorff said, and then he saw the four men seated in the waiting area to his right, opposite the desk.

"Yes, sir," Agna said. "These men here are from The Bureau. That right, gentlemen?"

"That's correct," Lannister said.

"Bureau?" Crandorff said, "What bureau?"

"Ha," Agna said, straightening his tie. "The F–B–I."

"My name is Special Agent Lannister," Lannister said, holding out his hand, "And these are agents of mine." He gestured to the men behind him, "Agents Caesar, Chavez, and Stanbridge."

"Y'all Mehsicans?" Runkle said, looking at Caesar and Chavez, who were quite obviously Black and Anglo-Saxon, respectively.

"Shut it," Crandorff said, giving Runkle a quick shake. "That's a black man, you idiot."

Lannister grimaced. Time was being wasted with these, these morons, he thought.

"Well, hell, I dunno," Runkle said under his breath. "Man says his name's Chavez, that's a Mehsican name to me."

Crandorff shook Lannister's hand.

"Pay him no mind," Crandorff said. "What can I do for you?"

"Lannister."

"Lannister, right. What can I do for you Agent Lannister?

"Well, Deputy."

"Hey, Agna, get over here would you and get this idiot in some clothes, would you?"

Tom Agna sped around the desk and grabbed the blanketed Runkle.

"Come on, you," Agna said.

"As I was saying," Lannister said.

"Right."

"Deputy, we've actually been chasing that man right there, Terry Runkle, for some time."

"Really?" Crandorff said. "Because I ran his name through the system on the way out here, and it came through pretty clean. Couple of misdemeanors some time ago but nothing crazy."

"Deputy, there are some databases you just wouldn't have access to in a standard cruiser."

"Oh yeah," Crandorff said, shrugging his shoulders. "I suppose that'd be about right."

"Anyways," Lannister said. "We would've had him earlier today, if Agent Stanbridge hadn't royally fucked up."

Crandorff peered around Lannister's head at Agent Stanbridge, whose own head was hung in shame.

"Him?" Crandorff said.

"Yes, him."

"So what can I do for you?"

"Well, Deputy, we need to interrogate your prisoner."

"Interrogate?"

"That's correct," Lannister said, articulating each word "He's involved in a very intricate plan, and we need to find out what he knows."

"Weeeeeell," Crandorff said, "I suppose I don't have a problem with that."

"Good," Lannister said.

"So long as I'm in the room with you fellas." Crandorff winked at Lannister. "I just want to observe a bit of y'alls' techniques. Get a little bit of FBI training and all that."

Lannister closed his eyes and muscled out the words "That'll be fine" through gritted teeth. They're all idiots, he thought. God help me.

XXVIII

Runkle, Crandorff, Caesar, Chavez, Lannister, and Bill were seated at a round wooden table in the interrogation room. The room seemed more suited for a card game than an interrogation. The décor would be best described as 1990s Dallas Cowboys fandom; there was even a mini fridge in the corner. Crandorff was snacking on a small package of salted peanuts.

It was 12:17a.m.

"Well, let's get to it," Crandorff said.

Lannister glared at Crandorff. Who's in charge here? He thought. He turned to Terry Runkle.

"Mr. Runkle," Lannister said.

"Yep," Runkle said.

"You're probably wondering why you're here."

"Naw I ain't," Runkle said. "That man o'er there 'rrested me, because I was chasing after a raccoon in my front yard."

Runkle leaned into a nonexistent microphone and said, "Let the record show that I was on my own property."

"Not why you were arrested," Lannister said, "Why you're in this room. Here. With us."

"Oh," Runkle said. "You and your lap dog and them two Mehsicans got some questions for me or something?"

Runkle motioned towards the agents.

"No. That's not it," Lannister said.

Crandorff perked up. He wondered, aren't we were here for questions?

"Well, what then?" Runkle said.

"I need you to do something."

"What's that then?"

"I need you to call someone."

"What in the fuck is all this?" Runkle said, looking at Crandorff.

"Better do what the man asks," Crandorff said. "The F–B–I."

"Who?" Runkle said.

Lannister held his arm out in Bill's direction.

"Agent Stanbridge, please hand me Mr. Runkle's sheet."

"I don't have it, sir," Bill said.

"What do you mean? You didn't bring it?"

"I, I left it at the agency," Bill said, thinking for a moment. "No no, you left it at–"

Lannister shushed Bill, and then he thought about it. He was the last one with the folder.

"Chavez," Lannister said, "Get me that folder, now."

"Sir," Chavez said. "Metamorphosis, changing tides of woven bugs, wonderful beauty," and then he vanished.

Crandorff jumped out of his seat, peanuts flew from his shaking hands. Runkle let out a high-pitched squeal, like an excited child who'd just seen a magician produce the three of clubs from his shoe.

"Where'd that Mehsican go?" Runkle said, bouncing in his seat.

"Sit down, please," Lannister said, motioning to Crandorff. "This is big. Bigger than each of you, and I didn't want it to happen this way, I would have preferred to keep both of you in the dark, here, but we are short on time."

Lannister stood, walked over to Crandorff, and eased the Deputy back into his seat.

"That man jus' dis'ppeared," Runkle said. "I never seen nothing—"

"Stop talking," Lannister said. "I've had enough."

Runkle stared at the sorcerer and swallowed with a thunk—the kind of noise a large rock makes when it's tossed into a pond by an obese redneck.

Lannister pulled out a cell phone, and he placed it on the table in front of Runkle. Crandorff and Runkle followed his every movement. They were stupefied. Awestruck.

Then Lannister reached in the inside pocket of his suit coat, and pulled out a piece of scrap paper. He placed the scrap paper next to the phone. Terry Runkle read the name Patricia, and looked at the phone number.

"Patricia?" Runkle said.

"Patricia," Lannister said.

"My ex?"

"Yes."

"Now what in the hell you want me to call Patty for?" Runkle said.

"It's bigger than you," Lannister said.

"What you want me to say?"

"Just call her and tell her that you're coming to New York. That you miss her."

"I can't go to New York," Runkle said. "I ain't got that kind of money."

Lannister reached into his coat once more and produced a flight voucher to New York City.

"You don't need any money," Lannister said.

Because Runkle was a moron, the phone number and the flight voucher impressed him more than the man who'd just vanished into thin air.

"Oh-oh-okay," Runkle said. "I'll call Patty."

Bill, breaking out of character, questioned Lannister.

"Sir," Bill said. "He's not supposed to make the phone call until 5:32a.m."

"I know that," Lannister snapped. "You think I don't know that?"

"I was just–"

Chavez materialized onto the tabletop. Everyone in the room jumped back, including Lannister.

"Sorry," Chavez said. "I missed." He handed Runkle's folder over to Lannister.

"Wha, what now?" Runkle said.

Lannister flipped the folder open, and he watched the sheet's thick red line flash and then turn orange.

"We wait," Lannister said.

And wait they did.

XXIX

Almost five and a half hours later, at 5:31a.m., Lannister nodded to Terry Runkle.

"It's time," Lannister said.

Runkle picked up the cell phone, and began to dial. The thick orange line inside the folder began blinking.

The phone rang. Lannister sat still, concentrating on the orange flashing line that determined so much.

The phone rang again.

Runkle looked up at Lannister.

Lannister held out his hand. Wait.

The phone rang once more.

A voice answered on the other end.

"Hello?" it said.

"Patty?"

"Who is this?"

Lannister watched as the blinking orange line began flashing green.

"Terry," Runkle said.

"Who?"

"Terry."

"Terry?"

"Yeah, baby. Terry."

"Terry?" Patricia said. "Are you fucking kidding me? I told you never to call here again. Ever."

The line went dead. The flashing green streak turned into a solid red stripe.

"Hello? Patty?"

Runkle turned to Lannister.

"She hung up."

"What do you mean she hung up?" Lannister said.

"She hung up. That's it. She don't really want me calling over there... it was a pretty nasty divorce."

What a waste of time, Bill thought, all of it. Another giant, pointless mess.

"The wheels keep spinning," Bill said, "just a cog in the machine, where nothing matters."

And then he vanished.

The Will

THE WILL

My mother's will was read on a Saturday morning during one of the largest snowstorms on record in Lansing. Snowdrifts piled against houses and parked cars as if the break of a perfect wave had frozen, decayed, and reconstituted itself into an endless white ocean.

I pulled over at the corner of Kalamazoo and Pennsylvania. The rental—a black sedan—listed to the right as its tires lost their grip and then regained traction. I wondered if the car was playing an amusing, low-stakes game with me. I could hear the crunch of the snow packing beneath the tires as my chariot eased to a stop. I hadn't been home in years. Didn't have to think about snow down south. I'd forgotten that pleasant fluff could turn on you, put you on the ground or crash your car—if you didn't pay attention.

After grabbing the key from the ignition, I cupped my bare hands over my mouth and exhaled in three short bursts: Hah–Hah–Hah. I took one final breath of the rental's warm air as I pulled the door handle and stepped into Satan's version of Narnia: Cap City in a blizzard.

My legs punched into the snowpack like pistons, but I felt only the slightest chill around where my knees were hidden. Fucking winter, I thought. I waded through the heavy, wet pack like some ancient human miraculously escaping the La Brea tar pits–like Atreu in the forest of despair.

The roads were empty. The city was barren. Abandoned buildings that I remembered from my last visit eight years ago had remained empty. Houses leaned. There was an absence of life. No other cars were parked at the gas station and none had passed me on the road, either. Tracks and prints lacked strength and longevity. Everything was white, and those things that had held out from the blanketing were slowly losing the war of attrition as the wind changed with every gust, and nooks in windows on forsaken buildings and dry triangles of concrete under the awnings of decrepit storefronts began their assimilation into the fold.

I opened the door to the Quality Dairy, the bell chimed, and I stepped onto the mat. I removed my wet hat and brushed my arms and shoulders, and then beat at my thighs with the soggy knit cap. I stomped each foot three times onto the doormat. I nodded to the clerk who sat behind a thick slab of bulletproof glass and walked over to the coffee machine.

There wasn't any coffee going.

I turned, scanning the aisle for maybe a second machine.

"Where's the coffee at?" I said.

"Huh?" the clerk said.

"Where's the coffee at?" I said, louder. "You got the machine," I pointed, "pot's here but no coffee going."

"Yeah," he shrugged his husky shoulders. "I didn't make any today."

"Didn't make any?"

"Nope?"

"Why the fuck not?" I said, shaking my head.

"Look man," the clerk said, "you're the only person other than me that's walked in here today, and I don't drink that shit."

"You still shoulda put some on, you know, in consideration for the potential customer that might, just might be interested in some coffee at eight-thirty in the morning when it looks like that outside."

I gestured towards the windows that spanned the length of the storefront. You could barely make the outline of the rental that sat no more than ten feet outside the window. The clerk shrugged his shoulders, again, and said, "You can put a pot on if you'd like."

"Oh, so now I gotta do your job?" I said, grabbing the decanter and placing it on the machine's port.

I took a filter from the stack, smashed it into the metal drip pot, and scooped three cups of grounds into the filter. I flicked the black switch at the top, and the machine began to whirr. Praise Forseti. There would be coffee.

Turning to the clerk, I raised my arms out like Christ hung out to dry.

"Jesus, that was excruciating," I said.

The clerk looked at me, and he fucking shrugged, again. Couldn't be bothered. And at the distance I was standing I couldn't be certain, but I'm pretty sure the fat, lazy sod rolled his eyes. He turned his attention back to the mini TV set next to the register.

As the coffee continued to brew, I walked up and down the three aisles looking at the packages of candy bars, beef jerky, chips, cookies, crackers, nuts, gummy bears and worms, and the wall of fridges, opposite the clerk's bulletproof enclosure (his stationary pope-mobile), filled with more sugary junk–sodas, energy drinks, fake juice, fake "real" juice, sports drinks, smoothies, diet juices, milkshakes, Starbucks Frappé bullshit.

You could seriously get your fill at a minimart these days. Everything in bright, alluring wrappers as if the contents were cause for celebration. The masses enjoyed the convenience of obesity. They enjoyed poisoning themselves, slowly, but in a socially acceptable manner, all the while growing bigger, growing weaker. This is a nation of molasses. I can't stand it. I want them to keep eating. I want them to suffer from their unyielding penance. Let them draw it out as long as they can, until that last meaty breath. Why not? They're doing it to themselves. I offer no sympathy.

I considered stealing something to show the clerk, in some petty way, how I felt about him, but I heard the whirr of the coffee pot come to a halt and decided against the whole vengeance through theft thing (although I'm certain that if I had taken a five-fingered discount on a few items, Hermes would have watched over me). Pouring the coffee, I paused while watching the piping-hot liquid tar fill my cup. I popped on a lid, grabbed the decanter, and made my way to the clerk's Plexiglas window.

"Hey, man, " I said. "I'm sorry about that, I've just had a rough morning you know, one of those kinds of days."

"Don't worry about it," he said.

I smiled.

"What?" he said.

I raised my arm above my head, brandishing the decanter of freshly brewed coffee, as if it were Thor's hammer and I was the God of Thunder himself.

"Your insufferable inaction has disappointed me, human!" I said, my voice roaring with false righteousness.

I swung my arm, hurled the decanter, and it shattered against the wall opposite the exit. I ran for the door as the clerk yelled, "Asshole. Asshole."

An eye for an eye, I thought, opening the door to the calamitous winter. The blizzard wind bit into my face like a hundred frozen piranhas–not that the piranhas were frozen, but that when they bit into me they–forget it.

I held my coffee at arm's length as I high-stepped through the snow to the rental, spilling large drops with each lunge. Snow forced its way into my boots and stuck to the fibers of my jeans like frigid magnets.

I tore open the door to the rental and threw the store clerk the finger before getting into my seat. I jammed the coffee into the cup holder and cut on the ignition. My heart was racing. I yelled come on, come on, as I deliberately pulled the car out of its parking space. After all, it was the blizzard of the century, and I wasn't going to risk getting in some dumb accident because of a hasty getaway.

The rental lurched, crunching over the snow, as I made my pathetic five-mile-per-hour escape.

I arrived at the lawyer's office seven minutes before nine, and I waited, drinking my coffee in silence. I hadn't seen my father in eight years. My mother had come down south a couple of years ago, to Savannah, where I'd resided for the better part of a decade.

The last time I'd been back to Lansing was to pay my respects at my uncle's funeral–my mother's brother. Uncle Rob had died from what the doctor had called a "massive heart attack," but what we just called a heart attack. My mother had told me it was as if someone had placed a grenade in his chest. All the vessels and arteries had burst. They looked like frayed wires, she said, his heart like a dog's old chew toy. Regardless of the medical accuracy of her summary, I got the message.

Uncle Rob was a good guy, a decent man. Somebody you might not exactly aspire to be like, but you also wouldn't be too upset if when it was all said and done you ended up resembling. After Rob went, my mother just kind of holed up in her house and let the months pass.

She divorced my father that year. He had it coming. Dad was a drunk—a real piece of work. He'd usually start around noon, taking a swig from his stash in the garage or down in the basement, and by the early evening he was gone. Sometimes he'd pass out on the couch, or if he got pissed or frustrated he'd make a scene, yelling, threatening, acting tough, and then he'd storm outside like a ghoul. His body would be crumpled, crippled by the booze and a lifetime of repressed whatever it was that he'd been holding inside for all those years. Growing up, those times were the worst. I was maybe fifteen or sixteen. I'd come home from school when dad had already been at the bottle for three or four hours, and he'd tell me to sit with him a minute. "Talk to me," he'd say, staring off into space. So I'd sit, and I'd talk to him how I imagined normal kids talk to normal fathers. When that didn't work, I'd speak in accents. I'd act Russian. I'd be Hercules. My imagination wandered, and whoever came out was whom dad got. He hated when I did that.

I remember thinking how pathetic he'd look, how sad. The man was toxic. Dad wasn't much for talking, and even when he tried his jaw would clench, and he'd bite his lips, as if his muscles were at war with his brain's synapses. I'd leave him there sitting on the couch, alone, his body all locked up.

I never thought dad would outlive mom, but after Uncle Rob died Mom just shut down. She quit her job at the law firm, after thirty years, divorced dad, got a small apartment downtown, and just stopped taking care of herself, I guess. Stopped living.

When she visited Savannah, she was thin and weak–she looked worn out, tired. It was the cancer. We spent most of that week on the balcony of my apartment, overlooking the square filled with Spanish moss below. With our feet up, we allowed time and the brutal humidity to pass over us. Accepting fate and circumstances, alike. Mom liked the trees, she said.

Mom went back to Lansing, where she held on for another five months. Then she died. I packed a bag and flew to Detroit, rented a car, drove to Lansing, broke that coffee pot on the wall of the gas station, made my slow getaway in this apocalyptic blizzard, and as I sat in the rental, with my hands gently waving in front of the heat vents, I thought about my mother.

She had worked for Müller, Lipin, and Camus her entire career. The same firm was handling her will, holdings, and any other post-mortem wishes she'd had.

I got out of the rental and stomped through the snow to the entrance, which had been both recently shoveled and, more recently, snowed over. I opened the door and stepped inside, brushing myself off with my hat and pounding my boots, remembering the curious rhythms of winter, before passing through another set of doors and into the reception area.

"How may I assist you today, Sir?" the receptionist said.

She was in her thirties–her blond hair was pulled back into a bun thing that rested just above the nape of her neck. She wore a suit that struggled to make her look unremarkable, and it would have succeeded if it weren't for her natural beauty–neutral business attire betrayed by the figure within it. You couldn't put Aphrodite in a pantsuit and expect it to hide anything, I thought.

"Hi," I said. "I'm–uh–here for my mother's will."

"And what's her name?"

"Helen J. Davis."

"Oh," she said, "You're Helen's boy?"

"Yep. That's me. I'm me. I'm Rich."

"I worked with Helen," she said. "I'm Cynthia, it's very nice to meet you."

You bore me with your innocuous formalities, human.

"Likewise," I said.

"We weren't very close, your mother and I," she said, "but nonetheless, we're all very sad not to have her around anymore."

She smiled, revealing a set of perfectly white and shapely American teeth.

"Thanks," I said.

"Anyways," she said, "I think your father is already here."

"And where would here be?"

"That way."

She pointed down the hall.

"Thanks," and I walked *that* way.

I knocked on a door, and a man on the other side of that door said, "Enter–" I finished his sentence for him. "The chamber of lawyerly pursuits Firstborn Son of Davis, for your presence is required."

"Rich, I assume," he said. "My name's Leonard Lipin." He extended his hand to me, and I took it. "My father's the one whose name sits between Müller and Camus on the side of the building."

Your namesake means nothing to me, peasant.

"Please, have a seat," he said.

He sat on the edge of the table and motioned with his right hand at a seat across the table from my father.

I looked over the old man. He was in a bad way. He looked wiry, and he was trying to hide the shakes by keeping his right hand in his lap. I could see his elbow twitching, though. He stared at the table, moving his left hand across the surface of the stained wood, preoccupied with the grain. He looked ugly–all picture, no Dorian. I see the test of time has brought you little grace, father. He stayed focused on his hand passing over the table. I walked down to the opposite end of the long table (a sizeable slab that sat at least twenty), and I took my seat at the head, opposite from Lipin.

"This seat will work just fine," I said.

"Suit yourself, Mr. Davis," he said, and he took his seat.

I placed my elbows on the table and rested my chin and cheeks on the knuckles of each hand.

"Let me start by saying," Lipin said, "that I had the pleasure of working with Helen for the entirety of her career."

Lipin scanned my father's face, which existed in a sort of mauled transience, and then Lipin's eyes met mine.

"And I can say," he continued, "Unequivocally, that Helen was one of the sharpest legal minds in the business."

He paused.

"Her capacity for legal strategy, for research and planning, for cunning courtroom preparation, and background investigation was unlike anything I'd ever seen before her and unlike anything that I'm likely to see from this day forward."

"And I know it's not my place, but after things got rough with the marriage and all that, I'd like you two to know that Helen showed incredible character during those years of turmoil by working harder than anybody else here, at this firm."

"She truly gave everything to this place, and on behalf of my father and his partners and myself, I'd like you two to know that she was truly a wonderful woman of purpose, intelligence, and character."

Lipin clasped his hands together at the edge of the table, proud of his words.

"Can we get this thing over with?" my father said. "Hey look, listen, I mean, if this is the end of the road, then I want to get on with it."

I gestured towards Mr. Lipin. See what I've been dealing with my whole life, Lipin? What we've been dealing with?

"Excuse me?" Lipin said.

"He just wants to know who's getting the money," I said. "Tell you what Dad, I'll save you the time and the worry and all that. Lipin."

"Yes?" Lipin said.

"I'm assuming my mother has given me all of her assets, her wealth, property, etc. is that correct?"

"Yes, sir," Lipin said. "That's right."

"I don't want it," I said.

"Sir?"

"Regardless of what's read, it doesn't matter," I said. "I've made up my mind."

I looked at my father, his face red and bulbous.

"I don't want it," I said, shaking my head.

"What?" my father said.

"You can have it," I said. "I don't want it."

"You sure you want," Lipin said.

"Yeah, yeah," I said. "I don't need it, I don't want it." I pointed at the old man. "Give it to him. I know what he's going to do with it, and I'm okay with it."

"You're going to have to sign some papers," Lipin said.

"Yeah, sure," I said. "Let's do that."

I signed on the various dotted lines, shook Lipin's hand, and left the room. I passed Cynthia the receptionist on the way out and smiled at her.

As I opened the doors, I gazed outside. The storm had worsened. The blizzard seemed to be raging from every direction. Chaotic ill will. Snowflakes so large you could hear them land, like fat bumblebees smacking into kitchen windows. Everything was white now.

Wading into the glacial fluff, I tucked my chin and ear against my right shoulder as the wind and snow bit into my cheeks. I jumped over a berm of snow that had recently blown into existence and blocked the path to the rental. The snow was heavier now, wet, and it tugged at my knees.

I looked at the rental, parked a few paces away. A small triangle of black that sat under the side-view mirror betrayed the rest of the car's new winter coat. You could hear the wind. You could hear the snow. I could see my breath. I looked up at the sky, and then all I saw was the white. My eyelids fluttered as they tried to protect their tenants from the onslaught.

I allowed my legs to go. I shifted my weight and fell back to the ground. My body thumped into the thick layer. The pack enveloped my head, and at first there was quiet. But then all I could hear was the snow, pieces of snow, avalanches of microscopic proportions sliding and eventually settling next to my ears. Finally there was silence, and the only feeling that cut through all that cold as the snow suspended me, weightless in my isolation, was warmth.

TETRA

The last three years I had hosted at Le Phoque, Paulo Embretti's most recent endeavor. I'd absolutely loved that job. It had been everything. More than a paycheck or social circle, I had a tiny piece of real estate in The City–a booth at a striking restaurant. A moderate space filled with handcrafted tables and chairs, amber lighting, and the sounds that accompany evenings filled with joy: clinking glasses, hearty laughter, good conversation. Every night, after the rush of service had dissipated and the restaurant was cleared, Chef Paulo and Mr. Dean would rattle off sales numbers and give out two vintages, one to the night's top earner and one to the hardest worker. Then came a beautiful family meal–wine paired with dishes from that night's menu. Everything that I loved about living in The City was attached to that job, and without it I felt alienated, orphaned. Surely there was another restaurant just like it, right? After all, there are thousands of restaurants in The City. But, like my dad used to say, "Nobody wants to get sent back down to the minors. Nobody wants to ride that damn bus, again." I gave that place my identity, and, in turn, it gave me back something refined, something better, a version of myself that I'd been waiting for my entire life. And then I got fired.

The circumstances surrounding my dismissal would be best described as unfair. I mean, that's what I thought of them then and that's what I think of them now. It was a Friday, and we had had one of *those* nights on the books. Stress levels were higher than normal that day, because Chef Paulo had fired his Sous that morning, a move I had celebrated (Quentin was a complete asshole), but at the time I was also unaware how far down the chain the dominoes would fall. An hour into service, the kitchen was already behind. Chef Paulo was on the line, and Mr. Dean was expediting. These two Dapper Dans had opened the place together, but it was obvious from the beginning of the evening that they were having a hard time deciding who was in charge of service. What should have gone smoothly became a mess. Even in the brief moments when I had walked back into the kitchen to tell the guys about a couple of Soigné tables, I'd heard them bickering about who was responsible for some miscommunication on a couple of tickets, why two of the ginger pork belly specials had been fired instead of three, and a moment when Chef Paulo actually told Mr. Dean to get back out on the floor where he "fucking" belonged. But, you know, it was business as usual in a way, so we all (the rest of us) did our best to act professional and get through what was clearly going to be a long night in the weeds.

By the third hour of service, reservations were behind thirty-five minutes. I told Michaela (my partner on the weekends) to comp drinks for the people waiting. I left her to run the host stand while I took a few seconds here and there to flip tables or run a couple of cocktails from the bar. Everything was behind and from time to time that was just how it went, and all you could do was smile and look for the light at the end of the tunnel and know that, even if you couldn't see it at the moment, it was there, somewhere past the darkness.

Michaela had been working with me for six months. So, you could hardly blame her for what happened, and really, you could hardly blame me. But in the end it was my fault (Mr. Dean's words, not mine). There was a folder that lived under our host stand with portraits of the important restaurant critics who worked and lived in The City. Everyday before service, whoever was hosting was supposed to flip through those photos, get acquainted with names and faces, and then notify the server, the bar manager, and the kitchen if one of them showed. Well, on the night that I was stripped of the only job I've ever loved, Michaela didn't recognize J. Miller from The Post. I'm not sure if it actually would have mattered at that point, because we were already so deep in the weeds, but, regardless of hypothetical scenarios, the reality was that he waited in the corner with his date for an hour. About the time that they had finally been seated, we began to flip the restaurant. It was a madhouse, and the servers, apparently, forgot to stagger their orders because everything came in at once. To try and help out, I sat people every five minutes, regardless of how long they'd been waiting—one table at a time, hoping that I could restore some of the natural rhythm and order to the performance. After another hour, it was obvious that my attempt at righting the vessel had been in vain. We weren't running in the fashion that we were used to (smoothly) and Paulo and Dean had both *clearly* underestimated the pivotal role that Quentin had played, a common occurrence for Sous Chefs it seems.

I abandoned Michaela, again, and started running drinks from the bar and food from the kitchen. However terrible the night had actually been going, this was my favorite part of the job, discovering an uncanny ability to move faster and think clearer through the thick fog of a shitty service. I had grabbed a couple of martinis from the bar and weaved my way through a crowd to Table 12, and when I began setting the drinks on the table, apologizing to the customers for the wait, I looked up and saw J. Miller. He was lazily sipping at his glass of water and looking both bored and dissatisfied. I addressed him, thanked him for joining us that evening, and I asked him if there was anything I could get him at the moment. "Our server would be nice," he said, "I haven't seen her in about twenty minutes." I told him not to worry, that I'd send her right over, and then I ran to the kitchen to tell everyone the awful news.

When I walked in, Chef Paulo was screaming at Mr. Dean. There were plates double and triple-stacked in the window, a line of tickets hung from the rail, and the chefs were standing by, idly. "We're not cooking another fucking thing until all of this shit goes," Paulo said, pointing at the window in front of him. I told Mr. Dean to give me the next tray, and on my way out the door, I turned around and said, "Oh, by the way, J. Miller is at table 12. I think he's been there for a while. So, you guys better play nice."

When Chef Paulo and Mr. Dean fired me, they said three things. One, J. Miller, or any other critic for that matter was not an "Oh, by the way," piece of information. Two, how long had he been there, and why didn't I know? And three, it wasn't my job to tell them how to interact with each other. "We've been business partners for fifteen years," they'd said. And then they let me go.

I guess I was feeling kind of down on The City, and the fish tank seemed to help (some). Aside from the job, nothing had changed, and I should have been able to bounce back relatively easily. Even with the horrible weather, The City was still dancing. During the last couple of weeks, I would peek out the living room window from my nest, down onto the street, and see people running around the neighborhood, going to the bars and restaurants, out on their happy, coupled excursions, being normal and (apparently) unaffected by life. Certain of their identities. But life wasn't really going on for me. I felt isolated. So I surrendered to whatever the universe was trying to tell me, and I started spending a lot of time in front of the fish tank.

The funniest part about it (if there was any humor at all in this dumb situation of mine) was that my roommates hadn't even noticed that I'd been spending all that time at home. Why would they notice? It's not as if they were ever there. There were three of them, roommates, I mean–Mike, Kelly, and Isis–and like plenty of young professionals in The City with jammed agendas, social calendars, and cell phones that never left their hands, they were hardly around. I mean Kelly and Mike basically lived with their SOs. Isis slept at home, but that was it. She'd come home, walk straight to her room, and close the door (hello, goodbye). You'd really only see her if she needed to use the bathroom or answered the door for the cute bicycle messenger guy that always brought her Chinese food. Also Isis worked early, so she was always up and out before anybody else.

The first time I spent the whole night on the couch watching the fish tank, I surprised Isis in the morning. She was on her bleary-eyed way to the shower. I was on the couch wrapped in my comforter to keep the chill off me–deflecting the irritatingly persistent gust that blew through the uneven edge of the window. I said, "Hi" as she walked out of her bedroom. Isis shrieked, like my presence was something to be frightened of at that time of day (frown). What was I doing up? Oh, I couldn't really sleep so I'd come out to the living room to look at the fish tank in hopes that it would be boring enough to knock me out (Ha-Ha). I kind of mustered this weak smile, and it must have made her feel awkward, because she just said, "Okay," and then took a shower, dressed, and left for work without any further interaction with that sad girl on the couch (me).

Our apartment wasn't that big, but it was definitely big enough when you were the only one who was ever there, with nowhere else to be. And when the weather looked like it currently looked, and time passed like it was currently passing, it was definitely big enough. For. Just. Me.

The fish tank wasn't even mine, either, it was Mike's, and I'd always wondered when he fed the fish. He'd been basically living at Victoria's since they'd started dating (Victoria was his "spectacular" girlfriend–he'd actually called her that once, spectacular). I got the answer to my question on the same day I'd surprised Isis, when Mike came home on his lunch break and fed the fish. Not working today, he said, and I shook my head and watched him tap, four times, on the plastic bottle of fish food, sprinkling the flakes into four different parts of the tank.

Mike was in realty. I've never been exactly sure what he did, but I know that when he first got the job he had a lot more money but was really stressed out all the time when he was home, and then he started putting together the fish tank, because he'd heard from a friend of his that watching fish would help him relax after a long day of hustling through The City. Now I was the one trying to get something out of that fish tank, and after two weeks I was starting to think that it might just be working.

Kelly literally hadn't set foot into the apartment in the last two weeks. I was certain of that, because I hadn't left (and, yes, I'm completely aware that's something I shouldn't be proud of). It's not like anybody ever complained about Kelly's absence, because she still paid her rent on time and when she had been around in the past we'd kind of realized that we'd had some poor judgment in letting her move in, because she had one of those personalities, you know *those* ones. Maybe you don't know. How do I explain it? Well, she was one of those types that you could only talk to for five minutes at a time (per week, really), and then after she was done shouting shrilly noises, you felt physically exhausted and needed some type of deep tissue massage and some scented oils and the sounds of nature to help you get through the rest of your day without replaying over and over again exactly how much you couldn't believe that she annoyed you, and then you couldn't believe she annoyed you *that* much, and then you couldn't believe that you'd been spending such a large portion of your day thinking about how much you couldn't believe that she annoyed you that much. She was pretty bad (but, you know, in that harmless kind of way). And, I have to say that as much as I'd accepted Kelly's absence in the apartment, she was punctual when it came time to send in rent. If nothing else, that's a silver lining, right? (Go Kelly).

The second day that Mike had come home around lunch to feed the fish, he'd asked me if I'd gotten a new job. I told him that Rosa, the bartender, had quit and they needed me to fill in for her schedule and that meant a split between lunch and dinner shifts. He asked me if I liked the change, and I told him that I was still adjusting. Then Mike asked me if I wouldn't mind feeding the fish, because it would help him out a ton (he'd actually used the words, "a ton," spectacular) if he didn't have to drive back across The Bridge every day to feed the babies (his words), and he'd give me twenty bucks a day. That would net me over five hundred dollars a month for my rent, if I did it every day. So, I mean, that decision was obviously easy to make, because I was, you know, unemployed (our secret). So now I fed the fish every day around two, and my unemployed, sorry butt only needed to come up with a thousand bucks to make rent by the end of the month, instead of fifteen hundred.

The first day that I took over food duty for Mike felt kind of weird, weird and harder than I'd imagined. It was exhausting to do anything (I know it sounds ridiculous). I knew that now I played a pivotal role in their survival, and it felt good to be needed. I lumbered up to the tank around the same time that Mike had come home the day before, and I just stood there. I was totally aware that all I had to do was grab the white bottle of flakes and feed the fish, but it honestly took so much energy to even lift my arms to the top of the tank and grab that bottle. Then I opened the three large, black plastic pieces on top of the tank that flipped open, and they should have weighed next to nothing but somehow felt like they were built from solid granite. It was pathetic how exhausting it was, and I caught my breath as I stared down into the bubbling water below. I tapped the bottle, and when the flakes hit the surface a couple of fish swam up to the top, and I saw them open their mouths in this funny, reversed bobbing-for-apples way. Like they were gasping for food. When I tapped the flakes out into a different spot in the tank, the little family of five that looked like black corn chips started nibbling at the surface. All the little families took their turns swimming to the top of the tank and eating. It was all very communal and friendly, almost cordial.

After that, I retreated to the couch. I looked outside (where it was still super grey and snowing), and I sunk deeper into my comforter. The last few little guys had gotten their fill, and then they kept going about their day just like normal. They went about it in a funny way, too. Their life took place in a miniature, submerged city of rocks and plants, and this giant log was their only skyscraper. The families moved together, yet stayed separate, swimming around the tank in a way that made them aware of each other but never let on that they were actually paying attention to anybody but themselves. Sometimes all the families would navigate the waters by carefully avoiding contact with one another, and other times they would occupy their few gallons of the tank while swimming in small, concentric circles–almost fearful about crossing the invisible barriers that existed within their rectangular, aquatic world.

That next week in the apartment wasn't much better. I was still sleeping on the couch, but you really wouldn't call it sleeping (at least, I wouldn't). Isis would get home and disappear into her room for the evening. It would go from dark to darker outside, there wasn't really any sunset or anything, a muted ray of grey light might attempt to poke through the overcast sky before ducking behind one of the nearby buildings. Then the light in the fish tank would click on, and it would glow this gorgeous blue (God, it was incredible). Seriously, I started believing that there were healing powers in that light that changed the entire aura of my living room. In those hours, my space felt like some Caribbean lagoon that was bathed in the twinkle of bioluminescent plankton, and I was floating, swimming in a soft glow. But then at three in the morning, the tank's timer would click again, and the light would go out. So I'd sit in the dark, alone, and the only glow that came into the living room was from the streetlights on Division, and the only thing I felt was the cold little whistle that came when a gust of wind pushed the broken window off its seal and the night air joined me in my misery. And I'd drown myself in my comforter and the other blankets I'd squirreled away over that past week, and I'd tell myself that maybe tomorrow things would be better, and the fish tank would heal me even more.

There was a nightly hope, but there really wasn't (it was all kind of half-hearted). I was horrendously blah-ed out, and I felt ill every time I even considered going outside. Deep cramps radiated under my lowest ribs, strong enough that I imagined them stifling the flow of blood to my vitals. I thought that maybe I was dying (which wasn't really the answer that I was looking for, but imagining dying as the reason for why I felt like I felt lent a strange, serene quality to all of it). But there's stuff going on out there, maybe you wouldn't be so bored and feel so useless if you went out there and tried having a good time with all those people. Oh gee, thanks, me, like I wasn't aware of all that? Look, we're just going to have to hunker down and hope it all passes, okay? Can you do that for me? I'm really not asking for much, am I? If you could just stop torturing me for a couple of days, then maybe the fish tank will be able to work its magic a little better, okay? Do you get it? I don't need *constant* reminders of how much stuff is going on in The City all the time, and how you think I'm worthless, because I won't go out there–or leave the couch. It doesn't need to make sense to you, okay? I just don't feel like it, and I don't want to know why yet, so please, please, give me a break.

On one of those days that next week I stumbled into Isis's room by accident (I thought it was the bathroom for some reason, which over the course of eight years had never happened, so congrats, Kristin, you're finally losing it). I reached over to turn on the light to the bathroom, and when I flipped the switch I rapidly came to the conclusion that I was standing in Isis' bedroom. I felt like I was losing complete control over my body (first the mind and then the body, or whatever people say about Alzheimer's–maybe I had that?). Or maybe it was something out of some Sci-Fi type movie where my intentions were always misinterpreted by my brain and my body's guidance systems ("Doctor, she can't come on this ship, she's ill"). I stood at the entrance to her room, and although it was one of the smaller ones in the apartment, Isis' space felt so much better than my own. There was a twin bed in the far right corner, with these gorgeous red sheets, and they looked so inviting. The walls were littered with bookshelves and photographs, like this incredible homage to all these people who had done fantastic things with their lives. And then this wave came over me, and I kind of just crumpled to the floor and started sobbing. That lasted until my eyes couldn't give any more.

The next thing I knew I was rummaging through Isis's stuff. I opened her desk drawers and looked through pencils and pens and paintbrushes and markers (keeping an eye out for maybe anything I could borrow), drawers filled with cameras and photography equipment, lenses, stuff like that. I flipped through her old photo albums I found underneath the desk in these two shoeboxes that had this collection from her childhood (first day of elementary school, family vacations to the beach, etc.). I sifted through her closet; letting the soft fabrics of dresses and skirts caress my hands. I even managed to try on a few dresses. I made sure to put everything back in its place (I didn't want to leave any evidence). Lying in her bed, I pulled a magazine from the pile on the floor next to the bed, and started reading a little bit about camera equipment. I imagined myself as Isis, in her bed reading about this Canon lens, that Nikon filter, and that felt nice, it felt good to be someone else for a bit. Her world hadn't transformed me in any physical sense, but as I lay there looking at the new space around me, I felt O-K (like whatever had come over me couldn't get through the frame of Isis's bedroom door). Well maybe not exactly okay, but it didn't seem to take as much effort to try on a couple of dresses as it did to feed the fish.

I spent the next day in Mike's room. Mike had a king sized bed, a hideous monstrosity that took up half the room, and a dresser. The dresser and the bed frame were both black, very chic, and he had black and grey sheets. Honestly, Mike's room felt like something out of some futuristic porn set where the set director decided things would look better if they spent the entire budget on two pieces of really expensive furniture instead of actually putting together a cohesive, plausible set. After lying in Mike's bed for the better part of the day imagining myself as him, I stepped over to the dresser and opened his sock drawer–which actually made me laugh (that hadn't happened in a while). I had no idea Mike wore so much argyle below the knee. Orange, blue, pink, purple, and green, you name it and the man had it. Socks, who knew? I searched through the rest of his drawers and saw sweaters and slacks and jeans, nothing out of the ordinary, nothing of interest– an unremarkable wardrobe suitable for a businessman. The top of the dresser was coated in this thin layer of dust. I wondered if he ever noticed that layer of filth and then thought to himself how he should probably just take the next step and move all of his stuff over to Victoria's place. I opened Mike's closet. It was completely empty. And I do mean completely empty. I couldn't believe it, not a single thing. I left Mike's room and went back to my spot on the couch and watched the fish tank for the rest of the day.

Mike's room had brought me down again.

It was sometime in the next two or three days (I don't know, leave me alone) that Mike actually came home. It was already dark out, again, and the blue lagoon had clicked on. He saw me on the couch and must have noticed that I needed some cheering up, because he told me that he had a present for me and looked all happy, like he was about to solve my problems (like he knew *anything* about my problems). Mike told me to wait right there (I'm not going anywhere, Michael, trust me on that one), and then he bounced out the front door. When he returned, he was holding a plastic bag filled with water. Mike said that he bought something for the tank, and I asked him why he needed another stick for the tank (weren't there enough inanimate objects in there already?). "It's not a stick, Kristen, it's an eel," he said, and then he effortlessly opened up one of the tank's lids and upended the bag and poured in the black, stick-looking eel. Mike spent some time cleaning the tank that night, which, believe me, was a process that I couldn't have even imagined mustering up the strength for, and then his phone rang (Victoria) and he left.

I don't even know where those next days went. A week might have passed. Two. I wasn't really paying that much attention (I was past the point of caring). The tank's magic of the previous weeks had seemed to come to an end. Blue lagoon clicked on, it was night, it clicked off, it was still night, the sun tried to come up, the fish swam, I fed the fish, the sun tried to go down, the blue lagoon clicked on, ad–fucking–nauseum. I spent long hours over those days (or whatever) lying in Isis's bed. I always made sure to make her bed before she came home for the evening (it was the least that I could do, and the most). I'd gone through her things more times than I care to count or mention, and the only thing that seemed to bring me any sense of normalcy was lying in the bed of a person who I used to feel embittered towards because of how much time she spent in her room. But there I was, in a room that wasn't mine.

I hadn't left the apartment in over a month (just thinking about that makes me hate myself). Things were getting progressively worse, that was obvious. I didn't know what to do anymore. It was awful, really. My limbs felt like they all weighed a hundred pounds. My body felt swollen, my hands and feet were constantly sore. I was hardly eating. I had retreated fully into the confines of my own mind. I'd look for Mike's eel every day when I fed the fish, and I could never find him (the little shit). There were the Black Tetras (with their little zebra faces and dark tailfins), the Blood Fin Tetras (my Aztec warriors, with their ashy-grey bodies and fins highlighted in war-paint), the Bumblebee Cichlids (these gentlemen had been appropriately named by Darwin or whomever), the two Sucker-Fish (Leroy and Belvin), and the other family of four (I couldn't remember what Mike had told me they were called). And then there was the elusive, invisible, nearly nonexistent, black stick of eely proportions that was nowhere to be seen. Ever. I'd named him Houdini. Although I hated it, it made sense that a guy I'd known since I moved to The City tried to do right by me (getting me a gift for his fish tank), and it ended up as if nothing ever happened in the first place.

Then sometime after that, I'd pretty much stopped eating altogether, and I hadn't ventured into Isis's room in over a week. I was spending all day on the couch, wrapped in my blankets, hurting. The dull aching had consumed my ability to feel anything else. But in the midst of all that pain, I thought maybe the answer lay in Kelly's room, so I managed to heave myself out of my prison and venture into her realm of superficiality. Try on her identity for size.

I leaned my forehead against her door, and I was shocked that I had sunk to the point that I was seeking answers from the uninhabited mess of a cheerleading, stretchy-pant wearing, giggle-bubble (but it was the last thing I could think of).

I opened Kelly's door and I found myself standing in a time capsule, a high school yearbook (her high school yearbook). There were all these multi-colored poster boards, tacky foam core with glossy three by five photos of spring breaks, dinners with friends, and field hockey (prom!). Medals from what looked like every sport you could ever play hung on pins and were draped over the gold-coated, molded plastic lumps on the tops of participatory trophies, throw pillows in places that didn't even make sense (they weren't even on the bed, just sitting, stacked in the corner), these hideous gold sheets and a green comforter, and there was a floor-to-ceiling shelf filled with shoes. I'm being serious; the entire thing was filled with shoes. I even have a decent collection of heels (not that I've needed them in the past month), but I was astonished that I'd failed to notice her obsession with shoes. The entire space made me feel worse than I already felt. I should never have gone in there. You shouldn't have opened the door, Kristen. You shouldn't have done that.

It took almost all of my remaining strength to close the door behind me. I was feeling so low. Like there was nothing left, and everything that I tried to take in from the others, Isis, Mike, and now Kelly, couldn't even imprint on a blank page, and at this point I had become exactly that: nothing. Dark ink, printed on the pages of my life, once recognizable, had faded and now left no trace. When I returned to the living room, taking my seat on the couch and straightjacketing myself in the duvet, I noticed a puddle of water on the floor in front of the tank. I followed the trail of water to my right and saw a curvy, black stick desperately squirming across the floor towards the front door. Houdini was gasping.

WHEN IT ALL WENT TO HELL

It's never easy to tell someone you love that they're acting like a cunt. It's a bit abrasive, I suppose. But hey, sometimes, for lack of better options, you just have to go all the way with it. Skip the, "Hey, could you not do that?" or, "What's your problem?" or, "Listen, you're pissing me off." Stop beating around the bush.

"You're acting like a cunt."

"Oh, fuck you, Jack, you're such an asshole. You have no right to call me that," Ricky says, her voice rising from a whisper.

"I have every right. When you do or say something, or whatever, that makes you sound like a six-year-old, I have the right to tell you that you're fucked in the head, thinking like a child, and acting like a cunt. I mean, as your husband, I'm almost required to let you know."

Ricky's pissed because, to use her words, I ogled a woman from across the bar.

"Who else is going to tell you?" I say, pointing at strangers nearby. "Him? Her?"

This is how it starts, sitting at some shitty airport sports bar called "Pucks," where the servers are wearing red-and-white-striped shirts and seem incapable of conveying any emotions other than ambivalence. There are a couple of business types gulping down some Sam Adams Seasonal, top forty on the radio, and I'm arguing with Ricky about some fantasy of hers that I'm cheating, or I'm still cheating, or I have cheated, or I'm a piece of shit, or it's my fault that this argument started in the first place, or that somehow I'm to blame for her insecurities. All because I glanced at another woman.

Here's a photograph of a man with a gun to his head, and he's seriously contemplating pulling the trigger. I finish my whiskey and stare at the bartender.

"Another?" She says.

"Yeah, thanks"

"You're not going to get me another?" Ricky says.

"Actually, dear, this is the non-cunt section of the bar," I say, "I believe the cunts are sitting over there." I point across the bar to three pig-faced button-ups who have been hitting on the bartender for the past however long we've been here.

"God you're such a fucking asshole sometimes," Ricky says. "I'm going to the gate."

"Yeah. Do that," I say.

I don't know what to say. I don't know how to just grab her by the shoulders and tell her that I love her, tell her that she's my best friend, tell her how much she means to me, because if I had any idea how to do that, then I sure as hell would. But I don't. I'm not built like that. So instead, Ricky gets the name-calling. She gets it, because she deserves it. She gets it because she's wrong. Irrational thinking's like a disease. Ricky's ability to focus on some inconsequential detail and convince herself that not only is that miniscule thing important, but also that it's a keystone to some arch supporting a conspiracy theory of hers, is uncanny. I've never seen anything like it. I've never known anyone like her. She's great. She really is. She's usually great. She's not great right now. Not at all. Right now she's shit. If she were a guy, I'd punch her in the face. She wouldn't even have to be a random guy–she could be one of my friends. She could be my buddy, Chris. If she was Chris, and he was acting like this, I'd deck him. I wouldn't even tell him that I was going to swing. I'd just punch him right in the nose. Watch his eyes well up and blood trickle out of his nostrils. See his expression change from hostile to hurt. The, "What the fuck was that for?" Well, sorry, Chris, but you were acting like a cunt, and I love you and all, but when you act like that I get to hit you in the face. Action and reaction. Consequence. Result.

But, Ricky isn't Chris.

"You want to close out, darling?" Bartender says.

"Shot of Jameson. Then, yeah," I say.

"Okay," she says.

It looks like she wants to say something about the argument that she's just overheard. It looks like she could have some amazing nugget of information that would help me, some words of wisdom that bartenders, for mystifying reasons, have hidden in their back pockets. It looks like she wants to say something, but instead she walks over to the register, hits the screen a couple of times, grabs a bottle of Jameson and walks back over to me.

"Here," she says.

"Thanks," I sit for a second before I knock it back.

"Where you headed?"

"Seattle," I say.

"Vacation?"

I laugh at that one.

"Fucking honeymoon," I say. "It's going to be great, I can tell already."

"Good luck."

"Thanks." I give her forty bucks, grab my bag, and I'm out.

She had a chance. Couldn't she tell that I needed something from her, some type of advice, some type of wisdom, something more than the standard, empty, "Where you going?" She must be dense. Yeah, she's definitely dense. Like when you see a woman suppressing tears, and a guy calls her a cunt, and the woman storms off, and you're watching the whole thing unfold, and the only thought that comes into your head is, "Oh, I wonder where he's going?"

Dense.

Airport dense.

I walk out of "Pucks" and start cruising towards Gate C 31, two terminals away. You've got to love O'Hare. And by got to love it, I mean of course that I don't. I don't mind the amenities—it's just the size of this fucking place. How far is my gate? How long will it take me to get there? Why don't you take the tram thing? Because there is no tram, that's why you don't take the tram. The tram isn't that hard to navigate. Yes, but in our current state, Jack, navigation has very little to do with it, and blind luck has everything. You can either walk there nice and slow and enjoy the monotonous airport scenery, or you can take your chance with the tram that you aren't sure exists, and even if it does you don't know in which direction to go. And considering the circumstances—Ricky, honeymoon, etc.—it would probably be in your best interest to make the flight. That's all you're required to do. Make the flight. Walk.

And here I am. Three in the afternoon, Friday, mid-February, drunk, walking through what seems to be a strange depiction of American life wherein everybody has some place to be, everybody really wants to get there, but they also have the time to buy crappy designer bullshit and eat slices of pizza, or calzones, or Thai food, or some moist, ten dollar croissant from Caribou Coffee, and stand in line as they pull out their phones and look like they're doing something interesting, act as if they have something, anything important to do, when the sad reality of the situation is what they're doing, *all* they're doing is trying to avoid talking to anybody. Avoid eye contact. Eye contact leads to conversation, and conversation means that you have to try to listen, or at least act like you're listening, or worse yet pretend that you care, that you give a fuck. Eye contact leads to the possibility that *you* might have to talk to *me*.

A woman in a pinstripe pantsuit walks towards me. Brunette. Cute smile, nice tits, and a strong walk. I'd fuck her. Eye contact? No. We pass each other. I turn my head. She's got a great ass. If only she'd taken the time to look at me, then we could have sparked a conversation that would have led her to discover that what she needs, what she really needs right now is to take me into the bathroom and fuck me. Why not catch some strange in the airport? That might change my mood.

How much farther is this goddamn gate?

I look at my watch. I've only been walking for two minutes? You've got to be kidding me. All right, eyes on the prize. Eyes. Focus. You're drunk. Not really drunk, good buzz going. You think that's why these people aren't making eye contact? Because they can tell that you're drunk? No. They're not making eye contact because they're assholes. That's why. It has nothing to do with you, you hardly exist to them, and they could care less that you're here.

I have to piss.

Bathroom.

Where's the bathroom? Restroom or bathroom? Restroom. Less vulgar. Subtle. What's the British version? Lou? Lew? Hey Lou!

Cuidado! Piso Mojado, sign at the entrance to the pisser. Short, bald guy with glasses standing there with a mop. He's not mopping.

"Why aren't you mopping?" I say, "The piso's mojado."

"Is that supposed to be funny?" He says.

"Yeah, I guess."

"Good one."

"Whatever, guy.

"Yeah, okay, sport," He says.

"Fuck you, man."

"Oh no, I'm offended now," He says, not paying me much mind. "How about you do me a favor and do whatever you're here for, please, and then just leave me alone?"

Fucking bald retard. He's probably retarded. That's why he's working in a bathroom at the airport, because he's retarded. I wonder what he's got. How did he even pass the airports' minimum employment standards? There has to be a test to become an airport employee, right? Background? Something. They have to have standards. We can't just employ fucking anybody, can we? An entire airport run by people with various chromosomal abnormalities would be mayhem.

I finish pissing and walk up to the sinks, where it appears an entire water polo match has just taken place. No thank you. I head for the exit. Oh hey, there's my new friend. Hey friend.

"See you later, retard," I say to my new friend.

"Have a nice day," he says, his lips barely open when he speaks.

Sometimes it's winning the ones that don't matter at all, that matter. Speaking of which, what time is it? Where's my watch? Watch is located on wrist. 3:17p.m. Gate is probably twenty-five minutes away, and the flight boards at 4:30p.m. If you get there too early, then you're going to have to face Ricky. It shouldn't be that big of a deal. She's got to be cooled down a bit by now, if not all the way. Just for calling her a cunt. You could have let it slide and called her nothing. Not gone down to her level. Not reacted. Not given her the ammunition to be pissed. But then what? Then you just take it? You just sit there and listen to her theories? Her conspiracy theories–weak, that's what they are.

How she doesn't believe that driving around helps you clear your head. How she doesn't believe that you're not going anywhere in particular, but that getting out of the house for a couple of hours is important. That you don't always go to the bar, but you drive past it, thinking about going in, but then you consider how pissed she'll get if you go in, so you keep driving past and go park in some shitty strip mall and watch traffic pass, and you listen to music and just sit there. No, you don't just take it. You tell her that she's out of her mind. You tell her that she's being irrational. You tell her to trust you. And then, when she doesn't, you tell her that she's acting like a child. Then she yells at you, so you call her a cunt. It seems just, though. Yeah, a bit harsh, but just–like when thieves in crazy countries get their hands cut off for stealing some bread.

And then I'm in another bar. This one's called O'Hare Bar and

Grill. Granite countertops, couple of TVs, little white napkins folded on plates. All you've got to do is have a couple more drinks, walk to the gate, and tell Ricky that you're sorry. Then you can enjoy your week in Seattle. She'll be in a good mood, and you can enjoy the trip. She'll be off of your back, we'll have make up sex the minute we walk into the apartment, and then you'll have a nice evening with some wine and some Chinese food, and you'll spend the night fucking and talking and being nice to each other, and things will be good. This is just one fight. Another.

"How ya doin'?"

"I'm all right, man. You?"

"Just fine. What can I get you?"

"I'll take a double Jack, rocks," I say.

This guy seems nice enough.

"Sure thing," he says. He pours. "Here you go."

"Thanks."

I drink.

"Where you headed?" he asks.

"Fucking Seattle."

"Don't sound too excited about it."

"I mean, whatever, I'm sure it's going to be nice. Grey, rainy, you know, the usual."

"I've never been," he says, "but from what I hear it's pretty nice."

I wonder how nice it is when you're traveling with someone who hates you.

"Yeah, it's supposed to be."

"Vacation?"

"Honeymoon," I say.

"Ah, I see, and where's the wife? Restroom?"

"Restroom!" I say. "A-HA!" I knew it.

"What?"

"Oh nothing, sorry. I didn't hear you right, what?"

"Is your wife in the restroom?"

"No. That's a good question? She left me sitting on my stool at Pucks."

He's silent for a couple of seconds, and he gives me a once over. Probably wondering what I did, or what she did, or what she looks like based on what I look like. His silence means he's thinking, he's thinking about Ricky, but he doesn't know that her name is Ricky. He just knows that she's my wife, so based on what I look like he thinks he knows what she looks like.

"Not worth chasing after?" He says.

How adamantly I respond to this question has a direct correlation to how attractive he imagines Ricky to be.

"Totally worth it," I say. "Just fed up, you know? Gotta clear my head."

"You clear your head like my father used to."

"Cheers."

I raise my glass.

"Well, how long you guys been married?"

"Not long enough for this shit to be happening," I say.

"It'll get better," he says, "it always does."

"And if it doesn't?"

"Well, then you and my old man will have even more in common."

He walks off to tend to a couple just down the bar. I can hear them. They sound chipper. I know they're together, because they have matching luggage–black rollers, same size, same zipper pattern–definitely a couple. Weekend getaway. Weekend jaunt.

Honey let's go to Barbados this weekend and mix with the locals and drink rum and lie on the beach and talk about our plans for our lovemaking next month.

I stare at my whiskey, and it stares right back. I gulp at it and start tearing at my beverage napkin. Beverage napkin. I rip small strips of the napkin off and then roll them into little wads. Try and flick each wad into the trashcan behind the bar about four feet away. Miss. Miss. Miss. Miss.

The bartender apparently finds me more entertaining than the weekenders on stools three and four. He makes his way back over.

"Where they going?" I say. "Barbados?"

"Fort Lauderdale."

"Never been. You?"

"Yeah, once," he says.

"What's it like?"

"Good enough to see it once and not be bothered to go back."

"So, why are they so, I don't know, fucking chipper?"

"Them?" he nods over to the couple, and they smile in return. "They're chipper because guy over there's hung like a moose, and she's got a vagina that's as small as a paper cut on a mouse's finger."

I remember why I like bartenders.

"Well, shit. If that's all it takes, then why the hell am I here talking to you instead of my wife?"

"No, you must have misheard me. I said *he's* hung. Like a moose," he says. "Big penis."

I choke out a laugh.

"You always this funny?"

"Only on Wednesdays," he says. A nice fat grin smacks onto

his face.

"It's Friday."

"Whatever. Details, my friend, they matter not," he says.

"What's that Confucius?"

"Who the hell's Confucius?"

"Some guy who said a bunch of stuff that some people consider important," I say. "Forget it."

"Wow, you sure did your research on that one."

"Yeah, yeah, yeah," I say, "So, what's your name?"

"Ben."

"Ben, Jack. Nice to meet you." We shake hands. He's got a firm grip, stronger guy than he looks.

"Yeah, hey, likewise," he says.

See, Ricky, I'm not an asshole. I just made a friend, a new friend. Granted, a friend in an airport, a guy that tends bar in the airport, a guy that I'm basically paying to talk to me, but a friend nonetheless. See, Ricky, if I was such a fucking asshole, then Ben here wouldn't have found me pleasant enough to keep talking to me. Sure it's meaningless, it's a tiny piece of nothing that will go nowhere and be nothing and turn out to mean nothing. But that doesn't matter, because right now, Ricky, it's something.

You're probably sitting in some black leather airport chair, Ricky, all worked up, hoping I die, justifying why it is that you hate me so much, and how it's my fault, and how I'm the asshole, and how you hope I don't ruin our honeymoon. And I'm above all that, because I'm having a drink with my new friend. I'm not sulking, I mean, not really, because I'm above it. I'm not going to sink down to your level. I refuse to meet you in the pits of anger.

I finish my whiskey.

"You want another?" Ben says.

"Yes, Sir." I think for a second. "Neat though."

 Ben pours.

"Here you go," he says.

"Thanks." I take another gulp.

The thing I've always loved about whiskey is that your first sip tastes just as good as your twentieth.

"Do you always travel this light, Jack?" Ben says.

"What are you talking about?"

He points to the two empty chairs at my side and then to the ground.

"The whole, no luggage thing," he says.

I look down at my feet. Oh, you have got to be kidding me.

"Shit, man," I say. "That's not good." I start laughing.

"Are you fucking around right now?" Ben says, "or did you really just lose your luggage?"

"No, Ben. I'm not fucking around."

I can hardly remember the past thirty minutes.

You're drunk, and you lost your luggage. What the hell are you doing? You're at the airport on the way to your honeymoon, you're drunk, and you lost your bag. Not only did you lose your bag, you, no, that's enough, you're drunk and you lost your bag. If it wasn't for Ricky going on and on about how she knows that you've been fucking around on her, then you wouldn't have gotten drunk, and you probably wouldn't have lost your bag. I mean, I'm sure people lose their bags in airports all the time anyways, right? Yeah, that's got to be why the lady on the PA system is always like, "Keep your bag with you at all times." You are truly pathetic. You have one job to do when you get to the airport and that is to hold on to your bag. If you don't let anyone mess with your bag, and you keep it with you at all times then you have done the simplest of things. Actually, you've basically accomplished all that is required of you. You, however, have managed to do the exact opposite of that, so congratulations.

"Well, you, err, we've got to find it," Ben says.

"Man, whatever. It's gone now."

"Look, Jack, I know you're a little lit," Ben says, "but you've got to find your bag. You can't just leave your bag in the airport, man. People freak out at that sort of thing. There are entire departments of security whose job it is to specifically monitor and respond to unattended bags."

Could you imagine that? If your entire job was just to watch for people who left bags in the airport? I suppose the job is necessary, but just the act of continuously traveling through the airport, scanning for abandoned bags. That job must be like what it feels like to look for Waldo's shoe in the "Land of Waldo's" page, eight hours at a time. Fucking Waldo, what a queer.

"Hey, you listening to me?" Ben says. "You've got to get that bag."

"Ben, honestly man, I don't even care about it anymore. I'm over it. I mean okay, if for some crazy chance I manage to track down the bag, me being hammered and all, and I do happen to retrace my steps, and the bag is still there, and it hasn't yet been confiscated by police, or TSA, or some stranger, then what? I can't exactly just pick it up and get on my flight."

"Why not? What are you talking about?" Ben says.

"Look, Ben, if the bag is still there, then that means that either nobody's fucked with it, or somebody has fucked with it, but they've left it where it is on purpose. Now if they haven't messed with it, then everything's cool. But if they have messed with it, put something inside of it, drugs, a bomb, whatever, then I'm not going near it."

"I don't follow."

"Because think about it. Right now, I got through security on my own accord and everything checked out, and since then, wait, I was, then I was at a different bar with my wife, and then I walked here, so, all I have to do is not leave here, and let the bag get found, and you can be my alibi, saying that I didn't put any drugs or a bomb in the bag, because I was with you the whole time."

"You're drunk," Ben says, "I'm calling security."

"Really?" I say. "Ben, I thought we were pals?"

"Yes, really."

The next few minutes resemble what I imagine the Three Stooges in Guantanamo Bay would look like. Ben gets on the phone, and within, I don't know, thirty seconds there's a security guard on my left, and he's asking me questions, and I'm less than sober, and I believe the security guard doesn't appreciate this. There are now four, blue-shirted TSA agents standing around me in a circle asking me to come with them.

"Why would you do this to me, Ben?" I yell back towards the bar. I laugh a couple of times.

"Sir, this is not a funny matter," says the guy who looks like the love child of Mahatma Gandhi and Stone Cold Steve Austin.

Ricky and I play this game all the time.

"Where did you last see your bag?"

"Honestly, Stone Cold Mahatma, I don't know."

"Sir," says the lady on my left, "if you could simply act like an adult for two minutes, then I'm sure that we can get this all figured out. But, if you carry on in this manner, you are not going to be able to fly today, and we're going to have to escort you out of here, possibly arrest you."

She's being condescending. Act like an adult. I'm acting like an adult. I'm letting it go. I'm not freaking out. I'm not caring about my bag and my things. I just wanted to finish my drink, not make a big deal out of everything, and then get on my plane. Just finish my whiskey, forget about my bag, walk to my gate, tell Ricky that I'm sorry, kiss her, and get on the plane. Now you're telling me to act like an adult? Fuck you, you fucking screening agent. Telling me to act like an adult.

"Look, I don't know where my bag is, okay?" I say, "Every bathroom in here looks the same, and I don't remember which one I was in. Now, I have to get going to my gate, because my plane is boarding soon, and my wife is waiting for me at the gate, and we're going to Seattle, as adults, which may surprise you."

"Excuse me?" she says.

"Yeah, we're going to Seattle as adults," I say. "As adults who have jobs, who get married, who buy plane tickets, adults who go on honeymoons. And this adult, has to go to get on that plane so he can go on his honeymoon with his wife, right now, you."

Wait for it.

"Fucking."

Oh my god. Her face.

"Cunt."

Her expression changes from annoyance to shock to hatred, like water cycling through the three states of matter in a fraction of a second. I smile at her. See, lady, you weren't expecting that today, were you? Well, neither was I, but Ricky can bring it out of me, she really can. I'm not blaming Ricky, lady. I can't blame Ricky, because I'm better than that. She doesn't have that power over me. I just want you to know, lady, that I really didn't mean to call you that, I'm just having a shitty day, and I wish Ricky would trust me, and I want her to know how much I love her, and all of that's been on my mind, and you just said the wrong thing that's all. I really didn't mean to call you that, lady. I hope you can understand. And it wasn't a personal attack, I mean I know how it probably looks to you, but it wasn't really. I'm just having a shitty day. And I feel a wave of energy go through my body, my muscles tighten, I feel hot, and then everything goes black.

I wake up. I'm in a room—a normal looking room—white-grey walls, grey short fiber carpeting, a metal-looking table, two chairs, no windows, just a cold silver door, and that stupid hospital lighting. My eyes burn. Why do my eyes burn? I'm naked. Why am I naked? Where are my clothes? They took my clothes. That's weird. Weirdoes. Who just strips people down these days? I suppose prisons do, detention centers, too. Okay, so I'm being detained, and therefore the lack of clothes would make sense. My eyes burn, why do my eyes burn? I spot my shoes in the corner. Another scan reveals my pants against the wall to my left. I see my shirt near the door. They stripped me down and then scattered my clothes around the room. Animals. There has to be a reason. Maybe it's some interrogation technique.

There's a camera in the corner of the room, in one of those little black bubbles. The kind you see at Wal-Mart. I stare at it.

"Really, guys? I'd like to talk to my wife, or my lawyer. Or, or, my mother."

The camera doesn't respond. I wasn't exactly expecting a response, an omniscient voice booming over a speaker that isn't there, "Sure thing, Jack, we'll get right on it." A few minutes pass, or at least what feels like a few minutes. I don't really know how long it's been. I'm disoriented. I feel ill.

I wonder what time it is? I missed the flight. You definitely missed the flight, that's not even a question. Did Ricky make the flight? Maybe she just got on the plane, and she figured that you got drunk in the bar, missed the flight, and you'll show up on the next one. They probably contacted her over the loudspeakers, "Ricky Sandowe, Ricky Sandowe, please report to the nearest gate and speak to an airline representative." She probably stood right up, ignoring the looks, walked right on over and said, "What's he done?" Ready to figure it out. Taking no shit, not caring about people's agendas, just finding a solution, and sweet-talking her way into getting what she wants. Of course, the loudspeaker could have also boomed, "Ricky Sandowe, Ricky Sandowe, your husband has just been arrested, tazed, stripped naked, and stuffed into a small room with no windows, please report." She would react the same. Give them hell, and get me out of here. It was just a fight. She's probably putting that female officer through hell right now about tazing me. She's demanding that I be released and no charges are pressed. Ricky's got my back.

I hear the door handle turn, and then a man in a white shirt and blue tie, with a healthy head of blonde hair walks into the room.

"Mr. Sandowe," he says, "my name is Thomas. I am second in command of the TSA here at O'Hare."

"Can I put my clothes on?

"Please do."

"Can you give me some privacy?"

"Just get dressed, Mr. Sandowe."

"Okay, fine," I say, waddling over to my pants, then my shirt and shoes. My pants are wet. Why, exactly?

"Now, Mr. Sandowe, do you remember why you're here?"

"Yes, I was going on my honeymoon."

"No, Mr. Sandowe, not why you came to the airport, why you're in this room."

"Yes, I do."

"Could you explain that to me, please. I just need to hear your side," he says.

"I was a bit drunk, the bartender noticed that I had left my bag somewhere, I told him forget about it, and then they were dragging me somewhere or something, and one of the women was being rude to me so I called her a cunt," I say, "and then I got tazed."

He glances down at a yellow notepad.

"Yes, that seems to be what I have as well," he says. "We have your bag, there was nothing tampered with, nothing found, you're clear as far as the bag is concerned. Aside from the act of leaving the bag, unintentionally, according to your bartender friend, the only thing we are going to charge you with is public intoxication. It's a misdemeanor and should only cost you a couple hundred dollars."

"That seems like bullshit."

"Does it? Mr. Sandowe. Let me tell you what could seem like bullshit, if you'd like to use that term in a more appropriate way. What would seem like bullshit, to you, I'm certain, would be if I decided to hold you here, in this room for the next six hours, I can have you cavity searched, and then I can take you down the hall and put you in a tiny cell, it's a lot like this room, but far less comfortable. I can hold you in that cell without a phone call for the next 48 hours, if I so please. Then I can have a few witnesses say that they saw you resisting arrest, pushed one of my staff members, which are a couple of allegations that hold some shitty consequences. After that, I can call CPD, and tell them that you assaulted one of my staff, and on your way to jail, Mr. Sandowe, CPD will kick your head in, a bit, not too severe, but enough to make you quite uncomfortable for the next couple of days while you await bond, because I'm positive that your wife isn't going to come back from Seattle just to bail you out."

Ricky left. Shit.

"Now, I ask you, Mr. Sandowe, which one sounds like bullshit?"

"Yeah, okay, I get it."

"Good," he says. He opens the door.

"Look, uh."

"Thomas," he says.

"Yeah, listen, Thomas, I'm sorry. Tell your lady that I apologize. I was acting like an ass," I say, "didn't mean for any of it to happen."

"Apology accepted, but I'm still issuing a ticket," he says.

"That's fine. I fucked up. I get it. So, are we done?"

"Yes, we're done," Thomas says.

"So, I can't fly today?"

"No, not today. Find a hotel for the night, and you can come back tomorrow," he says, "just try and act a bit more like, oh, I don't know, like you're a nice guy." He smiles at that one.

Oh, Thomas. You want me to act like a nice guy? Well gee wiz, I guess I will.

"I am a nice guy," I say. "Just having a shitty day."

"Okay, well, this has been riveting, exciting, enthralling, there are too many adjectives to possibly describe it, so now I'm going to leave, which means that you have to come with me. Okay?"

"Okay."

I feel a bit, eh, whatever. We exit the room and turn right down the long hallway. There's absolutely nobody around, no windows, I count three doors in the entire seventy some-odd feet we walk, the back channels of the O'Hare labyrinth. He stops and opens a door on the right and grabs my bag from the room. He places the bag at my feet.

"So, Thomas, this it?"

"That's correct, Mr. Sandowe."

"I feel like I should hug you or something."

"Don't fucking touch me," he says, calmly.

He flashes his card against a small black box, pushes the door open with his left hand, and extends the right to me. I shake it. Why not? He's all right. I step out into the terminal, terminal three, and the door shuts behind me. I'm still a bit drunk. Not much has changed. People are still walking around with determined blank stares, suspended, hollow. I follow the signs that say "Hotel." I glance at the departures screen. It's a bit after six.

Ricky's phone goes straight to voicemail. Of course it does, she's on a plane. She's on her way to Seattle. You're not with her, because you're an idiot. She's on the plane, talking to some stranger, telling them how her husband was, "Supposed to be here with me, but he decided to get drunk and arrested before our flight." Stranger likely consoles her and tells her that it's not her fault, tells her that I'm a piece of shit and in the wrong, and I shouldn't have argued with her, and if I am cheating, then I should come clean. Actually, now that Ricky tells a bit more, I probably am cheating on her. And Ricky's probably eating it all up, sitting there smiling, knowing that this is exactly what she wants to hear from stranger, smiling at how little they know about our situation, but smiling because within the span of thirty minutes Ricky's convinced them that I'm one hundred percent wrong. One hundred. And after an hour of this Ricky tells stranger, "Thanks for listening, I really needed to talk to somebody," and stranger will tell her no problem, it was their pleasure, and you're such a nice girl, and Ricky will have gained stranger's trust, and stranger will exert negative energy onto me. Stranger will think poorly of me, and stranger will tell their friends about me, and their friends will dislike me, and none of them will know shit, except that somewhere in Chicago is a guy named Jack who's cheating on his new wife, and Jack's also an asshole. And he's also a drunk.

Decent room, nothing crazy, but it's nice enough. I turn on the TV. I flip through a few channels. Basketball, news, weather, sitcom. I land on this documentary about the life of a girl who spent her childhood trapped in the basement by her crazy father. Didn't learn how to talk until she was twelve. Hadn't seen daylight since birth, basically blind. Got out after her father had a heart attack in the kitchen of the house, he'd called 911 and then died. The EMTs went into the house, found daddy stiff on the floor, and then heard a grunting sound from the basement. It's six years later and the kid has finished middle school. It breaks my heart that shit like this happens. The beginning isn't all that feel-good, but when they show her at the end holding up her middle school diploma, I mean, come on.

I try Ricky's phone again. Voicemail.

"Hi Ricky, I'm sorry. I didn't mean for all that to happen. I should be in Seattle with you right now, but I'm not, and I know it's my fault. I've got a flight tomorrow at three, and I'm spending the night in the airport hotel. So, look, I'd like to talk to you, but if you don't want to call me back tonight I get it. I'll see you tomorrow. Love."

And that's it. It's eight o'clock, and I'm on the bed, staring at my cell phone, waiting. Staring at the TV, thinking about the cell phone, waiting. It's better if she doesn't call back tonight. She got a cab to the apartment, and she's in the bathtub reading, trying not to think about me. And she's probably doing a good job of it.

And she doesn't call, so I let the TV drown me. I order room service. A cute hotel employee named Shailene knocks on my door and drops off my burger, we chat for a second, I eat, and that's it. That's the night. I sleep.

Take two at the airport. Everything's the same as it was yesterday, except I don't have Ricky in my ear, and I don't have any whiskey in my system. I pass through security with no problems and get to my gate. Then it's a waiting game. I spend the next forty minutes people-watching. There's an elderly couple in the seats across from me–they're mildly entertaining. They're in their mid-sixties, plain clothes, plain looks–plain lives I'm sure. The man is reading Time Magazine, and she's reading Great Expectations. Every five minutes that pass this guy is tapping his wife on the arm, showing her something in Time, and she smiles at him. She stops reading, smiles, and goes back to her book. Nobody says anything. They seem comfortable in their silence.

"Flight 3120 to Seattle is now boarding," the speaker says. I'm up, standing, waiting for my zone to be called. I'm in the plane. I'm in my seat. Everyone gets settled in for takeoff. Cabin check. Announcements. Taxi to the runway. The man at my right is staring at me. He extends his hand.

"Leonard Neeves," he says.

Oh hi Leonard, you must be interesting. You must be important.

"Jack Sandowe," I say.

"You fly often, Jack?" he says.

"An average amount."

"Well, I'd like to say a prayer before we take off," he says, "would you like me to include you?"

Oh how thoughtful of you, Leonard, how perfectly kind of you to include me in your prayer. How great, how grand, how wonderful.

"If you'd like," I say.

"Are you a man of God, Jack?"

We are still taxiing to the runway, and I already have to explain my thoughts to this Dockers-wearing Baptist? Why?

"I wouldn't exactly call me that. I'm more of a free thinker."

"Having the Lord in your life enables you more freedom than you think," he says.

"Please," I say. "Leonard, I'm having a terrible couple of days. If you could. I just need some space, okay?"

"That's fine," he says. "Not exactly my type of person anyways, I figure."

Exactly, Leonard, I am not that person. I don't want to talk to you. I have no interest in your story. I'm not interested in you. I could care less about you, your God, your family, your high school football days, what your average score is in golf, what you do for work, any of it. I simply don't care.

So, he's quiet for the rest of the flight. I'm tempted to order a whiskey, but I don't. Ricky will appreciate a sober knock on the door, an apologetic knock.

I look around the cabin at the people in the seats around me wondering if any of them happen to be undercover Homeland Security agents. There are two women seated across the isle. Are there female undercover agents? That sounds sexist. I'm sure there could be female agents, because all it would take to be an undercover agent is a crack shot with a handgun, a badass attitude, and maybe some light hand-to-hand combat skills. Most of these UCs have to be ex-military or ex-police. I discount the women as possible candidates. They don't seem to be surveying things with interest. You'd figure that if there is an undercover on this flight, they'd be quiet, interested in their surroundings, looking at people, tuned in to the people around them. There's nobody to my right that fits the profile. Hell, I probably look like the best candidate. Jack Sandowe, undercover airplane guy. No, it'd be more like Jack Sandowe, undercover Homeland Security Agent. Wait, I'd need to have a cover story, and it would have to seem mundane, inconspicuous. Jack Sandowe, elementary school band teacher. "You're a band teacher? That's so interesting." I know, isn't it? I just love music, and the kids are so much fun at that age, so eager to learn. "What's your favorite instrument to play?" I love all of them. "You can play all of the instruments in the band?" Yes, I'm pretty much what you call a savant, except I'm not stupid or deficient in any other area of my personality or mental capabilities. "Wow, that's impressive." I know, because not only can I play all the instruments in the band, but also I have a tazer in an ankle-holster strapped to my right leg, and my service weapon holstered under my left armpit.

It's not really a glamorous job, though. You'd just be flying around all the time. City to city, airports, planes, shitty food, boring people, people like Leonard. Ordinary people who want to tell you their story, want you to listen to them. I'd rather teach band. Could I still have a service weapon if I taught band? "Listen, Kevin, I want you to play me C Major, top to bottom, and if you don't do it correctly," and then I'd whip out the gun. I'd have the best band in the country.

The plane lands. We taxi. We stop moving. The seatbelt light dings. Everybody stands in that awkward half-bend, waiting for their turn to grab their bags from the overhead, unable to simply sit for a couple more minutes, thinking that if they somehow position their body in some odd way, like the early years of homo-erectus, it will increase the speed with which they can exit. They stand. They make the occasional noise, grunt, and scoff, indicating that they can't believe how slowly the people eight rows ahead are moving. Dexter Businessman standing in front of me seems close to yelling at people a couple of times. His body sways with anxiety, pulses with impatience. His head keeps swiveling back and forth, as if his waiting requires so much effort that his neck is having a tough time supporting his head. You poor thing, Dexter, you must have so much important stuff to do. You must have some deal that needs to get signed, or a loved one in the hospital who is going to die any minute, and if you don't get off this plane right now, they're going to die, and it's all because of that mother three rows up with two kids and that giant tote bag, trying to leave. She's the reason that you're not going to be able to say goodbye. You should say something. You should let her know how much you hate her right now. No? Don't want to? Say something. Do it. Don't hold it in Dexter, that's bad for you.

He stays silent. I grab my bag and exit the plane.

"Have a nice trip," the flight attendant says.

"Thank you," I say.

I step outside of the airport, and it's a mild day, no rain, some clouds, but the sun is shining. I walk up to the row of cabs parked along the curb. The ride into the city is just fine. Not much traffic. The cabbie seems competent. He's a patient driver, which is a nice thing to experience in a major American city. I still haven't spoken to Ricky. I hope she's at the apartment.

I give the cabbie an extra twenty to show him that I appreciated his silence during the drive. The apartment is in the center of the city, three floors above the street and right next to Chuck's Coffee, a restaurant named Au Vin, and Milk, the latter being a bar that judging from the exterior looks as if it has seen better days. The apartment belongs to Ricky's friend, Gale. Gale and Ricky met at The University of Colorado.

Gale is an interesting woman, great body. She works as a consultant that deals in the financial sector and gets hired out by her firm to fly pretty much anywhere in the world to help companies reconsider how wisely they're using their money. In her free time, Gale enjoys smoking extremely strong weed and telling stories about, "This one time when I was high I was like, doing this, and then, I was staring at this thing, and it was really funny." Repeat said story on and on. Gale is currently in South Africa telling a high-powered company that they need to do whatever it is she thinks they need to do, hence the apartment. Gale thought it would be nice if we got to visit Seattle on our honeymoon, considering the fact that neither of us had ever been. Gale thinks very highly of Seattle. I don't have an opinion on Seattle, but I'm sure that Gale thinks highly of it, because she found it suitable to recommend her best friend experience her honeymoon there.

I'm at the main entrance of the apartment building. I press the button for apartment 3-G. The speaker clicks on.

"Yes. Who is it?"

Oh come on, Ricky, you know who it is.

"Hello wife, it's your lovely, caring husband," I say.

"Hmmmm," she says, "I'm not sure if I have one of those."

"No, you do," I say. "In fact, he's standing outside of the main entrance talking to you through an intercom at this very moment."

"Does this lovely, caring husband of mine do things like apologize when he's acted like a complete asshole?"

"Yes, he does."

She wants me to work for it. And I certainly will.

"And what does he have to say to his lovely wife who has enjoyed the first night and first day of her honeymoon alone, just fine?" Ricky says.

"He has to say that he's sorry, that he didn't mean to call her those things, that those things were uncalled for, and he was overreacting, and it would have been easier if he hadn't been so defensive, and that he would like his wife to consider that he thinks the world of her, and that she's absolutely gorgeous, and that all he's been thinking about since she left him sitting on a bar stool in the airport is her, and that he really hopes she takes all of this into consideration."

There's no response. I wait. Maybe I can will her into letting me up.

"Ricky, you there?" I say.

There's no response.

Then the door buzzes.

I push the large, cold steel door open and hop up six sets of stairs. There's a shot of energy in my legs. I'm a little impressed that she let me up so quickly. I thought she'd make me work for it a bit more. Of course, she has all week to make me work for it. Or, maybe she's already over it. Maybe she understands that I wouldn't have called her a cunt if she hadn't accused me of cheating on her for the however-many-ith time. Maybe it's a wash. Maybe we're even.

I knock, and Ricky opens the door. And there she is.

Ricky's something to look at. There are these things about her that are so perfect, and, if they're not perfect, they're, at least, so perfectly unique.

Ricky has deep brown hair, in some light it looks jet-black, but in others it can shine a look–almost hazel. Her eyes are green, angular, and soft, and they do this thing, they have a tendency. She looks at you and makes a connection. She can speak with her eyes. The way she looks at you, you understand. And then she uses her eyebrows to highlight words, to hammer home a point. Like accents on letters. They can move, twitch, bend, and curve. Ricky's eyes are great, but they don't even touch her mouth.

She has the sexiest mouth. Warm, pink, elastic lips that rest beautifully on a wonderful set of teeth. Natural, beautiful teeth. No veneers, no major intruders or protruders, but instead just a bouquet of white, normal looking teeth that form this smile. This smile looks great in pictures, it looks great in person, it looks great when she's getting away with something, and it looks great when she's happy. It's the type of smile that is infectious to the point of controlling. She smiles, and you become happy. Looking at her smile is like looking at a thousand great books on a bookshelf; you know there is so much going on, and you can simply be happy that you are in its presence.

Ricky's wearing a grey, faded Stooges t-shirt that I bought her at a thrift store a few years back, a pair of grey slippers, and my favorite white cotton undies. She's holding a glass of red wine. Her hair looks jet black in the apartment's light, and it's down in a wavy mess around her shoulders.

"Hey," she says.

"Hey." I put my bag on the floor of the hallway and shut the door behind me. Ricky starts a lazy back-pedal. Her eyes are sharp, angular, and they're fixed on me. She smiles. I could die.

"You want some wine, Jackie boy?"

"Yeah. I'd love some," I say.

"The bottle is in the kitchen. Pour yourself one."

Ricky backs into the couch and flops down. I step into the kitchen and pour a glass of the red she's opened.

"So," she says, "how'd that whole mess you caused for yourself at the airport turn out?"

"It could have gone worse, I suppose. They let me off kind of easy."

"What's easy?"

Ricky is sprawled out on the couch. Her left arm hangs lazily off its side, and loose in her clutches, a glass.

"I got a ticket of sorts. It's a misdemeanor. Just have to shell out a few bucks and it'll be all over with."

I walk out of the kitchen and sit in a wooden desk chair. Ricky rolls onto her side, and rests her head on her hand. She sips.

"And so, the reason that you weren't with me on the plane yesterday, is because you thought it would be just, I don't know, a bit more fun to get a ticket for, I'm sure, being way too drunk and acting like an asshole in the airport?"

"Look, Ricky. I'm sorry. I really am."

Ricky smiles. Her eyes bend. She shows me that she knows she's won, or made her point, or proven to me what she wanted to prove to me.

"I know you are," she says. "I just want you to know that if I didn't love you so much, I wouldn't be here any more. If I didn't, I wouldn't have put up with you for as long as I did before we got married. And," she pauses, "you have to realize that I've put up with a lot of shit to keep this thing of ours going."

The last thing that I can do right now is tell her how crazy she was acting before I got drunk. I want to tell her, but I'm not going to.

"I know, Ricky," I say. "I don't even want to think about yesterday, I really don't. I want to forget the whole thing. Don't want to think about our fight, you flying here alone, me getting fucking tazed. I don't want to think about."

Ricky laughs.

"You got fucking tazed?"

"Yeah," I say. "One word. Brutal."

"Did you shit yourself?"

With that, she starts to giggle.

"No, but I pissed my pants."

"So, you, you woke up with wet pants?"

I think about it for a second. "No, actually, I woke up naked."

"Naked?"

"Not a thread of clothing to be seen."

"So, how'd you know you pissed your pants?" she says.

"Oh, right before the interview or questioning or whatever, I put my pants on and discovered I had left myself a little souvenir."

"Wait," she says. "The guy undressed you?"

"No. I had apparently undressed at some point before regaining full consciousness."

Ricky laughs.

"Why didn't he tell you to get dressed before he started asking questions? Before he even walked in the room?"

"I don't know, Ricky, the guy was a weirdo, maybe it was a power thing, maybe he saw my dick and thought, 'that's a good looking dick, I'm going to keep this one naked for as long as possible.' Maybe his dick had been severed in a terrible accident when he was twelve, and he wanted to look at mine for as long as possible, because it had been so long since he had seen one. Maybe–"

Ricky squints, and she purses her lips. Her head cranes.

"Getting worked up?" she says.

"No," I say. "Okay, fine. Yes, I am. Look, I don't want to fucking talk about it? Is that okay with you?"

"Okay. That's it."

Ricky sets her glass on the wooden coffee table as she stands. She walks over to me and sits sideways on my lap. Even though she's almost naked, her legs are warm; I can feel their heat. She grabs my right arm just above the elbow, and her other hand snakes behind my back, moves up from the base of my neck until she grabs a handful of my hair. She smiles, her lips move towards my left ear.

"I'm sorry too, Jack," she says, and then she bites.

"Off with it," I say, kissing her neck.

And we have sex. It's slow and passionate and fast and sweaty, and Ricky's practically an acrobat so we're all over the place, and we bite and scratch and nibble, and Ricky comes and she looks incredible while she does, and her body shakes and her lips quiver, and I come too but I'm certain I look like a guy whose just been hit in the head with a shovel and then had his mind erased. Then we lie in bed. I stare at the ceiling. I'm breathing heavy, and Ricky's curled up on my side. Ricky's silent, save for small breaths. I hear a car honking outside. We've been married for five days.

Morning light comes through the window to the right of the bed, and I'm up. It's a weak light, more of a subtle grey glow. It's misting, or it's sprinkling, or it's grey and wet–that's what it's doing. It's the first actual look I get of Gale's apartment. The bedroom is nice, not bad at all, actually. Forest green walls, light brown wood dresser and tables, spacious, giant book shelf on the wall opposite of the bed next to the bathroom door. The decorations are limited, but when there is one, it's quality. There are two paintings from some Haitian artist, a couple of Polynesian sculptures, and some type of old dagger hanging on the wall next to the bookshelf. It seems that Gale's ability to get really high hasn't stopped her from creating a comfortable living space. I walk to the bathroom and take a shower. I towel off and get dressed. Ricky's still asleep, so I make my way into the kitchen and throw on a pot of coffee.

The rest of Gale's apartment is equally as simple and nice as her bedroom. The kitchen is modern, and the living room is a soft sky blue and filled with wooden furniture. The main decorations are books and magazines. There is one photograph on the wall directly opposite the couch. It's a pretty big print, or at least big for what I'm used to seeing in people's homes, and it's got this guy that looks like a young Al Pacino lying on his back in a field of grass, with one hand resting on his chest, and he's smiling. It's nice.

I grab my coffee and sit down on the couch. The rain has picked up a bit, and I can hear it slapping against the cast iron table out on the balcony. I leave the lights off in the living room and sip my coffee in the grey. Gale doesn't have a TV. That's strange. A stoner without a TV, there's probably a story behind that: "This one time when I was high, I was like watching TV, and then I was staring at this book, and I just thought wow, books are so much more interesting than TV. It was really funny." Glad to hear it Gale. The rain keeps slapping outside.

It feels good to know that Ricky and I are okay. The pressure from the wedding has passed, and the stupid argument that resulted from the airport debacle is done with. We apologized and made up. The rest of the trip should go smooth. You aren't going to be away from Ricky for too long on this trip, so she certainly can't accuse you of cheating on her while we're here. She can't go fucking crazy on you. What are you talking about? Of course she can. She can get anything in her head. She sees you looking at some lady walk by on the street and that starts the conversation, "Oh, do you like how she looks?" and the next thing you know she's bringing up something from a month ago, or two years ago, or talking about Stacey–Stacey is my ex, we dated for four months before I met Ricky–who I haven't seen or heard from in over seven years. Ricky can lose her shit if she wants to. Hopefully she wants to keep it together while you're in Seattle, or better yet, keep it together for the next few years. That would be nice.

I flip through the pile of magazines on the coffee table: Time, Newsweek, Backpacker, and Outside magazine. Hardly interesting right now, maybe I'll read one later. I lie back on the couch and look out onto the balcony and watch the rain. I drink my coffee, refill my cup, and drink again. I can hear Ricky start to stir in the bedroom. The shower starts up. I don't move. The shower stops. Time passes through the gentle lethargy of the soggy, dim morning. Ricky walks into the living room.

"Hey," she says. Her eyes make her look as though she's been drugged.

"Morning. Sleep all right?"

"Yeah, but I feel groggy," she says, leaning into the word graaw-gy.

"I'll throw on another pot of coffee."

"Breakfast?"

"Let's grab something out," I say.

"Perfect," she says. She leans in and pecks me on the cheek and then walks back towards the bedroom.

We wind up at a diner just down the street. They've got a nice little bar, a couple of booths, and a couple of lifers filling up coffee and taking orders. Ricky and I sit in a booth right next to the door. Our waitress walks over. She looks almost exactly like Rodney Dangerfield with long hair and big tits. Ricky and I break into big smiles as she nears our table. She is not smiling.

"What can I get you?"

The waitress hands us menus.

"Two coffees, two waters, and an orange juice please," Ricky says.

"You want a minute to look it over?" Rodney nods at the menu.

"Please," Ricky says.

Mrs. Dangerfield waddles away. I start to chuckle.

"Oh my god," Ricky says, "What creature was she on the Island of Dr. Moreau?"

"She must have had the operation that made her look like Rodney Dangerfield and Bruce Vilanch right after she returned to the mainland."

Ricky laughs. She's smiling.

"That's exactly who she is."

"Right before she escaped the island, she managed to eat Brando," I say.

"You're terrible."

"I know."

"What are you getting?"

"Well, I was thinking about getting the biscuits and gravy," I say, "but I don't to want tempt our Orca friend into devouring my plate before it reaches the table."

Ricky shakes her head. Clears her throat. Down-Syndrome Jeff Daniels approaches.

"What would you like?" she asks.

"I'll have the bowl of oatmeal with an English muffin on the side," Ricky says.

"Okay. You?" Our new friend points her pencil at my face.

"I'll take two eggs, over easy, side of bacon, and some wheat toast."

"That it?"

"That's it," I say.

And that is it. Ricky and I sit in that booth for the better part of three hours. We talk about travel and what we want to do with the wedding gifts we don't like or want—the coffee maker that has a terrible spout that spills everywhere when you try to pour any amount of coffee from the decanter at any speed that is considered faster than dribbling, the giant planter that Tara—Ricky's second cousin—decided would look great in our foyer, the plant is not entering the house because we don't have a foyer. We talk about her mother's latest boyfriend, who seems to have simply been purchased, whose greatest attribute is that upon opening his mouth everybody within a two-mile radius seems like they just split the atom. Ricky talks about where she wants to move in a couple of years: New York or New Orleans. I tell Ricky that we should consider moving out of the country, see if we can completely alter our existence by drastically changing our comfort levels and force the issue. We talk about the highlight of the wedding, the delightful treat of my best man, Sam, calling me a fag and Ricky a whore and watching Ricky's mother's expression change from displeasure to contempt. I try to convince Ricky that there's no actual reason for why we don't own a pinball machine. She spends ten minutes arguing that—

The door chimes.

A beauty glides through the diner.

A glance, and through a hushed breath a vacuum of sound.

A look of loathing, eyebrows like hatchets.

A fight about betrayal.

Acknowledgements

The Author would like to thank a number of people who were involved in bringing this project to life: Josh Izenberg, for being thoughtful and, most importantly, kind while delivering his opinions early on in
the process, and for continuing to accept bottles of Maker's Mark as
payment for his efforts; Brett Marty, for being the exact opposite of Josh
but nonetheless effective, and for being a true soundboard for creative
ideas and, in general, hilarious; Henry Dombey, for his encouragement,
generosity, and hunger for all things energy and life and I hate that, no, I
love it, we need to do that more often, let's never go back there; Laurine,
for marrying Henry, putting up with me, and showing me day in, day out
what it means to work hard; Tricia, for going on walks with me to help me
clear my head and then buying me two beers and, oh, we might as well
get a pitcher or two, I mean Martin said he's on his way; David, for buying me beers as well; Peter Wilson-Tobin, for helping to edit these stories
and discussing all things words; Jocelyn, for conversations about process
and life; Jamie Killen, for being the best blurb writer in the game and one
of the greatest human beings out there; Mom and pops, for everything
that you do and the endless well of love; Kara Hemsworth, for not only
being an artist I believe in, but also for providing the killer artwork in this
collection; To my brother, Alex, who is a constant motivator in my life and
for whom this book is written, I say One Love; My family at Baker Street,
The City of San Francisco, and anyone that has influenced me positively;
I want to give a shout out to Ray Ray and Big Steve. Thank you.

About The Artist

Kara Hemsworth graduated from The Ohio State University in 2009 with a Bachelor's in Art and Technology and continued her education at Austin Community College in 2D Animation. She has had a passion for character design and animation for as long as she can remember and believes a strong fine art foundation was the key to becoming a well-educated and integrally strong artist. Kara is gearing up to enter the animation industry. Feel free to contact her with any freelance work, contract jobs, or career moves. "I'm open to anything!"

Kara uses adobe software such as Toon Boom Harmony, Flash, PSP, Ai, and Ae. Her blog, www.KaraHemsworth.blogspot.com displays her work process, flow, and ideas.

Full color prints of the artwork are available on:
karahemsworth.blogspot.com
whenitallwentohell.com

Follow Kara on Instagram @KarahemsworthArt

"JUST SAY A HAIKU ~~WITH THESE SLIT YOU MINUTE~~
AND YOU'LL GO WHERE YOU WANT TO
IN JUT ONE MINUTE ~~CHECK IN (CHECK UP)~~ AT THE OFFICE,

"I HAVE TO GO ~~HANDLE ON SOME OTHER MATTER~~," BILL SAID, AS
HE STARTED WALKING AWAY FROM FRED. "5:32 AM, ~~CROSS FORGE~~.

"DON'T FUCK IT UP."

BILL WALKED ACROSS RUNKLE'S LAWN, STEPPING OVER AND AROUND
~~SCATTERED~~ AUTOMOTIVE PARTS STREWN ABOUT ~~THE YARD (HE NOTICED THE FRONT HALF OF A 67 MUSTANG, A CAR HE'D OWNED IN HIS 30'S)~~, HEADED DOWN THE
SHORT DRIVEWAY AND OUT TO THE STREET. STANDING IN THE
DIM GLOW OF THE STREETLIGHT ABOVE, BILL RECITED A HAIKU
AND VANISHED INTO THIN AIR.

FRED SCAMPERED UP A TREE IN RUNKLE'S YARD THAT FACED
BOTH THE KITCHEN AND THE TRASH CANS. ~~RECEDED~~ THE CLOCK ON THE
~~KITCHEN~~ MICROWAVE IN RUNKLE'S KITCHEN READ 11:09 PM. FRED
GLANCED ~~UP~~ AT THE ~~TRASH~~ CANS, LICKING HIS LIPS, AND THEN
HE ~~LOOKED~~ ~~SCANNED~~ (LOOKED OUT ACROSS) THE ROAD AND YARD FOR ANY SIGN THAT BILL WAS
~~SEARCHED~~ SPYING ON HIM. ~~HE~~ NO SIGN OF BILL. HE ~~TURNED~~ (LOOKED) BACK TO
THE CANS. "SOON," HE THOUGHT, ~~AND THEN HE BLOOD STARED BACK AT THEIR WINDOW~~ TO KITCHEN.
ONLY ONE MINUTE HAD PASSED. ~~FRED READ~~

AS BILL ASCENDED TO THE AGENCY, TAKING DUE DILIGENCE
TO HOLD ONTO HIS TOP HAT IN MID-FLIGHT, HE QUESTIONED WHETHER
HE'D MADE THE RIGHT DECISION. ~~RACOONS WERE NOT TO RECEIVE
RECEIVE UNSUPERVISED DELEGATION~~ RACOONS WEREN'T TRUSTWORTHY, AND
YOU SHOULD ~~NOT~~ AVOID DELEGATING TO A RACOON, UNLESS COMPLETELY
NECESSARY. AT LEAST, THAT'S WHAT THE AGENCY'S MANIFESTO ON
ANIMAL DELEGATION, SUBSECTION 81-52.03 READ.

"AN AGENT MAY FIND HIS OR HERSELF IN A PICKLE FROM TIME
TO TIME WHEREIN TWO OR MORE ~~ONGOING~~ (OF AN AGENTS') CASES NEED/REQUIRE
INTERVENTION IN PRESENT/FUTURE PROSECTION ASSIMILATION, CON-
CURRENTLY. IN TIMES SUCH AS THESE THE AGENT MUST USE HIS OR
HER BEST JUDGEMENT AND AVAILABLE RESOURCES TO INSURE PROPER
MITIGATION IN HIS OR HER ABSENCE WHICH MAY INCLUDE THE
DELEGATION OF OCCURANCES TO THOSE ANIMALS/CRITTERS WHICH THE
AGENCY HAS DETERMINED, THROUGH THE EXPANSE OF TIME, TO BE
UNTRUSTWORTHY. THESE ANIMALS INCLUDE FLIGHTLESS BIRDS (INCOMPETENCE),
RACOONS (IMPULSIVITY & LACK OF INHIBITION), AND ~~THE COMMON DOMESTICATED~~ HOUSECATS (APATHY). ~~THE~~ TEMP-
ORARY EMPLOYMENT OF ANY THREE OF THESE ANIMALS CALLS FOR A ~~DIRECT~~
REVIEW OF THE AGENT'S ACTIONS ~~WITH REGARDS~~ BY A PANEL OF HIS OR HER PEERS AND THE ~~TO THE MARK~~

TERRY RUNKLE'S CASE HAD BEEN FAST-TRACKED TO A ~~HIGHER~~ PRIORITY STATUS BECAUSE OF HIS EX-WIFE, PATRICIA. PATRICIA HAD BEEN AND ~~CURRENTLY~~ STILL WAS TOO GOOD FOR TERRY. THEY'D BEEN MARRIED RIGHT OUT OF HIGH SCHOOL. BOTH CHILDREN LIVED WITH PATRICIA IN NEW YORK CITY, MANHATTAN, UPPER WESTSIDE. THE KIDS, SCOTT AND JUNE, WERE TOO YOUNG TO REMEMBER THEIR FATHER, AND SINCE SHE'D LEFT, TERRY HADN'T REALLY MADE ANY EFFORT TO ~~STAY IN~~ CONTACT ~~WITH~~ THE KIDS OR PATRICIA. THEY'D LEFT FOUR YEARS AGO, AND TERRY THOUGHT ABOUT THEM MAYBE ONCE A MONTH. THEY'D CROSS HIS MIND WHEN HE WAS STANDING AT HIS KITCHEN SINK WASHING DISHES, LOOKING OUT THE WINDOW ~~IMAGINING~~ IMAGINING THESE TWO KIDS RUNNING AROUND THE YARD OUT FRONT. TERRY WOULD PICTURE PATRICIA LAYING IN THE GRASS, READING, THEN HE'D THINK HOW NONE OF THOSE THOUGHTS FELT GOOD, BECAUSE THEY WERE GONE FOR GOOD AND HE KNEW IT.

PATRICIA ~~WORKED AS~~ HAD WORKED AS HIGH SCHOOL TEACHER OF POLITICAL SCIENCE AND INTRODUCTION TO ECONOMICS WHILE SHE'D BEEN MARRIED TO TERRY. ~~SHE'D MANAGED TO GET HER MASTERS, DEGREE IN POLITICAL SCIENCE, A~~ SINCE THE DIVORCE SHE'D FINISHED HER PhD., AT COLOMBIA UNIVERSITY, SPECIALIZING IN MODERN CAMPAIGN STRATEGIES AND INFLUENCE THROUGHOUT THE REGION KNOWN AS "THE BIBLE BELT," IN THE UNITED STATES. ~~HER EXPERIENCES~~ ~~COMPANY IN POLAND TO HAD GIVEN HER THE~~ PATRICIA NOW TAUGHT AT COLUMBIA, AND ~~SHE WAS~~ HER COLLEAGUES RESPECTED HER WORK AND INTELLECT. PATRICIA SPENT HER TIME IMMERSED IN HER WORK, AND ~~TAKING~~ RAISING TWO KIDS. ~~AND SHE'D~~ PATRICIA HAD JUST ~~BE~~ RECEIVED ~~AND THAT SHE'D BEEN STUDIED STUDIED~~ AN OFFER ~~BY~~ FROM A MAJOR POLITICAL PARTY TO HELP WITH CAMPAIGN STRATEGY IN THE BIBLE-BELT FOR THE UPCOMING NATIONAL ELECTIONS. THE MONEY WAS GOOD ~~AND THIS~~ AND PATRICIA WAS SERIOUSLY CONSIDERING THE OFFER.

THE BUREAU NEEDED PATRICIA TO DECLINE THE ~~OFFER~~ OFFER. FUTURE PROJECTIONS INDICATED ~~PLANS FOR THE~~ HER OVERALL INFLUENCE ON THE CAMPAIGN AS BEING THE REASON FOR THE PARTY'S VICTORY. TERRY RUNKLE WAS GOING TO FIND PATRICIA'S PHONE NUMBER NEXT TO A STRATEGICALLY PLACED ~~AIRPLANE~~ FLIGHT VOUCHER TO NEW YORK. ~~AND~~

~~FRED FOCUSED, AND IMAGINED A LARGE~~

"BUT DOES IT WORK?" CRIED A SMALL CRIPPLED RACCOON FROM THE CROWD.

"OF COURSE IT WORKS," FRED YELLED.

"PROVE IT," SAID THE CRIPPLE.

"PROVE IT," YELLED ANOTHER.

"PROVE IT, PROVE IT," THE RACCOONS CHANTED.

"I SHALL," CRIED FRED, ~~AND~~ FLIPPING THE VISOR OF THE SMELLMET DOWN.

FRED GESTURED TO THE CROWD TO MOVE BACK, AND AT HIS BECKONING, THEY PARTED.

FRED ~~IMAGINED~~ FOCUSED. HE THOUGHT OF TRASH, GARBAGE, REFUSE. HE THOUGHT OF THE SMELLMET'S POWERS. HE ENVISIONED A SMALL PILE OF GARBAGE BEFORE HIM, AND THEN HE STUCK OUT HIS PAWS AND EMBRACING THE POWERS ~~OF THE~~ THAT CURLED THROUGH HIS TINY BODY HE MADE THE PILE GROW. AND GROW IT DID.

THE TRASH PILE BECAME A HEAP, AND THE HEAP BECAME A MOUND. THE MOUND GREW, MORE NOW, AND IT BECAME A DUMP. THE RACCOONS LOOKED ON IN DISBELIEF AS THIS, THIS GOD MANIFESTED A LANDFILL'S WORTH OF GARBAGE FROM THIN AIR, FROM NOTHING.

THE PILE GREW AND GREW, SOARING TOWARDS THE HEAVENS.

DEPUTY CRANDORFF THREW ANOTHER CAN OF BUD OUT THE WINDOW. ~~HE WAS THREE OR FOUR. FOUR~~ CRANDORFF WAS A SIMPLE MAN - NOT A SIMPLETON, JUST SIMPLE. HIS DREAMS AND ASPIRATIONS WERE EXACTLY WHERE THEY SHOULD BE. FOR A HIGH SCHOOL GRADUATE WITH A STEADY JOB IN THE FORCE (THAT PAID QUITE WELL, BENEFITS, ETC.), A MORTGAGE, AND A WIFE WHO LOVED HIM AND THAT HE LOVED TOO. EVEN THE UNNAMED BAR-BE-QUE JOINT THAT HE THOUGHT ABOUT OPENING SOMETIME DOWN THE ROAD, WOULD BE SIMPLE - SOME COUNTER SEATS, A COUPLE OF BOOTHS, NOTHING FANCY. DEPUTY CRANDORFF HAD LITTLE INTEREST IN BEING A PART OF A GRAND PLAN, ANY PLAN, REALLY, OTHER THAN HIS OWN PLANS FOR A HAPPY LIFE. UNFORTUNATELY FOR THE DEPUTY, HE ~~WAS DRIVING~~ HAD JUST TURNED DOWN SHMALTZ ROAD

"DON'T GIVE ME EXCUSES," LANNISTER SAID. "I DON'T WANT EXCUSES."

"NOT TO MENTION THE CASELOADS," SAID JULIO CAESAR.

"YEAH," CAESAR CHAVEZ SAID.

"SIR, DO YOU HAVE ANY IDEA HOW MANY CASES I HAVE ON MY PLATE RIGHT NOW?"

"STOP. STOP IT RIGHT NOW," LANNISTER SAID.

BILL GLASS WANTED TO SPEAK UP, HE WANTED TO VOICE HIS OPINION. HE WANTED TO LET LANNISTER KNOW THAT HE AGREED WITH THE CAESARS, BUT HE STAYED QUIET.

"ENOUGH SHIT. ENOUGH WHINING," LANNISTER SAID. "THIS IS HOW IT'S DONE. THIS IS THE SYSTEM, AND IT'S ALWAYS BEEN AND IT ALWAYS WILL BE. SO, YOU NEED TO..." HE PAUSED FOR EFFECT, "FIGURE... IT... OUT."

A FEW HEADS HUNG, DEJECTED. OTHERS NODDED. BILL WAS RELIEVED. HE'D HELD HIS TONGUE.

"OKAY. MOVING ON," LANNISTER SAID, "WHO'S ON THE RUNKLE CASE?"

"SIR," BILL SAID, STANDING FROM HIS CHAIR.

"GO," LANNISTER SAID.

FRED THE RACOON HAD LET HIS IMAGINATION GET THE BEST OF HIM. HE WAS IN A CHILD WORLD OF HIS OWN. HIS IMAGINARY SMELLMET, THE OF UNWORTHY CITIZENS GATHERED BELOW HIM LIKE THE PEASANTS OF ANCIENT ROME, YELLING, REACHING, IN AWE OF THE POWER BEFORE THEM. FRED WAS FINISHING HIS EPIC SPEECH.

"THERE WILL BE NO MORE HUNGER. THERE WILL BE NO MORE FIGHTING. THERE WILL BE NO MORE FAILED ATTEMPTS AT LID-LIFTING ON MODERN CANS. THERE WILL BE ONLY COMARAGUE FOR ALL. ON DEMAND. SUCH IS THE POWER OF THE SMELLMET!"

JERRY RUNKLE ROLLED OVER IN HIS SLEEP, ALMOST DISTURBED BY THE SQUEAKING OF A RACOON.

"SQUEAK SQUEAK SQUEAK SQUEAK" WENT FRED.

~~FRED FOCUSED, AND IMAGINED A LARGE~~
"BUT DOES IT WORK?" CRIED A SMALL CRIPPLED RACCOON FROM THE CROWD.
"OF COURSE IT WORKS," FRED YELLED.
"PROVE IT," SAID THE CRIPPLE.
"PROVE IT," YELLED ANOTHER.
"PROVE IT, PROVE IT," THE RACCOONS CHANTED.
"I SHALL," CRIED FRIED, ~~AND~~ FLIPPING THE VISOR OF THE SMELLMET DOWN.
FRED GESTURED TO THE CROWD TO MOVE BACK, AND AT HIS BECKONING, THEY PARTED.
FRED ~~IMAGINED~~ FOCUSED. HE THOUGHT OF TRASH, GARBAGE, REFUSE. HE THOUGHT OF THE SMELLMET'S POWERS. HE ENVISIONED A SMALL PILE OF GARBAGE BEFORE HIM, AND THEN HE STUCK OUT HIS PAWS AND EMBRACING THE POWERS ~~OF THE~~ THAT CURSED THROUGH HIS TINY BODY HE MADE THE PILE GROW, AND GROW IT DID.
THE TRASH PILE BECAME A HEAP, AND THE HEAP BECOME A MOUND. THE MOUND GREW, MORE NOW, AND IT BECAME A DUMP. THE RACCOONS LOOKED ON IN DISBELIEF AS THIS, THIS GOD MANIFESTED A LANDFILL'S WORTH OF GARBAGE FROM THIN AIR, FROM NOTHING.
THE PILE GREW AND GREW, SOARING TOWARDS THE HEAVENS.

"DEPUTY CRANDORFF THREW ANOTHER CAN OF BUD OUT THE WINDOW. ~~THE MOTES THREE OF THE TRAILER. BEING~~ CRANDORFF WAS A SIMPLE MAN - NOT A SIMPLETON, JUST SIMPLE. HIS DREAMS AND ASPIRATIONS WERE EXACTLY WHERE THEY SHOULD BE. FOR A HIGH SCHOOL GRADUATE WITH A STEADY JOB IN THE FORCE (THAT PAID QUITE WELL, BENEFITS, ETC.), A MORTGAGE, AND A WIFE WHO LOVED HIM AND THAT HE LOVED TOO. EVEN THE UNNAMED BAR-BE-QUE JOINT THAT HE THOUGHT ABOUT OPENING SOMETIME DOWN THE ROAD, WOULD BE SIMPLE - SOME COUNTER SEATS, A COUPLE OF BOOTHS, NOTHING FANCY. DEPUTY CRANDORFF HAD LITTLE INTEREST IN BEING A PART OF A GRAND PLAN, ANY PLAN, REALLY, OTHER THAN HIS OWN PLANS FOR A HAPPY LIFE. UNFORTUNATELY FOR THE DEPUTY, HE ~~WAS DRIVING~~ HAD JUST TURNED DOWN SHMALTZ ROAD

"DON'T GIVE ME EXCUSES," LANNISTER SAID. "I DON'T WANT EXCUSES."

"NOT TO MENTION THE CASELOADS," SAID JULIO CAESAR.

"YEAH," CAESAR CHAVEZ SAID.

"SIR, DO YOU HAVE ANY IDEA HOW MANY CASES I HAVE ON MY PLATE RIGHT NOW?"

"STOP. STOP IT RIGHT NOW," LANNISTER SAID.

BILL GLASS WANTED TO SPEAK UP, HE WANTED TO VOICE HIS OPINION. HE WANTED TO LET LANNISTER KNOW THAT HE AGREED WITH THE CAESARS, BUT HE STAYED QUIET.

"ENOUGH SHIT. ENOUGH WHINING," LANNISTER SAID. "THIS IS HOW IT'S DONE. THIS IS THE SYSTEM, AND IT'S ALWAYS BEEN AND IT ALWAYS WILL BE. SO, YOU NEED TO..." HE PAUSED FOR EFFECT, "FIGURE... IT... OUT."

A FEW HEADS HUNG, DEJECTED. OTHERS NODDED. BILL ~~WAS~~ ~~DEFEATED.~~ ~~GLASS~~ RELIEVED HE'D HELD HIS TONGUE.

"OKAY. MOVING ON," LANNISTER SAID. "WHO'S ON THE RUNKLE CASE?"

"SIR," BILL SAID, STANDING FROM HIS CHAIR.

"GO," LANNISTER SAID.

FRED THE RACOON HAD ~~BEEN~~ LET HIS IMAGINATION GET THE BEST OF HIM. HE WAS IN A CROWD WORLD OF HIS OWN. HIS IMAGINARY SMELLMET, THE ~~PARADE~~ OF UNWORTHY CITIZENS GATHERED BELOW HIM LIKE THE PEASANTS OF ANCIENT ROME, YELLING, REACHING, IN AWE OF THE POWER BEFORE THEM. FRED WAS FINISHING HIS EPIC SPEECH.

"THERE WILL BE NO MORE HUNGER. THERE WILL BE NO MORE FIGHTING. THERE WILL BE NO MORE FAILED ATTEMPTS AT LID-LIFTING ON MODERN CANS. THERE WILL BE ONLY GARBAGE FOR ALL. ON DEMAND. SUCH IS THE POWER OF THE SMELLMET!"

JERRY RUNKLE ROLLED OVER IN HIS SLEEP, ALMOST DISTURBED BY THE ~~BROKEN~~ SQUEAKING OF A RACOON.

"SQUEAK SQUEAK, SQUEAK SQUEAK" WENT FRED.